A COMPROMISING POSITION

DIANE MERRILL WIGGINTON

JEWELED DAGGER PUBLISHING COMPANY

https://www.amazon.com/author/dianemerrillwigginton

© Copyright 2022 by Diane Merrill Wigginton

Designed by Keidi Keating

First edition

ISBN — Compromising Position eBook 978-1-946146-10-6

ISBN — Compromising Position Paperback 978-1-946146-11-3

Follow Diane Merrill Wigginton at

BookFunnell: https://BookHip.com/FFJRKAT
Twitter: https://twitter.com/wiggintondiane
Facebook: https://www.facebook.com/AngelinasSecretBook/
Amazon: https://www.amazon.com/author/dianemerrillwigginton
Linkedin: https://www.linkedin.com/in/diane-merrill-wigginton-926b89159
Bookbub: https://www.bookbub.com/profile/diane-merrill-wigginton?follow=true
Goodreads: https://www.goodreads.com/author/show/8355606.Diane_Merrill_Wigginton

Acknowledgment and a huge thank you to

Uvi Poznansky: Main Editor

Keidi Keating: Final Edit and book design

Catherine Borkowski: Florida Area Technical Adviser

A special thank you to Barbara Woods and Sylvia Luehr:
for their final-final read-through and editing.

Dedication

I wish to dedicate this book to the dreamer,
the planners, and everyone in between.
Thank you to everyone who has patiently waited
for this book to come out, and to those who
have helped me through the last few years.
Life can get complicated, and sometimes
it can be downright heartbreaking.
I dedicate this book to my children,
and my grandkids, and a special
dedication to our son, Alec.
May he find peace and comfort
In his loving Father's arms.
RIP

CHAPTER 1

The boardroom smelled of freshly brewed coffee, expensive aftershave, and desperation as Catherine Lawrence entered the room and took her seat near the head of the table.

Tiny prickles of anxiety raced through her when a cell phone went off, vibrating loudly across the polished boardroom table. The young intern sat on the opposite side, his face flushed and his eyes darting about as he grabbed the offensive device, turning it off and discreetly tucking it inside the pocket of his gray suit jacket.

Catherine sat up a little taller in her seat. She was dressed in a navy-blue, pinstripe business suit, pencil skirt, white blouse, and navy pumps. A pair of diamond studs sparkled in her ears and a simple diamond heart-shaped pendant hung on a silver chain, solely for decorative purposes. But the antique gold wedding band that she twisted absently around the ring finger of her right hand had a deep sentimental value. It once belonged to her deceased grandmother and she looked down at it, realizing what she was doing. The twisting of the ring was a nervous habit she picked up years ago. It usually calmed her but today it didn't.

Catherine's long auburn hair was pulled back into a tight bun at the back of her head and it felt restrictive as she shifted in her chair. In fact, everything about her current situation felt uncomfortable.

Her boss, Russell Tillman, cleared his throat loudly and began to speak. "I've called you all here this morning for an emergency meeting. See, it has come to my attention that my poll numbers have dramatically fallen — let me restate that. My numbers have plummeted in the last few weeks and I am very concerned — again, let me restate that. I am furious!" he said, raising his voice as his eyes darted around the room, landing momentarily on Catherine before moving on.

Russell Tillman was clearly agitated and nothing short of someone's head served up on a silver platter would suffice.

Bringing her hand up to her mouth she cleared her throat loudly, in preparation to say something, but was cut off when Russell ignored her and continued to speak.

"I want an explanation for the falling numbers! I don't want excuses or platitudes. I want cold hard facts and I want them now!" he bellowed. Standing at the head of the oval boardroom table, his eyes landed on his current campaign manager, Chase Stoneman.

Catherine held her breath. She hadn't seen Russell this worked up over anything since the murder case they'd worked on four years ago went up in flames. It was the third day of their case when a second-year defense attorney introduced a surprise witness that disputed their DNA evidence. The case was quickly thrown out on a technicality, a mistake that neither of them could ever forget.

The current campaign manager straightened his spine, sitting a little taller in his chair, his tan face turning the color of a tomato. "Sir, I can explain—" he began to say but was cut short by his angry boss.

"I said no excuses, Stoneman, and I meant it!"

"If you would just give me a private moment of your time," Chase begged, looking very uncomfortable under the scrutiny of his incensed candidate.

"Personally, I believe I have given you more than enough of my time. Certainly, more than you have proven yourself to be worth, Stoneman. And all I have gotten in return are a bunch of lies, a bit of deceit, and a truck load of horse shit!"

Catherine took another deep breath, shaking her head with disapproval. When Russell went off on one of his long, lengthy, profane filled rants it was difficult to rein him in. The image of giant brass balls hanging from Russell Tillman's nether region, well concealed beneath his perfectly tailored trousers, flashed across Catherine's mind and she shook her head to dispel it.

"Why is it that, over the past month and a half, the polls show my numbers steadily declining and you have done nothing to stop it?" he glared at Chase. "And why the hell do we find my numbers at their all-time low since I began this campaign?" he yelled, slamming his fist down hard upon the boardroom table, causing a reverberating noise to bounce off the windows.

Catherine noticed several interns wincing in fear and cringed inwardly. He was losing control, and she knew that he needed to dial it back but how would she help him see this fact?

Clearing her throat rather loudly once again, she deliberately reached for a glass of water while catching Russell's eye. Catherine hoped that she wasn't overstepping the boundary of their personal and professional relationship. After all, she hadn't yet been officially named the new campaign manager.

Russell glanced in her direction but then quickly averted his eyes. He obviously didn't want her advice, at least not yet.

"I'd love to hear an explanation," he said.

Everyone was now staring at Chase, the one person who should have had the answer.

In Catherine's opinion, Chase Stoneman was a vain, opinionated blowhard who thought very highly of himself and should never have been appointed as the campaign manager in the first place.

His Latin heritage was evident by his full, dark lashes and broodingly handsome features—but that was where his appeal ended for her. He had a smooth smile, and even smoother pickup lines. A real lady's man. He had even gone so far, once upon a time, to deem himself the man with all the answers.

Except in this instance, Catherine thought.

Chase looked like a drowning man without a life preserver, and by the look in his eyes, he was going under for the third time. He looked desperate as his face flushed crimson. He attempted to smile but the expression didn't quite make it all the way up to his eyes.

One could imagine the wheels in his head feverishly turning as he attempted to come up with a plausible explanation for the declining poll numbers. Unfortunately, he could think of nothing.

Russell Tillman growled and slammed his fist down hard once again, causing Catherine to jump this time as Chase gave him a pleading look.

Russell's eyes turned icy, and Catherine expelled the air from her lungs that she'd been holding. She knew that look. She'd seen it before. That was the look he got just before he exploded like a volcano.

Frantically wanting to get Russell's attention, Catherine loudly cleared her throat again, then began to throw out a quick hand signal by sweeping one finger under her nose several times.

They'd developed their own hand signals in court while working together for years because it was impossible to stop in the middle of a trial to converse with one another.

She was attempting to tell Russell that he was making too public of a stink over this matter and that he needed to move on. But Russell refused to be reined in, and deliberately cut his eyes away from her after signaling her with a negative shake of his head.

"Pick up your things and get out of my sight. You are finished in this town, Stoneman." His voice took on a determined, resolute tone as if the simple mention of Stoneman's name left a bad taste in his mouth. "And don't let me catch you hanging around one minute longer than necessary or I will have you thrown out."

You could have cut the tension in the room with a knife as Tillman and Chase locked eyes for a long, strained, silent moment.

Chase blinked first, then looked away, unable to reasonably dispute Russell Tillman's reason for sacking him.

Chase slowly got to his feet, aware that everyone in the room was staring at him as he straightened to his full height. He gathered his things from the table, tucking them into his satchel, and slipped his cell phone into his pocket.

"I'm truly sorry that I let you down, Sir. If there is any way—" he began to say.

"There isn't," Russell said, cutting him off as he folded his arms across his chest.

"Of course," Chase added as he walked around the table, taking the long way to the door in an effort to avoid going past Tillman. He paused in the doorway as he propped it open with his foot. He allowed his gaze to land on the two women sitting across from one another at the head of the table.

Chase's eyes landed upon Catherine Lawrence first and then Patricia Grant, Catherine's arch nemesis and the very bane of her existence since the day she'd been hired. The two women glanced at one another from across the table before looking away.

Patricia Grant turned her eyes back towards Russell, lifting her chin just a little higher while wearing a confident smile upon her perfectly lined lips.

With a cynical smirk, Chase chuckled. "I'm just sorry that I will miss the fireworks between the two of you," he scoffed, allowing the door to close slowly behind him.

Everyone watched Chase as he walked to his office and closed the door. Russell signaled for the two guards on duty to follow him. Tom and Ben would see to it that Chase left the building without incident.

Russell broke the awkward silence with a forced smile.

"Well, now," he said, taking a deep breath as if finally relaxing for the first time since he'd walked into the building that day, "it feels good to be free of that dead weight. Let us get down to the real business at hand." He paused for dramatic effect, picked up his coffee mug and took a long drink before placing the cup back down in front of him. "I have had my eye on this young woman for quite some time, I know her as well as one knows their own right hand," he said without hinting as to which woman he was speaking of.

But then he smiled and graciously looked down at Catherine.

"Miss Lawrence, will you stand up here next to me and do me the great honor of accepting the recently vacated position of campaign manager? I believe you are the one who will see us all the way through to the Governor's office."

It took Catherine only a moment to respond as she took a hold of Russell's outstretched hand and allowed him to pull her to her feet.

"Mr. Tillman, it would be my great honor to be your new campaign manager."

One person, and then another, began to applaud.

Catherine had been fairly confident that the position was hers. After all, she and Russell had known each other more than four years professionally. And his wife, Angela, was her roommate and best friend from college.

"I just want to say how honored and humbled I am to be given this opportunity. I look forward to sitting down with each of you to discuss your role in this campaign," Catherine said as she allowed her eyes to go around the room before landing upon Patricia.

Unlike everyone else at the table, Patricia had a forced smile on her lips.

Catherine made a mental note: *Don't turn your back on Patricia Grant when she has something sharp in her hand.*

"This meeting has run a little longer than I intended. You are all dismissed. If anyone has any problems or concerns," Russell said with a wry grin, "I suggest that you take it up with the new campaign manager."

Catherine watched everyone grab their things and file out of the room before she leaned over to pick up her purse. Russell leaned in towards her and cleared his throat. "Catherine, my office. I need to discuss a few matters with you before you get started."

Touching his arm to keep him from walking away, she answered, "Of course, sir." "You know that theatrics and drama play well in the courtroom but they don't play well in the boardroom."

"I couldn't help myself," Russell said, giving her a boyish smile and a wink.

"I saw two interns holding back tears, Russell. That was really unforgivable," she sighed. "You really need to make amends and do something nice for all of them."

"I know, I know," he answered, sounding regretful. Then spotting Patricia waiting for him at the door, he acknowledged her, "I can give you two minutes and two minutes only, Patricia. I have a meeting scheduled with my new campaign manager," he said as he turned and smiled at Catherine.

"Make this up to the staff, Russell. It's important for morale."

"I promise," he said, crossing his heart, just before turning and leaving the room.

Leaning over once again to retrieve the pen she'd dropped, she called out, "I'll only be a minute," as she stood back up. That's when Catherine watched Patricia saunter from the door, swaying her hips as she stepped directly in front of Russell. Catherine shook her head.

"This is going to be a very long campaign season," she muttered under her breath. "A very long campaign season indeed."

CHAPTER 2

*P*ulling her silver convertible into the garage, Catherine put the top up and climbed out before walking into the house and straight to her bedroom. It had been a long day, and she was ready to unwind and relax.

She placed her Chanel heels in their usual spot in her perfectly organized closet, before she walked out to the kitchen to open up a bottle of chilled Chardonnay. A glass of wine was a real treat for a work night—Catherine took a sip as she walked into the living room. She would take a moment to relax and celebrate her accomplishments.

Switching on the television, Catherine sat down on the couch and listened to the news playing in the background, not really paying attention to what was being reported as she enjoyed another sip. The white noise of the news commentators talking back and forth was soothing, like having someone else in the house with her.

Normally, every minute of her evening was carefully scheduled but tonight she would enjoy her moment of victory with a lovely glass of golden liquid and simply zone out.

Catherine had done it; she'd done what she'd said she would do in her fifteen-year plan. She took a deep breath and released it slowly, savoring the accomplishment. It hadn't taken her as long as she thought it would to get to this point in her life.

Ten years ago, Catherine's grandmother, Alice, became very sick. When the diagnosis came, everyone was shocked. Cancer.

It was especially heartbreaking for Catherine since her grandmother took the place of her own mother when she ran out on her and her father just after Catherine's second birthday. Her father moved back to New Smyrna, Florida, and in with Alice, leaving Catherine in his mother's capable hands as he made a living to support the three of them in Daytona Beach.

Then Alice became increasingly ill and Catherine became the devoted granddaughter. She would sit by Alice's bedside for hours doing homework or reading out loud. And when Alice received the diagnosis that her cancer was terminal, she prepared Catherine for the future the best way she knew how. They made out a meticulous plan for Catherine's life to follow when she was gone.

Writing out a five, a ten, and a fifteen-year plan seemed to bring Catherine's grandmother great comfort, so Catherine went along with it. The roadmap for Catherine's life also brought Catherine significant comfort in the end when her grandmother was gone. But fate had another cruel twist to deliver to Catherine, and just nine weeks after her grandmother's funeral her father was killed in a head-on collision with a drunk driver on his way home from work.

At the age of nineteen, Catherine was alone, bereft, and devastated.

Tears ran down Catherine's face as those old feelings of pain caused her heart to tighten in her chest.

Wiping her face with the back of her hand, Catherine looked over at a picture on the side table of the three of them together. She began twisting the gold ring on her finger before tipping her wine glass to her lips and taking a deep sip. A small chuckle escaped her lips as she took another deep swallow of her wine. She had so many wonderful memories associated with the day that picture had been taken.

It had been a brilliant, sunny, July day, and the water had glistened like it had diamonds sprinkled on the surface. At least that's what it looked like to her five-year-old mind. Her father had gotten off work early that day and they had picked up Kentucky Fried chicken on their way to the beach to watch the sunset. It was one of those perfect days that stuck in your mind forever. Catherine would never forget how the three of them sat there laughing, eating their meal, watching the dolphins play in the waves. She could still recall how the evening sun had felt on her face. The sunset that day had been so vibrant and stunning. At that moment in time, her life had been perfect.

Catherine had done it. She had made the life plan a reality. She'd stepped into the political arena, so to speak. It wasn't her as the candidate, but it was the political arena nonetheless. She would unwind for fifteen more minutes before resuming her tightly scheduled nightly ritual.

Her list of things to do ticked off in Catherine's head: Run on the treadmill for twenty minutes before moving on to a seven-minute shower. Then, devote seven minutes to picking out her outfit for the next morning, and twenty-five minutes to prepare and eat dinner while checking emails, which naturally led to planning out the next day. She estimated that she would need an hour for that with her new responsibilities. That would leave her thirty to forty minutes at the end of the evening to focus on the local news and take notes as she sat in bed. Then it would be her favorite time of the night when she could read a good book for thirty to forty minutes before turning out the lights.

She knew that Russell expected her to put together an entirely new agenda by Monday morning. Was she crazy for stepping into such an impossible position after the momentous disaster Chase left them in on his way out the door?

She took another sip of the fruity drink, enjoying the way that it played across her tongue before she swallowed. Taking a moment to admire the wine, she realized that it was both crisp and mild as she took yet another sip, relishing the feeling of calmness she experienced while the cool liquid slid down her throat.

A heavy sigh escaped Catherine's lips as she looked out the sliding glass doors at the crashing waves upon the shore. Her oceanfront condo was nestled upon the dunes of New Smyrna Beach in Florida.

People bragged about Florida's gulf-coast sunsets, but Catherine preferred the deep purples and blues of the glorious sunrises. She was an early riser, always had been. There was something so magnificent about greeting the day with the first rays of dawn as it broke over the horizon, giving Catherine a feeling of hope and optimism.

But tonight, she would enjoy witnessing another of Florida's most spectacular occurrences: a rolling dark, majestic electrical storm, complete with thunder and lightning. They were brought on by the heat of the warm May evening, with temperatures hovering around eighty-three degrees. To someone who has never experienced one before, the spring storms could seem like the horsemen of the apocalypse arriving, throwing lightning bolts across the evening sky as some sort of foreboding. Yet Catherine had come to love these storms even if it hadn't always been that way. When she was a small child, the storms terrified her.

As a true Floridian, she knew to stay out of the unpredictable storm and appreciate the spectacle from afar. And as a spectator, she enjoyed God's splendors in all its magnificence from the safety of her condo.

A three-pronged, jagged streak split the night sky, causing Catherine to jump when the loud crack of thunder boomed, rattling the windows. Setting her glass of wine down on the coffee table, she reached behind her head and began to remove the pins holding her hair back into its tight bun. Shaking out her thick, auburn hair, Catherine took a deep breath and held it as another bolt of lightning lit up the sky. Then, letting it out as the thunder boomed, she allowed the excitement and tension of her workday to flow out of her.

She counted to herself after the lightning flashed again.

"One-one-thousand, two-one-thousand, three—"

The thunder boomed, rattling the wine glass she had poised upon the glass-top table. The storm was less than two miles away.

Catherine imagined pirates getting caught up in a storm like this and it made her shiver. They would be at the mercy of the powerful waves that pounded the shores and their ship.

Catherine picked up her glass and took a sip of wine, savoring the taste and texture again while telling herself that she was perfectly content and happy in this moment of her life.

But somewhere in the back of her mind the words rang hollow and she knew that they weren't true. There was something missing in her life but she just couldn't quite put her finger on what it was—or maybe she just didn't want to examine things too closely, for fear of finding that her life was somehow lacking.

It was true that she hadn't been on a date in over two and a half years, nor had she attempted to have any real relationship since her dreaded freshman year of college. Ever since then, her fifteen-year plan and current lifestyle didn't allow for distractions. Besides, there was neither the time nor the space for any other person in Catherine's life, especially now that she was taking on the responsibility of running Russell Tillman's campaign.

If everything went smoothly, this governor's race could be a pivotal moment for her career. It could eventually be the beginning of her own political career.

Catherine glanced down at her watch. It was a crystal Tiffany's watch with a delicate brown leather band. The face of the watch didn't have numbers, just tiny diamonds where numbers should be. The hands of the timepiece were held in place by a perfect little emerald set in the center. It had been a birthday gift from her grandmother during her senior year of high school, and Catherine rarely took it off except to shower or swim.

Catherine's thoughts shifted again to the time when she had sat at her grandmother's bedside, doing homework as Alice had slept. Alice had been overcome with fatigue from the chemo treatments. Catherine remembered how scared she'd been. Shortly after that, Alice had insisted that Catherine promise to stick to their plan, no matter what happened to her. Oh, how she'd cried while making up some silly oath, swearing to her grandmother that she would rather die than not complete their plan.

Several tears ran down Catherine's face once again and she wiped them away as she recalled the contented smile that had been on Alice's face when she had leaned down and kissed her on the head to seal their pact. Then Alice had closed her eyes and fell into a deep sleep, from which she never awoke.

Completing her Master's degree in record time, Catherine knew in her heart that her grandmother had been watching over her. She was thinking about the first time she met Russell Tillman. When she went through the interview process at his office, the two of them pretended that they had never met before. Angela and Russell had been dating for a year by then and the three of them were already tight.

The interview took place in a large boardroom, and there had been four other people on the interview panel, including Russell. Her nerves had been a mess that day.

Catherine was staring off into space, lost in her own thoughts, when suddenly she heard a loud rat-a-tat-tat at her door, which pulled her from her daydream.

Wiping the tears from her eyes she jumped to her feet.

"Ugh, coming," she called out, staring at the wine glass in her hand.

Catherine made a split moment decision, tipping the glass back and draining it of its contents before setting the empty glass down on the coffee table in front of her. Then, she crossed the room to the front door.

"Who is it?" she called out while peering through the peephole.

"G'day to ya," came an unfamiliar, husky voice. "I'm your neighbor next door. I just moved in yesterday and wanted to introduce myself."

Looking at the attractive man through the peephole, Catherine saw a well-formed, chiseled chin, and could tell that he was quite tall. His blond hair was windblown as if he'd just stepped out of the ocean. When he leaned down as if trying to see through her peephole, she noted that he had the bluest eyes she'd ever seen.

"Hello, are you still there?"

"Yes. Just a moment," Catherine called back, quickly checking her reflection in the mirror above the credenza by the door. She fluffed her hair and made sure that her lipstick wasn't all smeared around her mouth as she licked her lips.

"Pardon me?"

"I said, just a minute," she said, trying to sound pleasant as she ran a dampened finger under her left eye where her mascara had smudged.

Of course, he has an accent, she thought as she opened the door with a smile and stepped out onto the front landing.

"Catherine Lawrence. It's a pleasure to meet you," she said, extending her hand to him. "Welcome to the complex."

Perhaps it was merely the wine going to her head, or maybe it was the way he stood there smiling down at her, but Catherine felt her heart quicken. "What can I do for you?"

"I knew you would be like the waters of the South Pacific Ocean."

"I beg your pardon?"

"I liken people to different bodies of water," he quickly explained.

"You what?"

"Each ocean has a different personality," he said to clarify. "The Pacific Ocean is warmer and inviting, but the color is muddied in places. The Arctic Ocean is cold and very uninviting, one might even say that it is not very appealing, but it's full of life. Then there is the South

Pacific Ocean, warm, inviting, and crystal clear. It has this purity to it. Why, the coloring of the water is some of the brightest blue I've ever seen in my entire life. There are even places that you can see thirty meters down."

"So, what does that have to do with me?" she asked, still feeling confused.

"I'm just saying that you are pure and clear, like the South Pacific Ocean. You don't hold your beauty back."

"Thank you," she said, puzzled by his strange explanation. "I think."

Jake looked past Catherine, into her neat, tidy little condo and whistled between his teeth.

"Crikey," he blurted out, "looks like something from Better House and Gardens."

Catching him looking past her, Catherine suddenly felt annoyed.

"Is there something I can help you with, Mr.—" she asked, leaving the question open ended on purpose, in hopes that he would take the hint and fill in his name.

"Oh, sorry, love. Where are my manners? Jake. Jake Ryan," he said, clasping her hand in his and giving it a firm shake.

Catherine felt a shock of electricity when he touched her and she jumped. "Ouch," she recoiled, pulling her hand back.

"Truly sorry about that," he apologized, letting go immediately. "Static electricity."

Catherine chuckled, "That tends to happen during an electrical storm. What can I do for you, Mr. Ryan?"

Jake quickly realized that Miss Lawrence was a no-nonsense kind of girl. He would have to work hard to bridge the distance between them.

"I am planning a little party next week with a few of my mates. It's a very casual event. We usually throw something on the barbie and pop open a few cold ones." Growing uncomfortable with her blank stare, Jake realized he hadn't actually invited her to join them as he rambled on. Clearing his throat, he said, "I wanted to invite you to join us if you're free."

"I'm not certain I understood—" she began to say.

"My friends and I get together and throw something on the barbie to eat," Jake repeated, talking slowly as if that would solve the language barrier. "Then we sit around the fire pit and play music and converse with sheilas and drink."

Looking at him as if he had suddenly sprouted two heads, Catherine took a moment to catch up with his meaning.

"I was simply trying to clarify...wait, did you just say sheilas?"

"Yes."

"And sheilas would be women?"

Jake nearly burst out laughing but restrained himself when he saw the look on her face.

Clearing his throat, "Yes," he replied. "Now don't go crook on me. It's a simple language barrier. I just wanted to invite you to join my friends and me for a little barbecue, as you Americans call it, Thursday evening."

"So, you do speak English. That makes sense now." Catherine said, shaking her head.

"Of course, I speak English. I'm from Australia, not Tanzania."

"Thank goodness. For a moment there I was worried when I was only able to understand every other word you said," Catherine said with a smile. "But I'm afraid that I will have to decline your kind offer, Mr. Ryan. You see, I just started a new position at work and I am terribly busy."

Feeling disappointed, Jake smiled graciously.

"If you should change your mind, my invitation is open to you. We will be hanging in our *bathers* and *thongs*, downing some *coldies*."

Clearly misunderstanding the use of the word *thong*, Catherine's face registered her shock.

"What?" she questioned, taking a step back as she reached for the door to close it on him.

Jake laughed, again realizing his mistake.

"Wait, love, honestly, I think we got off on the wrong foot. I truly didn't mean to offend!" He tried to apologize while pointing at his feet. "I should have said flip-flops. In Australia, we call them thongs."

Catherine stopped, a flush rising to her cheeks, and looked at his feet before she chuckled again, feeling completely foolish. That's when she spotted Jake's swimsuit hanging over the railing behind him.

"Are you wearing anything under that towel?" she asked, narrowing her eyes with suspicion.

Following the direction of her eyes, Jake turned, looking over his shoulder at his swimming trunks hanging casually over the railing and before he could turn around to answer, the door was being shut in his face.

"I'll say, G'day to you, Mr. Ryan!" Catherine said as she quickly closed the door in his face. "Oh, the arrogance," she growled under her breath, leaning her back up against the closed door. "He thinks he's so irresistible with his rugged good looks and sexy accent."

"I'm standing right here, and I can hear you!" came Jake's muffled words from the other side of the door. "Oh, c'mon love. I'm sorry. I didn't realize I was offending you. That's just what we do after surfing where I'm from. I would have gotten my ears clapped if I walked in the house with sand and sea water dripping from my shorts."

"I'm ignoring you, Mr. Ryan!" Catherine called back, pushing away from the door as she headed for the other room to retrieve her wine glass.

"I'm sorry for the misunderstanding."

"I have an accent and I'm too good looking for my own good," she said in a low murmur to herself, mimicking his Australian accent. "The nerve of him, assuming every woman has no willpower to resist a man standing at her door without pants on. As if I would simply fall for him—Augh!" she scornfully uttered, setting the wine glass down onto the granite counter with a tad too much force and breaking the delicate stem off. Growling in frustration, Catherine picked up the broken pieces, cutting her pointer finger on a jagged edge of glass. "Oh, darn it," she gasped, sticking the injured finger into her mouth.

CHAPTER 3

*t*he "Blue Martini" was experiencing a great deal of success as one of Daytona's trendiest Martini bars. Young professionals and those who were on the prowl for someone new could be found in the swanky establishment every weeknight. Known for their famous drinks like the *Pink Flamingo* or *Morning Sex*, the place started buzzing every night around seven.

Patricia Grant had ducked out of the office when it seemed likely no one would notice her leaving and had arrived while there was still parking available near her favorite night spot. She was not averse to flirting with Trevor, the want-to-be model working as a parking lot attendant, in order to get a reserved spot. But Patricia also knew that he'd recently started dating Jesse, one of the cocktail waitresses who was working her way through college at Florida State University, school of medicine, and Patricia did not want to draw her attention. Although Jesse was a huge flirt herself, Patricia knew that she really only had eyes for Trevor and flirting was what servers did to encourage patrons to tip a little more generously.

Patricia had walked straight to the bar, ordering from Miguel, the bartender, who knew which martini she liked without making her say any of the names that were created as a fun thing to encourage tourists to loosen up. She took a sip of her drink and smiled at Miguel before making her way to a tall table against the back wall of the room. Pretending to be unaware of the heads that turned as she crossed the room, she hiked her pencil skirt up a couple of inches in order to climb onto the bar stool in her slim fitting dress. She managed to seat herself without exposing more than a momentary glimpse of slim suntanned thigh. Looking out from behind thick fake lashes, she glanced around to see who might still be watching.

Sitting all alone on a tall stool at a table against the wall, her vantage point allowed her to look over the entire room as well as see who was entering the bar through the tinted window.

From a distance, Patricia Grant appeared poised and collected as she sat there sipping her martini on that stool. But inside, the strikingly beautiful woman was a jumble of nerves. She drummed her perfectly manicured nails on the table, and for the third time in the span of five minutes, glanced at her phone. Irritation caused a crease to form between her brows. Taking a deep breath,

Patricia jiggled her right leg as she absently stared into the crowd of people mingling about.

Allowing her mind to wander, Patricia found her thoughts drifting to Catherine Lawrence. What was it about Catherine that made people respect her? Patricia thought to herself. She was equally as beautiful as Catherine Lawrence, possibly even a tad more so. Her luxurious, waist-length, bleached blonde hair had been ironed and hung straight down her back as she fidgeted, pushing a stray strand of hair over her shoulder. Her almond-shaped, dark brown eyes were meticulously lined and always had that well-rehearsed, come-hither look. High cheekbones framed her delicate face along with lush, full lips that could entice any man to do her bidding, or so she believed.

Patricia placed an elbow upon the table, resting her chin upon one thumb in a contemplative manner as she turned towards the window and looked out. Men that had strong constitutions and willpower were her favorite kind to play with. The thought of them fighting their instincts, trying to stand resolute against her pull, telling her no just before they gave into the pressure she placed upon them was the best, she thought, as a smirk played across her full red lips. They were no match for her womanly wiles as she strategically played with their emotions to outwit them. It required cunning and skill on her part. Miguel the bartender happened to glance in her direction at that moment and couldn't help but wonder what that smirk was about. He turned back to his customers, dismissing Patricia from his thoughts. Too high-maintenance for me, he thought. Women like that could chew a guy up and spit him out before he even realized what was happening.

Checking the time again, Patricia let out a sigh and took another nerve calming sip of her martini. It really was quite good. She raised the glass towards Miguel and went back to her thoughts. Patricia knew she was intelligent, witty, and clever. In her mind, she was the whole package. So, why had she never been asked by any of her many conquests to marry? She had done well in law school, and felt she should have had at least one good divorce settlement by now. She was a good companion, amiable and fun. And there was no doubt that she was beautiful. Some might even say that she was a bit twisted, but in a good way.

Patricia had grown ambitious, maybe too ambitious for her own good, taking a few wrong turns down life's bumpy road. Her moral compass was definitely broken, if she was being honest with herself.

"I've made it just as far as Catherine Lawrence," Patricia hissed under her breath, still lost in thought, questioning where she had gone so wrong with Russell Tillman. "I should have been his campaign manager, not her!" She pursed her lips together, shifting to lean on her other hand.

Drumming her nails on the table top again, she pondered further while her thoughts and insecurities haunted her. She thought she understood men. She had rarely been wrong when it came to predicting what they would do or say, but she had learned an unwanted lesson today.

Patricia's troubling childhood sprang to the forefront of her mind as she stopped the incessant click-clack of her fingernails. She blamed her beautiful self-centered mother for the endless parade of potential stepfathers throughout her life, starting when she was just seven-years-old. All of them thought she was cute at first, showering gifts upon her early on to win her mother's affections. Later, the gifts became more extravagant and personal as she blossomed into a young woman during high school. That was when she learned the true potential of her power over the opposite sex.

Patricia knew that the right look or pout of her lips at just the right moment could turn men into putty in her hands. A smile could have them begging for more. Men were simple as far as she was concerned. They were more likely to use their money, status, and position of power to get what they wanted from women. She had simply learned how to turn the tables on them. The 'aha' moment for Patricia came one day when she was nearly eighteen. That was the day that she decided to use the only weapon that she had in her arsenal—sex—to bend men to her will. A short-lived relationship with a married man earned her the tuition needed to start college without having to worry about a summer job.

From her first day as a freshman in college, Patricia wanted for nothing. From classmates to professors, she manipulated anyone who could either further her degree or just make her life easier. The only time she used her actual intelligence was when she was pushed into a group project with other women. Women never became her friends, but they did realize that she was actually smart, something she hid from most men, who could be so easily intimidated. Turning her loose on the world had been a huge power trip and she had spent the next eight years earning her degree as she perfected and honed her skills even further.

"And perfect them I did," Patricia muttered out loud, into her drink.

She lived in a very comfortable, two-bedroom beachfront condominium in a gated community and drove a metallic red Stingray Corvette convertible. Her walk-in closet was filled with designer clothing, handbags, and jewelry—all gifts from adoring admirers, who had since moved on.

The fact that Patricia had the degree and glowing references from her professors was a testament of her sheer determination and willpower. But references merely got her a foot in the door of the jobs that she desired. Keeping that job was another story.

Until today, Patricia had thought that there was nothing she couldn't obtain if she put her mind to it. It was hard for her to understand how that mealy-mouthed Catherine Lawrence had managed to steal the golden position of campaign manager right out from under her.

"I put so much time and effort into grooming that man," she muttered under her breath as if she were the only person in the room. Then she took another sip of her drink to calm her jangled nerves.

Only two days before, Russell had all but promised that position to Patricia during their inner-office meeting. They'd been discussing the campaign when she strategically placed her hand upon his thigh. Then she gave him a look. The one that had never failed her before as she glanced up at him through her thick lashes, with slightly wistful eyes as she chewed on her lower lip. It was perfect. Hell, she had even known that he was firing Chase before anyone else did. Yet something must have gone wrong.

But what had gone wrong?

After today's announcement, when Russell called Patricia into his office, she was certain he was going to at least apologize for his terrible decision. Boy, was she wrong.

"I'm very concerned that you have misinterpreted our relationship, Miss Grant." Russell said, "People have begun to talk about us. I can't afford to have this campaign derailed by a scandal."

"Whatever do you mean, Russell?" Patricia questioned innocently, her eyes growing large as she batted her long, false eyelashes at him.

"That, right there, is a good example of what I am saying, Miss Grant. The familiarity with which you use my name and look at me is part of the problem. While in the office, I'm going to have to insist that you call me Mr. Tillman," he said. "It's important to me that we keep things very professional."

"I understand," she replied solemnly, lowering her head. But Patricia wasn't sad at all. In fact, she was angry, and that was a dangerous position for Russell to be in, because Patricia was likely to do whatever it took to get what she wanted. Even if it meant cutting off her nose to spite her face, as the old saying went.

Switching tactics, she decided to use the oldest trick in the book. Guilt. The crocodile tears began to roll down her cheeks and she calculated that Russell would feel bad for making her cry. Then she would wrap him around her little finger like she'd done to every other man that had crossed her.

Russell merely handed her a large box of tissues and told her once again, in a clipped voice, that he was sorry if he'd led her to believe that she was getting the job. Then he dismissed her for the day.

Patricia had been torn between stomping her foot or throwing something at his head. In the end, she'd decided to play the long game and bide her time. Only now she was going to have to do something truly despicable and underhanded to get what she wanted. That much was clear to her.

Patricia would have to employ the help of a certain person that truly got under her skin as well as sabotage Catherine Lawrence at every turn.

"I need to find her Achilles heel," she mused.

This whole situation was exhausting. It really made her head hurt. Patricia had settled upon a plan, with the perfect patsy to be her fall guy. He was crucial to this plan.

Patricia needed someone who could get to Catherine and spy on her when she wasn't in the office. She needed some dirt to discredit Catherine when the time was right.

Patricia knew the gubernatorial race would be a fierce one for Tillman and she wasn't about to blow his chances at winning because she'd set her sights on sharing that Governor's mansion with him. Her plans didn't include Miss Catherine Lawrence, or Russell's wife, Angela.

Patricia had always felt that Angela Tillman looked down her nose at her and had resented the woman since day one.

She was lost in thought when Chase suddenly appeared, leaning down to whisper in her ear, "I hear you're looking for trouble?"

His words dripped with sexual intent as he smoothly stepped around the table and took the seat across from her.

It's game time, Patricia thought as she switched on the charm, flashing Chase her award-winning smile while arching an eyebrow at him. She knew this look drove him crazy.

Dropping one shoulder forward as she lifted her chin ever so slightly to give off a strong, confident air, Patricia grinned.

"Chase, darling, I'm always looking for some kind of trouble. I guess it really just depends on what you had in mind?" she purred. "The only real question you need to ask yourself is can you afford me?"

Chase opened his mouth to answer, only to be cut off by her.

"More importantly, do you have enough gas to make it interesting? Hmm?" She raised an eyebrow while flashing him a wicked, playful smile.

Sparks danced in her eyes as her grin widened, giving Chase the distinct impression that she was merely playing with him.

Meeting Patricia's challenge, Chase smiled back with a slightly larger grin. This was his favorite part of the game, the chase.

Now who was the hunter and who was the prey? That was the fun part. Figuring that out was half the battle—but with a woman like Patricia, the stakes had just gotten higher.

"Well, I suppose that depends on the lady. What does the lady want?" Chase asked.

The pawn moves forward and the game begins, Patricia mused happily to herself.

"Well," she drew the word out, adding a sultry tone, "I suppose you heard who took your old position at work?" She let the question hang in the air between them.

"It was always going to be one of you, Patricia," Chase retorted dryly as he turned to look at the people walking by just outside the window.

Patricia felt herself tense, worried that she had suddenly lost his attention.

I will not lose him now.

After all, she was the master of manipulation and she knew how to bring him back around.

She gently touched his arm with one hand while reaching out with her other to turn his face towards hers. Patricia gave Chase a coy look, playing the roles of mother, friend, lover, and companion in one glance. After all, that was what all men secretly desired, she thought.

She switched to a more sympathetic tone as if she understood all of the pains he had ever suffered.

"Chase, darling, what Tillman did to you today was terribly wrong. He's a coward for ambushing you in the meeting the way he did. He should have faced you behind closed doors and worked it out like a real man. Believe me when I say, darling, that I have always been impressed by how confident you are. You would never have done anything so despicable to another colleague, now would you? Anyone could tell that you are not that kind of a person just by looking at you. I know you to be a real man of action, Chase Stoneman. Someone who wouldn't sit idly by and take such abhorrent treatment from anyone, not even from Russell Tillman."

Chase opened his mouth to say something but was cut off by Patricia as she continued her commentary.

"Oh no! You are a man of action. A man who would see to it that this miscarriage of justice was answered properly. That is truly and honestly the only reason I've called you, darling. I felt so bad for you. And I wanted to be the one to help you take back your self-respect after Tillman stripped it away so cruelly today," Patricia said, laying the sympathy on good and thick.

Chase's eyes shifted back to hers without turning his head. Patricia knew that she would soon have his full attention. Now she just needed to sweeten the pot, so to speak.

"You might have been replaced today but I want to make sure that you are not forgotten," Patricia said as Chase tried to pull his arm away from her.

Reading his body language and feeling him pull away, she could tell that she was losing his interest. She gripped his hand tightly.

"Had it of been me who took your place, I would have insisted that Tillman made a very public apology to you. I know Russell doesn't want to be known for being a bad tempered, hothead."

"Says who?" Chase scoffed. "The man thrives on—"

"Says me," she cut him off. "I've come to know Russell very well over the last few months and—"

"Oh, so it's Russell now," Chase cut in, "When did the two of you become so cozy?"

Taken aback, Patricia stammered, "Well, we—I mean, he—"

"We—he, what, Patricia?" Chase asked angrily, turning away from her again. "Are the two of you an item, Patricia?"

"No! Of course not, Chase. It's just that—" she stammered again, unsure of what to say next to convince him that he needed her.

"Spit it out, Patricia. My time is very valuable to me and right now you are wasting it!"

"Please, Chase, I'm on your side and I want to help you. Won't you look at me?" she pleaded.

He slowly turned to look at her.

"What do you need from me, Patricia?" he asked in a bland tone. He felt as if she were trying to play him, which made him angry. But in the end, nothing mattered more to Chase than to reclaim his dignity and self-esteem as a thought sprang into his mind. He just might end up in bed with this flirtatious blonde bombshell sitting across the table from him.

Leaning his chin upon his hand, Chase tried to look interested in what Patricia was saying. After all, she'd never given him the time of day before, a fact that made Chase question her motives. He began to think she considered him beneath her. He knew somewhere deep down that Patricia had set her sights on Tillman from day one. But for now, it seemed that he was somehow valuable to her and he didn't care why. This was something he would use to his advantage while playing along with her little game. He certainly was not fooled by her sudden interest in his welfare.

She must think me a complete idiot if she thinks I'd fall for her lousy little performance, Chase thought. She was up to something and he would play along until he figured out Patricia's endgame or he took her to bed a few times and he became bored—whichever came first. Either way, he would consider it a win.

"Well, I think that you should start following the new campaign manager around and observe her movements. If Tillman gets into any kind of trouble, little Miss Goody-Two-Shoes will be the one doing damage control. Plus, if you are following her, you can dig up some dirt for me to use against her when the time is right. Something might pop up," she added very innocently before covering her mouth with her hand as if she suddenly realized what she'd just said.

"Oh, I'm sorry, that was inappropriate, but you get the idea. When you get anything on her, you will let me know, won't you? It's a win-win for both of us. Right?" Patricia added with what she hoped looked like a sincere smile. "Everyone wins, and we all go home with what we want. She will be out on her ear, and you get your vindication. Right?"

"What do you get out of this deal, Patricia?"

"What?"

"I asked, what do you get out of this?"

The music played on as they sat in silence a moment. Patricia was spinning her wheels trying to think of an appropriate answer that didn't sound terribly self-serving.

"That's simple, darling. I want to see that you are compensated for your humiliation and Miss Lawrence ends up out on the street looking for a new career path while I take her place. You will be able to show your face again without being subject to ridicule and possibly work in this town once again. Isn't that enough?"

Chase continued to study Patricia, and his scrutiny caused her to fidget in her seat. Finally, the suspense became too much for her. She blurted out, "What do you say, Chase, are you in or out?"

Her words made her sound unsure of herself for the first time that night. Chase knew that he had the upper hand and he was going to press his advantage, if it was the last thing he did. He leaned back in his chair and continued to study Patricia, just to see her squirm. When the music ended, he knew that she was ripe for the picking.

"So, what do you think, darling? It's a dumb idea, isn't it?" she finally said, appearing to second-guess herself. "I should just stop overthinking this whole—" Patricia babbled before reaching for her purse.

"No, Patricia. It's a good idea," Chase said, placing his hand over hers to keep her from leaving. "But what do you get out of this whole deal?" he asked again, knowing that she hadn't given him a straight answer. "And before you try to feed me that watered-down explanation again, I need you to know that I suspect that you are full of crap."

"Why, the satisfaction of helping you regain some semblance of your dignity back. The added bonus is putting that boorish, stick-in-the-mud in her place. Isn't that enough for you, Chase?" Patricia replied innocently, still trying to sell him the same old story.

The saying, 'Like a moth to the flame,' flashed through Chase's head.

"I have to hand it to you, Patricia Grant. You are really quite devious," he said somberly. "And I will let this go for now because I am such a good guy. I think I might even get started this weekend, provided," he paused for dramatic effect, "I receive the right kind of incentive."

"Chase Stoneman, whatever do you mean?" Patricia asked, hoping that she sounded naïve enough to get out of the tight spot she suddenly found herself in, knowing exactly what Chase was hinting at. There was absolutely no doubt in her mind, and she really didn't like the look he was giving her. It made her feel cheap, somehow. Somewhere along the way Chase had turned the tables on her and gained the upper hand, and she had lost control of this situation.

Where did I go wrong? Patricia pondered.

A sinking feeling settled in the pit of her stomach and she knew that she would have to swallow her pride and pay the tab in full before the night was over.

Placing a warm hand upon her leg beneath the table, Chase winked and smiled brashly at her.

"Oh, I am fairly certain that you know exactly what I am getting at, but just in case there is any confusion, let me spell it out for you—"

Patricia's smile quickly faded as she took a deep breath and let it out.

"Don't bother," she said flatly. "Down and dirty in the parking lot or did you have something else in mind?"

"What kind of crass individual do you take me for, Patricia Grant? And don't you act as if you've never thought about us together before," Chase said, "I know I have."

"I need another drink," Patricia said as her tone took on a bland quality.

Chase lifted his hand to flag down the cocktail hostess before she passed them by.

"We need two more of whatever the lady is having," he said, practically crooning the words. "Then we will be closing out the tab." His smile widened.

The waitress gave Chase a knowing wink and glanced at Patricia before disappearing into the crowd. She returned a few minutes later with two *Between the Sheets Martinis*, and the bill, which she presented to Chase with a flourish.

Patricia swallowed a sigh as a sardonic smile once again crossed Chase's lips. He folded up a couple of bills and tucked them between the scantily clad waitress's breasts. "I added a little something extra for the college fund, Jesse."

Pursing her lips together, Jesse blew Chase a kiss and said, "Thank you very much, Mr. Stoneman. As always, it has been my pleasure to serve you." Then she winked at them both. "You two have a lovely evening."

Bringing two fingers to his brow, Chase grinned and saluted the young lady. "Oh, I intend to, Jesse. Until next time."

By this point, Patricia was truly regretting her decision to involve Chase Stoneman in her little scheme.

This is going to be a very long evening, she thought, taking a long sip of her Martini in an attempt to calm her jagged nerves.

"Drink up, my dear, so we can get onto the main event of the evening."

A groan of exasperation escaped Patricia's lips, covered up by the loud music as she brought the martini glass to her lips, in hopes that the liquid would do its job and dull her senses.

The expectant smile stayed permanently pasted to Chase's lips.

"Did you say something, darling?" he asked, raising an eyebrow.

With a sweet smile, Patricia began to say, "No darling, but I was thinking—"

Quickly, Chase put a finger to her lips.

"Now there is no need for you to trouble that pretty, little head of yours with any more thoughts tonight. I'll take it from here." The forced smile on her lips vanished as Patricia contemplated just how much pressure it would take to snap a finger with her teeth. Then with a calculated shake of her head she pushed the image out of her mind, reminding herself that she needed him.

"Of course not, Chase, darling. Whatever you feel is best," she simpered, while pushing her disgust for him further down with another long sip of her drink.

"Good. Now finish up so that we can go," he insisted, bringing her hand to his lips and placing a wet kiss on the back of it. "I am getting excited just thinking about us."

Lord help me, I think I'm going to be ill, Patricia lamented as she turned to gaze out the window, rolling her eyes, while he kissed her hand a second time.

CHAPTER 4

*C*atherine was so wound up about her new position that she couldn't sleep. Her raw nerves and to-do lists were never-ending. Everything kept running through her mind in an unceasing loop. Finally, she gave in to the voice screaming at her to get up and do something. Throwing the covers back, she climbed out of bed and padded to the bathroom to splash cold water on her face. Then, walking out into the kitchen, she started a pot of coffee and waited for the first cup to be ready before heading back into the bedroom.

It was four-thirty, Saturday morning. She was groggy but awake. Taking a seat at her desk which faced the large, wall-to-wall window that looked out towards the ocean, she allowed her mind to focus on the task at hand. There was no light yet coming over the horizon, and Catherine stared into the pre-dawn darkness.

With a strong cup of coffee in hand, she began to work on the reorganization plan that had been going around and around her head for hours. Come Monday morning, she was going to shake everyone up with her brilliant strategy. The only problem was, she didn't exactly know all of the details of that plan yet.

Just as she had always done in college and in life, Catherine first drafted a rough outline. She would ponder her plan, weigh the pros and cons of every move, then make some calculated decisions before finalizing the details. This had always worked for her in the past. She simply had to focus her energy and not allow herself to get distracted.

Two hours passed as she diligently laid out the plan. Everything was coming together as the sun began to lighten the sky. Catherine stopped working to stretch her legs and pour herself another cup of coffee.

Standing in the kitchen, her stomach complained loudly, and she pulled the refrigerator door open and peered inside. Its meager contents consisted of a nearly empty, expired carton of milk, half a stick of butter, a shriveled-up orange and an apple in the same condition, and a jar of garlic-jalapeno green olives with exactly four olives left swimming around in half a bottle of juice. Half a bottle of Chardonnay, two pieces of bread, and a half-eaten box of Sweet and Sour chicken brought home over a week ago from the takeout place two blocks away sat on another shelf. *This is truly a sad state of affairs*, she thought to herself.

Slipping a slice of bread into the toaster, Catherine looked out the window while she waited for it to pop-up. Four sandpipers ran up and down the beach with the tide and a seagull dove into the water to retrieve a fish. She loved the quiet solitude of dawn. It always made her feel renewed.

Absently, she twisted the gold band around her finger as she stared out to sea.

She caught sight of a lone surfer carrying his board out towards the early morning surf.

Who was that? Catherine wondered as she squinted against the early sunrise. From this distance, he seemed familiar—but she couldn't put her finger on why. With the rays of dawn in her face, she tried to separate his silhouette from the shapes of the rising waves. He had a handsome, lanky build, with long arms and legs that reminded her of her attractive neighbor. Oh yes, it was Jake from next door.

Catherine wanted to look away and ignore the fact that he even existed, but she couldn't. His graceful gait and the ease in which he carried himself were mesmerizing. She heard the toaster pop, yet she still stood there gazing out of the window at him as he casually dropped his towel and kept walking straight into the water without breaking his stride.

Once waist-deep in the water, Jake seemed to soar over the waves with such ease and grace that Catherine found herself wondering if he was actually human or some mythical sea god pretending to be human. She shook her head to clear Jake from her mind. What was it about him that had her so annoyed last night?

Jake paddled out a bit further before turning around. Still straddling his board, he leaned over, furiously paddling away from a large wave headed his way, then jumped up in a flash when the wave picked him up and jettisoned him towards the shore.

Catherine held her breath, anticipating Jake tumbling off his board as the wave seemed to engulf him, swallowing him and the board whole. In a blink, Jake shot out of the wave on the other side, still perched atop his board and unharmed.

Turning away, Catherine popped her toast back down and waited twenty seconds before popping it back up and spreading warm butter on top. A part of her wished she could be as free as Jake Ryan, able to enjoy the early waters of her beloved beach, rather than simply staring out at it from the window.

"Maybe later," she said out loud, slumping her shoulders forward as she headed back into the other room to finish her task. "When my work is done. Work first, play second," Catherine repeated the well-rehearsed words she'd learned from her grandmother.

Sitting down at her desk, Catherine took another look out the window at Jake in the water. She could see her reflection in the window and smiled sadly. Lifting her chin just a touch as if she were looking down her nose at herself, she asked, "Who are you and why is this job so important to you?"

A split second passed before she answered, "I'm Catherine Lawrence and it has been my dream to enter the political arena for years." Lowering her chin now to reflect upon the answer she'd just given, she said, "Are you sure that's your final answer?" Shaking her head, Catherine leaned forward, resting her chin upon her hand. "You mean, this is the promise that you made to your deceased grandmother and now you feel that it is the only path you are afforded, you overachiever."

Looking out the window toward the ocean again, Catherine searched for the figure of Jake on his board, but he was nowhere to be found. Somewhere deep down she felt a pang of regret. Taking a bite of the toast, Catherine began to type on her keyboard as she ignored the outside world.

"No one else can close the door that God has opened for you," she quietly said under her breath. That was something that Grandma Alice had said to her many times before her death.

"I miss you, Alice," she whispered, "and wish you were here with me now."

She drafted a plan for the coming week, listing her pros and cons before pressing save. Six hours, four cups of coffee and one slice of toast later, her tasks were finished. Everything that had been keeping her awake was written down and organized on the computer screen before her—a comprehensive plan that she could take to Russell on Monday morning. It was her roadmap of how they were going to win the gubernatorial race and put Tillman in the Governor's Mansion. Catherine's world was righted once again and she felt she was back in control.

Remembering the meager contents of her refrigerator, her stomach grumbled loudly. Catherine realized that she would have to go shopping before she starved to death.

She could see the headlines now.

'Spinster dies alone in her condo. No one discovered her corpse for three days.'

She had been so preoccupied with work, that she'd neglected to do the grocery shopping and was now regretting it.

Her stomach grumbled once more. Throwing on a pair of jogging pants, a sports bra, t-shirt, and lightweight running jacket, Catherine slipped her feet into her running shoes and laced them up. Tucking a debit card into the zippered pocket of her jacket, she pulled a hair tie from her pocket and put her hair up into a high ponytail.

Catherine locked the front door behind her and placed her earbuds in, setting her phone to Janet Jackson's

Rhythm Nation. Then, she slipped it into the band on her arm and headed out. The rhythmic, heart pounding beat always got her feet moving and her blood pumping as she walked down to the end of the condos to stretch.

Catherine did twenty-five lunges before beginning her four-mile run, then hit the grocery store on her way back, just a few blocks from her condo.

Carrying her groceries, she adjusted her reusable bags under her arms as she walked along the boardwalk. She climbed the three steps as she headed down her row of buildings, admiring the beautiful ocean and the birds flying overhead. The heavy contents of her overflowing bags blocked her view slightly as she continued towards her door.

She was giving herself a mental pat on the back for a good workout when something caught on her foot and she tripped.

"What in the world!" she cried, just before crashing to the ground at the same time as the surfboard toppled over with a mighty clatter.

Hitting her knees hard, Catherine's bags of groceries flew out of her hands and scattered upon the deck. The apples and oranges were still rolling about when all of a sudden, Jake opened his door.

Jake quickly stepped out onto the deck, with a towel wrapped about his waist. He squatted down next to Catherine who was still down on all fours.

"Crickey, love, what happened here? Are you hurt?" he asked, lifting her to her feet, the surfboard leash still wrapped around her foot.

Her eyes worked their way up his torso, along the plush green towel hugging his midsection. Catherine couldn't help staring at his well-formed abs and chest before making her way up to his concerned eyes.

"Obviously I fell," Catherine said. "I think I got a splinter."

"Let me see," Jake insisted, taking her hand into his. "It's small. I can take care of that in a snap."

Staring up into his deep blue eyes, Catherine could feel herself drowning in the depths of them, unconsciously resting her other hand upon his dampened chest to steady herself.

It wasn't until a few seconds later that she realized she was staring dumbfounded, when he said, "Are you alright, Catherine?" a second time.

She took a step back as her eyes traveled downward and noticed Jake's muscular thigh peeking out from the side of his towel. "Yes." She cleared her throat. "I'm perfectly able to remove a splinter."

Quickly bringing her eyes back up to his face, Catherine noticed his dampened hair clinging to his head. Diverting her eyes from him, Catherine bent over to retrieve the apples and oranges scattered about.

Then Jake squatted down next to her to retrieve a couple of lemons that were threatening to roll off the step, causing Catherine to gasp as his leg darted out from the towel again. She stood up abruptly.

Jake stood upright, handing her the bag of groceries. "What is the matter with you?" he asked before noticing her eyes looking skyward. "What are you looking at?" He tipped his head back to see what she was looking at before realizing that there was nothing there.

Bringing her eyes down again, Catherine found herself gawking at Jake's perfectly formed, muscular chest and stomach. She felt her cheeks flush when she noticed that his towel was still parted, showing off a very lean, muscular leg. Shaking her head to clear her sudden, illicit thoughts, Catherine covered her eyes as Jake turned back around to retrieve another bag of groceries from the ground.

"I tripped over that...that...thing over there," she stammered, pointing at the offending leash laying in her path. She felt embarrassed to find herself tongue-tied.

Jake couldn't help himself as he gave a small chuckle.

"Didn't anyone ever teach you to watch where you were going?" he teased.

"Didn't anyone ever teach you to put your things away so that people didn't trip over them?" she quickly fired back, irritated that he found the entire situation amusing. "And while we are talking, I truly need to know. Do you ever wear clothes?"

"Oh, sorry, love. I was just getting out of the shower when I heard this loud commotion in front of my door." Jake gave her a sloppy grin. "I didn't realize there was a dress code when coming to the aid of a beautiful neighbor. I'll keep it in mind for the next time I come running."

Ready to fire back another nasty retort, Catherine glanced down at the ground to see her carton of eggs broken and dripping yellow ooze onto the ground. "Oh... no! My eggs," she cried, bending over, picking up the carton to see if there were any eggs that could be salvaged.

The distress in her voice drew Jake's eyes to the ground as he adjusted his nearly-slipping towel.

"I'm sorry about that. Really, I am. No worries, I'll replace them," he insisted. "And I'll clean up this mess as well."

Taking a deep breath, Catherine immediately dropped the carton back down on the ground with a heavy sigh. Then she stood up, stepped around the mess, unlocked her door, and entered her home with a quick glance back at Jake over her shoulder.

CHAPTER 5

*C*atherine stepped into her new position with elegance and style. She found she was perfectly comfortable giving directions to the large group of people under her. Everyone except Patricia Grant, who refused to fall in line.

There wasn't anything too obvious about Patricia or her attitude that Catherine could put her finger on. It was just a nagging, intuitive feeling that left her uncertain about Patricia's motives, especially when a sappy sweet smile was plastered to her perfectly painted lips.

Catherine had studied enough deceitful people in her life to know that there was something off about Patricia's behavior. Something was brewing just beneath the surface. Catherine felt as if she needed to have eyes in the back of her head, and it was becoming quite tedious. Someone mentioned to her that Patricia had tried to stir the office against Catherine. But as far as Catherine was concerned, it was simply office gossip. Nothing had come of it, so she'd left it alone.

Catherine took her eyes off Patricia so that she could flip through Russell's schedule for the next week. Then, her phone rang. By the time she hung up the phone, Catherine sensed that someone was standing behind her and turned to see Patricia.

"Is there something that you need from me, Patricia?" she asked, blocking her view of the laptop screen.

Patricia took a step closer and smiled.

"No, thank you, Miss Lawrence. I have everything I need."

Catherine took a deep breath, trying to control her fury. She didn't know what Patricia had been searching for, but apparently, she had seen what she needed from Russell's schedule. How could she have been so foolish?

Closing that page, Catherine watched Patricia saunter off. The woman was practically skipping back to her desk.

Deciding that no real harm had been done, Catherine pulled up the latest poll numbers.

Four weeks had passed, and already Tillman's numbers were up by twenty points. Russell was over the moon and couldn't stop praising Catherine for it.

The Medicare and Pensions speech she had written when she'd first taken over had turned the tide. Catherine and Russell both knew that if Patricia had written the speech, the results would not have been the same. It all tied into the immigration and unemployment problems Florida had been experiencing. Given his constituents in South Florida, Catherine tirelessly prepped Russell to address the concerns of those demographics before his upcoming speech as well.

Mindy from the HR department approached Catherine's desk, drawing her attention back to the present.

"Boss, I just had a few matters to discuss with you. Is now a good time?" she asked.

"Sure, Mindy. It's a perfect time. Do we need to go into my office or is this good?"

"We are going to need privacy. The matters I need to discuss with you are a little sensitive."

"Certainly," Catherine said, leading the way into her office, closing the door behind them. The room had a large glass window that looked out over the rest of the office so that she could keep an eye on the comings and goings of everyone.

Taking a seat behind her desk, they got down to business.

Her meeting with Mindy concluded, Catherine prepared to go home for the night. It had been a productive and fulfilling day and she was mentally exhausted.

Catherine's current schedule didn't always allow her to make it home by seven, yet she always looked forward to her workouts on the treadmill, located on the back veranda. The cool damp breezes from the ocean made the workouts bearable while the velvety hues and shadows of the sunsets were a motivating factor.

Tonight, Jake was about twenty yards away, bent over his slate patio table, working on his surfboard. His perfectly chiseled back muscles jumped as he rubbed a bar across his surfboard. He switched sides, walking around his board now as he faced her.

Catherine watched as his muscles flexed and his shoulders beaded with sweat. It hadn't gone unnoticed by her that every day that week he had been without his shirt as he paraded in front of her each night. She found it distracting and even dangerous. Just the night before, she'd missed a step and nearly fallen off her treadmill. His torso had glistened enticingly in the sun, displaying his glorious, Adonis chest and well-tanned six-pack abs.

"Who wouldn't be distracted by all of that?" she murmured under her breath before reaching for her phone to turn the music up louder, averting her eyes when he looked up in her direction.

"Does he even own a shirt?" she mused, dabbing her forehead with a towel before turning the speed up on the treadmill to distract herself.

She could not afford to think about any man in her life right now, especially that one. It was bad timing. And besides, a man like Jake Ryan would *not* be a good fit for someone who was running a governor's campaign, Catherine thought. Then she saw him waving at her.

Instantly she went weak in the knees, nearly stumbling on the treadmill a second night in a row. Fortunately for her, she managed to hit the right button, slowing the machine down enough to keep her feet from becoming tangled up and tripping like a fool.

She checked the time to see if she had worked out long enough before grabbing her bottle from the holder and taking a sip of water. She gave him a nod, acknowledging his presence, never dreaming that he would take it as a sign to come over.

Jake had a hopeful look on his face and Catherine noticed that he ran inside after waving to her. She recalled the afternoon that he'd teased her, asking if she had pajamas with pinstripes on them. She hadn't found his humor funny at all. His awkward attempts to joke with her fell flat.

"Hey there, Catie," he called out, deciding that she looked more like a Catie than a Catherine.

"Mr. Ryan," she nodded coolly.

He laughed at her formality.

"There is an entire beach that you could jog on, why the treadmill?"

Catherine stepped off the treadmill, looking up at him as perspiration dripped down the side of her forehead. She kind of liked the way he called her Catie.

Her grandmother had been the only other person in her life to have called her Catie. It sounded nice when he said it, which made her smile.

"So, you do smile."

"Of course, I smile. Everyone smiles."

"It's just, well, I've never really seen you smile before. Oh, by the way, before I forget, here are the eggs I owed you," he said, offering up a carton of eggs as a peace offering. "I'm sorry again for leaving the leash of my board out and tripping you and for not getting these to you earlier but I could never catch you at the right moment. So, tell me, why do you run on the treadmill instead of the beach?"

She was trying to catch her breath. "Think nothing of it, Mr. Ryan. I've forgotten all about the matter with the eggs," she said, taking them from him and placing the carton inside the sliding glass door before turning back around to face him. "I have my reasons for the treadmill, and I don't feel that I know you well enough to share that kind of story with you," she added, scrunching up her nose at him.

"Oh, come on, how can you say such a thing? I thought we were friends."

She shook her head. "Is that how you would describe our relationship, Mr. Ryan?"

"Jake, please, I insist."

Easing past him, Catherine grabbed a larger towel.

"Alright, Jake. I need to cool off," she said, walking towards the water.

"I'll come with you."

She looked at him over her shoulder. "You don't have to do that."

"But I want to. Besides, it gives you a chance to tell me the story of why you prefer to run on a treadmill rather than utilize this amazing beach."

Her cheeks burned and her heart-rate quickened as he ran to catch up to her. "Really, the story is a bit embarrassing. I don't like to talk about it. Don't you have a board to wax or something?"

His nearness excited her. She wondered if he could hear her heart racing.

"But I really want to hear the story. You can trust me, I won't laugh. I will even take an oath that I will never retell the story to another living soul, if you like," he said, crossing his heart. "Come on, you can't begin a story and not finish it."

She glanced at him over her shoulder as she reached the ocean's edge, then turned around, sliding out of her spandex pants, to reveal a pair of bikini briefs. Her T-shirt followed revealing a matching top. She deposited the clothing items along with her towel upon the sand.

Jake froze at the water's edge, momentarily stunned by her actions before recovering. He quietly whistled between his teeth as Catherine pulled the tie from her dampened pony-tail, allowing her auburn hair to fall down her back before walking into the water to cool off.

Jake stood admiring her shapely figure, athletic legs and the fullness of her bottom. Instinctively, he crossed his arms over his waist, a move he had been doing since seventh grade. One arm went straight down in front of the middle of his shorts and his other arm grasped his elbow. It made him look casually cool, or so he'd decided years ago, while covering up anything that should arise.

Catherine looked over her shoulder again and saw Jake was still standing there.

What did he want? she wondered as he continued to stare at her.

Choosing to ignore him and the awkwardness of the situation, she dove into the ocean, cooling off her overheated body in Florida's evening waters. The waves lapped lightly over her arms and belly as she stood up, letting the water bead down her skin. Each wave was like a soothing balm as it washed over her, throwing a salty mist up into the air. Each time, one wave receded and another one rolled in, quickly cooling her and causing goosebumps to form on her skin. Catherine took a deep, relaxing breath for the first time that day, allowing her stress to wash away with the water.

"So, am I going to get to hear that story or not?" Jake asked, breaking into her moment of calmness.

She jumped back, startled by the sound of his incredibly husky, sexy, Australian accent. Was it her imagination or did he sound differently when he was so close to her? Despite his closeness, Catherine didn't have any real desire to step away.

"Mr. Ry—"

"Jake," he interrupted, cocking his head at her.

"Jake," Catherine said as his name rolled off her tongue. Something about him thoroughly confused her thoughts, causing her to feel strangely giddy when he was around. She found herself mesmerized by his beauty.

"Jake," she began again, sounding very pragmatic, "it's a rather embarrassing story. Let me just say that the treadmill gives me the opportunity to enjoy working out while admiring the beach in any weather condition," she said with a smile.

Jake took a step closer to her and she resisted her instinct to touch him. Instead, she gave him a stern look.

"What are you doing?"

Smiling from ear to ear, Jake was definitely flirtatious.

"Just admiring you."

"Do you have to do it so close to me?"

"Please," he begged, "If you tell me your story, I'll tell you an embarrassing story." Jake grinned boyishly, looking down at her.

She took a deep breath. Catherine liked his boyish charm and smiled back.

"It's really a stupid story but if it means that much to you, I'll tell you."

"You know, I kind of like really stupid stories," he said with a simple smile that showed off his beautifully white teeth. "Would you like to sit on the beach and dry off for a while? You can tell me the story—or not. It's entirely up to you."

Jake was just too handsome for his own good, Catherine decided, walking to the spot on the beach where she'd dropped her clothes. She pulled her spandex leggings back on after drying off with the towel, then pulled her shirt over her head and wrapped the towel around her shoulders to catch the water dripping from her hair. The quickly cooling air made her break out into goosebumps.

"Alright. So, I have promised you a story and a story you shall get," she said, feeling a need to share something intimate about herself with this man.

After all, what was the worst that could happen? she thought. *He could laugh but then again, she probably would chuckle too, if it had happened to someone else.*

"Only if you don't mind telling me," he answered. "No pressure."

Sitting down on the white sand, untouched by water, Catherine couldn't help feeling pleased that Jake sat next to her, close enough to warm her with his body heat.

"I already think you're a really good storyteller," Jake said, "because the suspense is killing me." He grinned, noticing that she had goosebumps. "Are you cold?" His concern showed on his face.

"Just a little but I'm fine," she insisted.

Suddenly, Catherine was anxious to share her story with Jake. She was feeling comfortable with him and wanted to trust him. "Last year when I— when I was running on the beach," her speech halted, "I began later than usual, and the sky had darkened, making it difficult to see where I was going on my way back to the condo."

She shuddered, and her cheeks flushed bright red as she took another deep breath.

"I was looking up at the night sky, admiring the stars, when a wave rolled in with a school of stingrays. That's when it happened."

"When what happened, Catie?"

"I jogged right into a school of stingrays—those nasty bottom dwelling marine creatures with their long, poisonous, serrated spikes at the base of their tails. I couldn't believe it at first. I realized my mistake immediately but it was too late to do anything about it. I fell to the ground. The pain was excruciating! I called out for help but it was late and no one was on the beach. Laying on the ground in pain and no one coming to help really makes you ponder your life." She smiled up at him and noticed that he wasn't laughing at her as some people had done when she'd shared her story before.

"So," Catherine continued, "About fifteen minutes in I remembered that I had my phone in my back pocket. I called 911 and described to them where to find me, but it still took them another twenty minutes to get to me. I felt like such an idiot." She looked down at her hands, resting in her lap, as Jake watched the waves roll in and out.

"That must have been awful. No wonder you don't like to run on the beach anymore." Jake reached a hand out to take hers.

"Well, there it is," Catherine said, looking up and gazing out at the water.

Jake placed a finger beneath her chin, forcing her to look up at him. "I'm not sure that I would go into the water after that kind of trauma myself," he said.

She blushed an even darker shade of red.

"I had to be hospitalized because I had been hit 15 times by the little monsters, and their barbs were still deeply rooted in my leg and foot. Surgery was the only way they could get them all out," Catherine added, turning her foot over to show him the scars.

He gently touched her foot, running a finger along the prominent scars at the bottom of her foot and her inner ankle, causing her to shiver. She wasn't sure if it was from the cold night air or his touch.

Jake reached out and placed a comforting arm around her shoulders.

"That really must have been a horrible experience for you. I'm sorry it happened. Thank you for trusting me with your story."

A few minutes passed while the two of them continued to look out at the ocean, watching the tide swell, before either one of them spoke again.

"Let me ask you another question, if I may," Jake says. "Have you ever been in love?"

"Yes. Sure, I have," she answered defensively.

"No. I mean really in love. The kind of love that makes you abandon all reason and throw caution to the wind. The kind of love that makes you trade logic for passion?"

Turning her head to the side, Catherine sat in silence for a moment, pondering his question.

"I knew it, you haven't," Jake said.

Suddenly feeling awkward, Catherine jumped up, wiping the sand from her leggings.

"Well, it's getting late, and I need to go in now. I have a very tight schedule to keep."

"I'm sorry. Did I say something wrong?" Jake said. "Don't go," he pleaded, reaching out to take her hand as Catherine took a step back.

"It isn't that," she said, dusting the sand from her backside and not really looking at him. "I really do have to stay on schedule, or my entire evening falls apart. You understand, right?"

Jake reached for Catherine's hand again but stopped short of touching her. Just like that, the relaxed mood had been broken, and Catherine retreated into herself. With a shy smile, she turned and quickly headed back toward her condo.

Jake ran to catch up, walking alongside her.

"A gentleman always walks a young woman home. My Mum trained it into me since I was a young boy."

"I wouldn't want you to go against your upbringing."

"Thank you again for sharing your story with me."

Catherine smiled.

"Goodnight," she said, before going inside.

"Goodnight, and don't forget to lock your door."

"I won't," she said, feeling light and giddy.

Jake stood on the sand watching her walk into her condo. She was an enigma. A delicate, intricate puzzle that would take time and patience to figure out.

Jake had never been the kind of man to stay in one place too long, let alone form an attachment. He preferred to keep things light and simple, moving often to keep the excitement from fading.

So why am I contemplating staying here now? he asked himself.

The last rays of daylight were setting on the horizon. Jake pulled his gaze away from Catherine's sliding glass door.

He walked out a few feet, sat down on the sand and looked out at the ocean. He wondered what made her different. He'd been drawn to her from the beginning, for some inexplicable reason, but how could he want the very person who was his polar opposite? There seemed to be no rhyme or reason to his feelings.

His phone rang.

"Jake Ryan. No, Stan, this is a perfect time to discuss whatever you need," he said, before pausing to listen.

"I wouldn't invest in that one. I've been reading up on that particular business's holdings and I don't believe that they are on solid ground yet. They are too new and haven't been tested yet. Anyone can pad the books, Stan. The real test is time. Well, you can do what you want. I'm just saying, I'd wait a couple of months and see how their numbers are then. You're welcome, mate. Sure. Anytime, my friend."

Getting up slowly, he dusted the sand from his shorts and began to walk towards his condo. He looked down, stopping to measure his footprint next to Catherine's in the sand. Her feet were so petite next to his.

As he passed under her window, he was surprised to see someone in a black hoodie taking pictures of Catherine through the thin curtains of her bedroom.

"Hey you!" Jake shouted, startling the man holding a camera in his hand. "Stop!"

The man took off running for the other side of the condos towards the parking lot as fast as he could, with Jake in pursuit. As Jake rounded the corner, he heard a car start up and speed off.

Rounding the corner of the building, Jake saw Catherine step out of her door. She looked startled.

"Who were you shouting at?"

"There was a hooded pervert snapping pics of you through the window," Jake said. He was irritated by the fact that he hadn't caught the guy.

"You really should pull your curtains closed," he admonished. "It's like a bloody peep show."

"I'll keep that in mind - next time I get dressed," Catherine retorted angrily before slamming the door closed and leaning against it.

"I'm sorry, Catie," Jake called to her through the closed door. "I didn't mean it; I spit the dummy. I mean, I lost my temper, but I wasn't mad at you," he continued as he leaned up against her door. "I was just angry that I couldn't catch the bugger."

Both of them stood in silence, leaning against the same door from opposite sides. Neither one wanted to end the conversation on such a bad note.

Jake could hear her heavy sigh through the door.

"I am sorry I spoke to you like that, Catie," he finally said quietly, before giving up and walking over to his own door.

With one last look towards Catherine's door, Jake shook his head and stepped inside, quietly closing the door behind him.

Catherine heard his door close and slowly opened hers, to see if he really had gone. A moment of regret pierced her heart before she quietly closed her door and went back to work.

CHAPTER 6

*T*he weeks progressed, and the entire office was busily working to raise money for the *Meet Your Republican Candidate* Ball. Tillman's ability to campaign successfully hinged upon the money raised by this last event and everyone in the office was expected to attend. Tickets were five-hundred dollars a seat, and there were over four-hundred tickets left to sell.

Catherine was focused on the campaign speech. She needed to touch upon three main talking points: Medicare pensions, immigration, and unemployment. She hired five of the best speechwriters to craft the message, but found herself constantly correcting small errors in their work. Her intensive work was beginning to wear on her.

With only two weeks left to fill the seats, Catherine was relying heavily upon her top lobbyists: Patricia Grant, her 'problem child'; James Newton, a Harvard undergraduate who majored in Political Science; and

Roger Phillips, a Tulane graduate with a Masters in International Relations and Diplomacy. Then, there was Sarah Fischer, an Oxford Masters graduate, who was the winner of both a Rhodes Scholarship and a Harry S. Truman Scholarship.

Catherine was heavily relying on these four people to reach out to the Republican members of the Floridian Congress, community leaders, and the elite to sell entire tables rather than one seat at a time.

The outcome of this one dinner would determine Russell's standing as the state's Republican candidate. The stakes were high as Catherine pulled her lobbyists together for a meeting.

"I've called you in today to discuss our numbers," Catherine said, very matter-of-factly. "As you know, we have only heard back from sixty percent of our Republican party elite and we are down to the wire for this dinner. What is going on, people? I need to know if you can pull this thing together and get our bacon out of the frying pan," she said, looking around the room to see three heads bobbing up and down as their eyes darted towards Patricia.

Sitting behind her desk, Catherine took a deep breath, putting a smile on her lips despite her feeling of dread.

"Great. Then all will be well and our dinner will be a success. Can you all leave me your call sheets? I'd like to go over them," she said, dismissing them with a nod.

Patricia, James, Roger, and Sarah all stood to leave, depositing their call sheets upon Catherine's desk. She looked up when she noticed Patricia's sheet. "Patricia, could you please stay behind a moment?"

With a curt nod, Patricia continued to stand in front of Catherine's desk as the door closed quietly behind the others.

"Please, take a seat," Catherine said politely, gesturing with her hand to a chair directly in front of her. "Can you please explain to me why you are so far below everyone else in performance?"

Patricia looked Catherine in the eye.

"Well, you see, Miss Lawrence, I have been so busy with my other duties that I haven't been able to make all of those calls. I think that I—"

"Let me stop you right there, Miss Grant. I hired a speech writing team so that you would have time to focus on making those important calls," she said, interrupting Patricia. "And what could be more important than filling the seats?"

"I was also sick for two days," Patricia explained.

"You mean, the two days you took off without a warning?" Catherine asked. "You had a stunning tan upon your return."

"First of all, I got the tan from the weekend before, and then I got food poisoning that Monday and needed Tuesday to recover."

"Well, thank you for clarifying that for me, because I just figured you were playing hooky for those two days—"

"Food poisoning is no joke, Miss Lawrence. I could have died."

"So, you went to a hospital and were treated in the E.R. then?"

"Well, no," Patricia stammered. "But it was serious—"

"So, you didn't go to the hospital? Were you treated by a doctor?"

"Ah, ah, no but I was in rough shape and—"

"And you forgot how to operate a telephone to let me know what was going on with you?"

"I was throwing my guts up. Literally."

"If you don't have a doctor's note or an E.R. bill that shows that you were truly at death's door and you didn't call out sick, then you were playing hooky. And if that is true, then I expect you to make up the time and the calls that you missed on your own time. Do whatever it takes. Stay late and come in early. Just as long as the rest of those numbers are called by the end of our work week, which is in two days," Catherine informed her with a pleasant smile.

"But there is no way I am going to be able to do all of that—" Patricia began before Catherine cut her off.

"I'm sorry, but you are going to have to be responsible and make up the time. I can't give you anyone else to help you with your work. They all have assignments already.

If we are going to pull this dinner together, on time, we have to work as a team. Everyone has been doing their jobs, while you decided to take a couple of days off. You let the team down, Patricia. Now you have to make up for lost time. I'm sorry but that is the way it has to be."

With a stomp of her foot, Patricia had no choice but to agree. She turned on her pointed little heels and made her way back to her desk.

Patricia called Sarah over to her desk, saying something to her that caused Sarah to look in Catherine's direction, a look of bewilderment on her face.

Getting up from her desk, Catherine motioned for Sarah to come to her office.

"I'm not sure what Patricia just asked you to do, but I need you to know that I asked her to do her work. I want you to do what you were assigned to do and let Patricia clean up her own mess."

Looking relieved, Sarah let out a sigh of relief.

"Thank goodness," she said, shaking her head. "I already had plans for this evening and didn't want to stay later if I didn't have to."

"No, Sarah. You don't need to stay late. And thank you for all of your dedication and hard work over these last few weeks. I don't know what I would have done without you. You can tell Patricia that she can do her own work and if she gives you any trouble, just bring it to me."

"Thank you, Miss Lawrence. That means a lot to me."

"You better get some lunch before it gets any later," Catherine said, opening her office door and walking Sarah out.

"Thank you again, Miss Lawrence. I appreciate it."

"Think nothing of it."

As the next week began, over three-quarters of the tickets were sold and the dinner was on track. The speech was finally finished and Catherine felt as if she could take a deep breath for the first time since becoming the new campaign manager.

"Lawrence, my office. Now!" Tillman's voice echoed through the building, silencing everyone.

Standing up and straightening her shoulders, Catherine looked around.

"Let's get back to work people. Nothing to see here," she said, walking towards Tillman's office, thinking to herself, *Except for a train wreck, with dead corpses scattered about in full view.*

After an hour and a half of discussing the numbers and reviewing the previous week's activities with Tillman, Catherine presented the next week's plan to him. She felt even more pressure to have everything perfect—even if it meant she had to stay at the office twenty-four hours straight. Catherine already felt like a noodle that had sat too long in a pot of boiling water.

Tillman walked Catherine to the door of his office, clapped her on the back and made a show of being happy. He smiled before shutting his door. After another thirty minutes of phone calls, Russell gathered his coat and said goodbye on his way out the door. He was going home for the day.

Catherine knew he was concerned about the upcoming dinner, but he was even more stressed out by what was going on at home.

Angela had asked him to sleep in the other room and was acting distant lately, Russell had confided in Catherine. She made a note to call Angela and find out what was going on.

Her stomach grumbled, and she felt sick as she realized she had missed lunch and barely eaten breakfast.

Catherine took a few minutes to inquire as to who had skipped lunch, then asked one of the interns to place a large order for sandwiches from the local deli. It was the least she could do for everyone picking up the slack and working through their lunch hour.

"How are you feeling?" Catherine asked Patricia.

"Fine."

"Can I get you anything?" she asked, her tone calm and measured. "Tea, a cough drop perhaps?"

Shaking her blonde head, Patricia turned her sultry eyes to Catherine.

"No, thank you. I will be fine."

"Great. I brought you a turkey avocado sandwich because I know it's your favorite. Oh, and Patricia?"

"Yes," Patricia answered, looking up at her.

"Don't even think about checking out early this evening," Catherine said, "because you and I will be staying late tonight."

"Of course. You're the boss," Patricia said, staring after her as she made her way across the office.

Catherine turned to address the office.

"Don't forget, people. Tillman is counting on each and every one of you to boost his numbers. It's up to you, and you, and especially you," she said pointing at certain people, "to take us to the Governor's office. We all have to do our part." She emphasized her point by turning around and looking directly at Patricia.

Patricia's cheeks turned crimson as she got busy making calls, ignoring the sandwich Catherine had placed in front of her on the desk.

Several people looked in Patricia's direction before going back to work.

Patricia seethed in silence at her desk as she glared at Catherine's back.

You may have won today's battle, Catherine Lawrence, she thought as she doodled across a piece of paper while she spoke to the person on the other end of the phone, *But I will win the war.*

Snatching up her purse from beneath the desk, Patricia looked around before pulling out her cell phone and dialing a number.

"We need to talk!" she said to the person on the other end of the phone. "I'll call you back in two hours when I'm in my car. And Chase, I want good news. Understand me? Good news!" Her sudden, harsh whispers drew looks from several people who turned to look at her.

Plastering a fake smile on her lips, Patricia hung up the phone without even saying goodbye, placed it back into her purse and casually slid it under the desk, as if she had simply been powdering her nose. She quickly picked up the office phone receiver and began dialing numbers again.

CHAPTER 7

$\mathcal{T}$he week closed with a triumphant bang. Patricia and the rest of the team pulled their numbers and managed to get the Republican elite to fill every last seat for the dinner. For the first time since taking over, Catherine felt confident that Tillman had a good chance at winning.

With only six weeks until the election, the polls showed Tillman's numbers not only climbing steadily but also surpassing his opponents by a large margin. The mid-September weather was predicted to be perfect for the *Meet Your Republican Candidate's* Dinner and Ball. It would be the last 'hurrah' before election day. The venue was at an aquarium, and depending on how everything went at Friday night's dinner, Catherine would have her first full weekend off through Sunday afternoon. Then it would be the big push to the end.

Someone in the office had asked Catherine if she was bringing a date to the event. She had given her usual retort, "Who has time to date?" But that answer was wearing thin even to her own ears.

It was 6:30 p.m. on a Thursday evening, and time for her usual workout, but Catherine was growing tired of the same routine. It was time to shake things up. She was feeling celebratory, which was completely out of character for her on a work night. So, instead of a jog on the treadmill, she decided to search for her favorite cubby in the dunes and watch the surf while flipping through a fashion magazine.

After all, she had earned a reprieve from her routine to relax and unwind properly. Tomorrow, she had penciled in gown shopping at three boutiques from 10 a.m. until noon. Her outfit had to be elegant yet professional, and not too flashy.

Catherine hated more than anything putting things off until the last minute but it couldn't be avoided. She'd had her hands full trying to save the campaign ship from sinking. She knew that the stores had just received new shipments for the upcoming social season and called ahead to have several new gowns held aside for her. It was nice to have connections, Catherine thought to herself with a smile.

She and Angela agreed to meet in the morning at ten to do the gown shopping together before getting a quick bite to eat and then get their manicure and hair appointments done together.

Catherine had promised Russell that she would talk with Angela and find out what was going on with her, since he had been unsuccessful at getting to the root of their problem.

Afterwards, she planned a walkthrough at the aquarium from four o'clock to check everything from place settings to food to the sound check. Her top four interns were supposed to meet her there as well. Catherine would pass out the assignments to them. The master list was already xeroxed and ready to go in her briefcase.

If all went according to plan, she could be out of there in an hour, giving her time to get ready and back in time to oversee the final preparations.

Kicking off her shoes as she walked in, Catherine grabbed the two magazines she'd picked up earlier so that she could get some idea of what types of dresses she might be looking for. She placed her shoes in their assigned spot in the closet and changed into a black bikini. Pulling on a white cover up, she grabbed her favorite flip-flops and chair, and locked the door behind her.

Catherine's private little cove was nestled among the sea oats, and she sighed deeply, breathing in the glorious sea air. There was nothing like it as far as she was concerned. It soothed her weary mind and rejuvenated her every time she visited it.

The Florida dunes were a series of little mounds and hills made by waves at night, but some of them were constant, made over time so they never really changed shape when the waters receded. From these mounds of sand, tall sprigs of golden reeds with wheat-like tops grew from the grass, known to all Floridians as sea oats. The sea oats growing on top of the semicircular dunes made perfect little cubbies for tanners, party goers, artists, and lovers in need of a little privacy.

Catherine had a favorite, secluded spot, straight outside her back door and a little to the left. It was nestled up alongside a small wall of mangrove bushes that led to the water's edge. It was the perfect place for someone like her who needed to escape the demands of the world, because it was so out of the way. She'd nicknamed it 'Catherine's little haven' the first time she threw a blanket down and rested her back up against the dune.

Settling down in her seat, Catherine got straight to business finding the perfect gown. After all, the day was quickly flying by and there would only be another hour and a half of daylight left. Catherine had yet to determine what a campaign manager's ball gown was supposed to look like. She groaned inwardly at the thought of what her nemesis, Patricia Grant, would most likely show up in. Something perfectly sexy, beautiful, and stunning. Her blonde hair would be perfectly coiffed and undoubtedly, she would be in the Republican Red. More than likely, it would be long, form-fitting, and completely inappropriate. Catherine knew there would be no outdoing Patricia for dramatics but maybe she could out do her in style and grace. If only she could figure out what she wanted.

Catherine began flipping through a copy of Vogue Couture and tried to focus on the gowns, when a far-off whoop of glee caught her attention. She looked up and there he was, Mr. Jake Ryan, and his perfect Greek god body. He was cutting through the water, seamlessly gliding in and out of the waves. His angles were one with the board as he crested the surf.

Catherine knew that she could've watched him for hours as he danced with his surfboard in the waves—his tanned, glistening form was so appealing and taut. She especially liked when he did a few tricky maneuvers in and out of the curls. Despite thinking the sport of surfing was silly, she couldn't help but feel impressed by Jake's skill and ease in the water as he commanded his board so effortlessly.

He was at least a hundred and fifty feet away from the shore when Catherine saw a four-foot fin rise up out of the water not ten feet behind his board. It was a shark. Without missing a beat, Catherine jumped up and ran to the water's edge. She wanted to get his attention without startling him or causing him to fall off the board. But how ? Should she yell? Use the whistle she always carried on her?

Catherine dug around in her bag and pulled out the whistle she'd carried since college. She began blowing it as loudly as she could. Once she had his attention she cupped her hands around her mouth so that her single word would reach him.

"Shark!"

The dorsal fin slowly slipped beneath the water. Catherine's shaking knees refused to hold her upright any longer as she sank down into the sand. Holding her breath, she clutched at her chest and watched Jake riding the wave.

Jake looked nervous, checking the water around him, as he made his way through the surf. He went over the sandbar and headed towards her, racing out of the water quickly with his board.

Catherine jumped to her feet and ran towards him.

"You're alive," she cried, searching his body with her eyes and hands for a mark.

"Whoa-oh," Jake chortled gruffly. "I'll be happy to get chased by a bull shark on a daily basis if this is the kind of reaction I can expect."

Splaying her hands against his chest, Catherine looked up, assuring herself that he was whole and intact.

"A bull shark!" she gasped, before paling. "They're dangerous, Jake. You could've been killed." Her knees began to shake again. She wrapped her arms around herself as a shiver shook her body.

"Aye. After I saw you screaming and pointing, I looked back and saw that there was something underwater, trying to take a bite out of me," Jake said with a chuckle. "By the way, nice job." He lifted her chin a touch so that their eyes met.

Catherine thought he was being patronizing and tried to pull away, but he held firm.

"Honestly, you saved my life."

Her heart skipped a beat, then began to race again as her cheeks flushed and she caught her lower lip between her teeth.

He grinned. "And I am grateful."

Catherine smiled up at him and took a step back.

"You know I couldn't let you go out like that. Too messy. The beach would be closed for days while they cleaned up the blood, guts, and all those body parts. Then there would be an investigation and they would have to hunt down that poor, defenseless bull shark and kill it. Not to mention, what an inconvenience it would be to me and what little leisure time I have, while they close the beach off."

"It warms the cockles of my heart to know that you have your priorities in the right place," he laughed, giving her a large grin, which mesmerized Catherine. "Of course, you have thought this all out ahead of time. How perfectly logical of you," he teased, cocking his head to one side.

Catherine couldn't help but notice that she felt light inside. She actually enjoyed Jake's teasing.

"Could I interest you in a little dinner or a stiff drink? My shout of course, since you did just save me life."

Catherine suppressed a smile at the slang he used to offer to pay for dinner, and the fact that she actually understood it.

"We both could use a stiff drink, but just one!" she warned. "My nerves are shot, and I have a busy day ahead of me tomorrow," Catherine said, quickly grabbing her blanket and magazines. "Follow me, I know the perfect place."

Catherine was surprised by her forwardness as she winked just before turning back around and walking up the beach with Jake following closely behind her.

Catherine directed Jake to sit in one of her reclining Adirondack chairs with a table between them. The seat he chose was right next to the treadmill.

She slipped inside to prepare their drinks, leaving the sliding door open. Catherine was always up for entertaining people and was well stocked with liquid refreshments.

"Name your poison?" Catherine called out.

"Whiskey on Ice."

"I think I can manage that order."

"You're my kind of lady," Jake called back with a chuckle.

"And I will have a Tom Collins with a twist of lemon," Catherine replied from just inside the door, a twinkle in her eye.

Catherine put a lit candle on the tray and carried it outside.

Jake raised his eyebrow as Catherine brought out the drinks on a beautiful tray and placed the five-wick citronella candle between them.

"I'm surprised to see you drink anything other than wine," Jake mused.

"Man can't live by bread or wine alone," she said, before turning to the task of lighting the tiki torches lining her patio.

"These will definitely keep those pesky mosquitoes away," she said, looking over her shoulder at him. Their eyes locked for a full beat before Catherine turned away.

When Catherine finished lighting the torches, she sat down, raised her glass and took a sip.

"So, tell me something about yourself that most people don't know," Jake said.

Catherine gave a little laugh, caught off guard by his direct question.

"You don't fool around, do you? Just straight to the questions. I respect that. Most people don't know that my mother left my father and me when I was very young. My Grandmother, Alice, raised me. She was a second mother to me. I lost her to cancer ten years ago, and then I lost my father a few months later to a car accident. There are those who say that death is final but I think they're wrong. The ones that are left behind grieve their loss long after they're gone." Catherine looked melancholy.

"I'm so sorry that happened to you."

"No, I'm sorry for bringing the entire mood of our conversation down," Catherine said.

Brightening up quickly, she added, "I can play the piano, and I took a couple photography classes in high school. I even won several awards for my body of work at the county fair when I was just eighteen. And now I'm the campaign manager for Russell Tillman. Ta-dah!" She concluded with a half bow from her seated position. Jake rewarded her with a round of applause.

With a slight lift of his eyebrows, Jake was impressed by her openness, and lifted his glass to her.

"Congratulations. Can I see your photos sometime?"

"Of course," Catherine responded, clinking her glass to his, "I have everything in a portfolio along with the ribbons I won that year. So, tell me something most people don't know about you, Jake Ryan?"

"Well, Miss Catie, most people don't know that I am the middle child. I have an older brother named Jesse and a younger sister, Jacqueline. But we all call her Jackie. I'm from Australia—"

"No. Really? I would never have guessed that by your accent," Catherine teased.

"Who's telling this, now?"

"I'm sorry, I couldn't resist. Please, go on."

"My Mum and Pops have been married since they graduated high school, and they are both the wisest, most down-to-earth people I know."

"Do you get along with your brother and sister?

"They're my best friends. We were always very tight growing up."

"That sounds lovely," Catherine said, looking out toward the ocean. "I was an only child, so I don't know the joy of having siblings. Angela and Russell are the closest I've come to that," she said with a sad smile.

"This Russell, he's your boss?"

"Sorry, of course you don't know who I'm talking about. Angela was my roommate back in college and is my best friend. She married Russell Tillman, who I worked with at the District Attorney's office for four years before he decided to enter into the political arena. I went with him and was just named his campaign manager. The two of them are like family to me. So, Jake, are you Democrat or Republican?"

"Nope, nope!" he cried. "My Pops taught me a good lesson when I was young, Miss Cate. When sitting down with a beautiful woman for the very first time, ye never speak of three things," Jake said, laying the accent on even thicker than usual as he held up one finger. "One, religion. God bless the Mother and all the saints," he whispered while making the sign of the cross, before holding up a second finger. "Two, football," adding, "Go Jaguars," under his breath, before holding up a third finger. "Three, politics!" he concluded with a smile before taking a sip of his drink.

"So, it's Miss Cate now," she said with a laugh. "No one has called me Cate since my grandmother." Catherine smiled, deciding that she not only liked the way it sounded when Jake called her Cate, she loved it. With a slight nod in his direction, she raised her glass to him. "I think I like it when you call me that. But don't let it get around or my tough gal reputation will be ruined."

"Then it's just between you and me, ah?"

"So, tell me more about these rules your father taught you?" Catherine questioned with a smile, kicking sand at his feet.

"Maybe later. When I get to know you better. There are certain things you don't discuss in polite company. Period," he concluded by taking another sip of his whiskey.

Catherine took a deep breath and a sip of her own drink.

"So, Mr. Ryan, enough about me. Tell me how you came to be a professional free-spirited waif, surfing every day. That is of course, when you are not in need of being rescued from a man-eating bull shark"

"Oh, it's a very serious, serious tale indeed..."

"No seriously. I want to know," Catherine insisted.

Throwing his hands up, Jake relented.

"Fine, I'll tell you, but if you breathe a word of this to the neighbors, I'll deny that I told you a thing."

"I swear, your secret is safe with me," she said, crossing her heart.

"I ran away from home and I'm hiding out here for a while. Just until I decide what I really want out of life. You see, it isn't always easy being the middle child, and sometimes you have to take a step back so that you can see things more clearly. My Mum always said that the blade of destiny has two edges."

"What does that mean?" Catherine asked.

"It means, Miss Cate, you can choose to stay or continue to search but you cannot choose to do nothing."

"Your mother sounds like a very wise woman. But what do you do for money?"

"At thirty-three, I have worked, saved and invested my money wisely, so I do alright for myself. I was an investment broker. Then I invested in my brother Jesse's business venture, and it has paid off handsomely."

"Well, that is good to hear. Nothing like a neighbor coming by to borrow a bucket of money to get through till the end of the month," she said, which made them both laugh.

"I like that. Is that an option?" Jake asked with a grin.

"I should say not."

"I was just checking." With a smile, Jake leaned over, cupping his hand over the side of her face.

"Don't tell anyone, but I keep my money under my mattress," he joked. "It makes for a lumpy night's sleep, but it's comforting to know where my money is."

"Wow. Good to know if I ever need to borrow a bucket or two," she laughed.

"I'm sure I won't stay here forever. There will be something that catches my fancy or something I want to work on. I just got burnt out and needed a break from life." Jake forced a half smile to his lips and Catherine could tell that there was something more to his story, but she didn't feel the need to pry.

"Speaking of mates," Jake said, swiftly changing the subject, "I'll be having a few come 'round tomorrow for a barbie, music, and such. I'd love for you to come and meet everyone."

"Oh, Jake, I'm so tempted by your offer. It sounds like it will be fun but I have a Candidates Dinner I'm running tomorrow night." Catherine cringed and began to fidget with her glass as she downed the rest of her drink.

"Are you alright, Catie?"

"No. I mean, yes! Of course, I'm fine. I'm really sorry, Jake, but I have to call it a night," she said, looking down at her watch. It was 8:30, only an hour behind schedule. "I'm so sorry, Jake. I'd love to meet your friends, but I have a very important event that I'm in charge of. It's an important fundraiser dinner that I really must finish preparing for," she said as she stood up.

Jake stood up as well.

"I really should go, then."

"I'm really glad that the shark didn't eat you and that you made it safely to shore," she said, blowing out the candle and putting the caps on the tiki torches before gathering up the glasses and placing them back on the tray.

"That really would have been terrible —" she sighed.

Jake took a step closer to her and laid a hand on her waist before capturing her chin with his free hand.

"Catie, don't forget to breathe. Everything is going to be alright."

Smiling up at him, Catherine took a deep breath and smiled, embarrassed by her silly reaction to being behind schedule.

"You're right of course. Everything will be great. I truly do wish that I could learn how to relax like you do. I would probably live longer," she said, staring up into Jake's face as it hovered over hers.

The heat from his body as it pressed up against hers was comforting. For a moment, she forgot why she was in such a hurry. Suddenly, Catherine wanted him to kiss her. His tranquil blue eyes were mesmerizing as his lips brushed across hers. The heat between them was undeniable and Catherine closed her eyes in anticipation of a kiss.

Touching his lips to hers, Jake gently pressed down harder and Catherine could see stars behind her closed eyelids. Pressing the back of his hand to her head to bring them even closer, Jake deepened the kiss as she wrapped her arms around his neck and parted her lips to allow his tongue to explore.

In a blink, Jake pulled back slightly as he smiled down at Catherine. "Everything is going to go well for you tomorrow. I just know it," he said, taking a step back. "Can I carry that tray in for you?"

She shook her head.

"No, thank you. I can do it. And thank you for the lovely evening, Jake Ryan."

"My pleasure, Miss Catie. If you get done early, my mates and I will still be around. The invitation is open if you can join us," he said.

"Thank you. That is so kind of you. Save me a hot dog just in case," she said.

He smiled down at her.

"I'll be sure to do that," he said with a nod. "Well, I'd better go so that you can get things done."

When Jake let go of her, Catherine felt a chill where their bodies had been touching. He leaned over and pulled the door open, allowing her to step into her condo. Then he handed her the tray.

"Don't forget to lock your door. You never know what kind of strange people are hanging around," he said, reminding her of the night he caught someone peeking in her window.

Catherine set the glasses into the sink and took a deep breath. Her lips still tingled from where they had touched Jake's.

Chase adjusted his high-power, infrared night vision goggles so he could see Catherine and her friendly neighbor more clearly. Patricia had been pressing him to dig up some dirt on Catherine but so far, there was nothing to report. Catherine Lawrence was just too squeaky clean.

He and Patricia dubbed her the Ice Queen.

"I guess she is beginning to thaw out after all," Chase murmured, packing up his equipment for the night.

CHAPTER 8

*C*atherine awoke the next morning feeling like she hadn't slept at all. In fact, she'd tossed and turned the entire night while an enticing, well-proportioned surfer was gliding through her dreams.

"Snap out of it, Catherine Lawrence! Today is an important day, and you have to be focused," she told herself as she climbed out of bed and headed towards the bathroom.

She was meeting up with Angela to go shopping for the perfect gown, then they would grab some lunch and get their hair and nails done at the little salon downtown.

Distracted, Catherine began making a list in her head. *Nothing dispels the thought of a man better than a well-organized list*, she thought. But her To-Do list was crowded by thoughts of last night and the way Jake's lips hovered over hers, making Catherine's heart pound frantically in her chest.

"What's wrong with me? Focus! You have to focus! Get your head in the game, Lawrence!" Catherine exclaimed.

Turning on her stereo and tuning the radio to her favorite '80s channel, Cindi Lauper's *Girls Just Wanna Have Fun* was playing. She began her morning ritual, confident that thoughts of Jake would swiftly leave her mind.

But they didn't.

Angela helped Catherine find the perfect gown for that evening's event in the second boutique they visited: A black and white floral pattern in organza that flowed gracefully over the skirt and to the floor, cinched tightly at the waist, with a modest, sweetheart top with thin straps that crisscrossed in the back. The waist gathered in the front with a large diamond shaped jewel. It was elegant, fashionable, and Catherine looked stunning in it.

Next, they stopped at a restaurant they both liked. Catherine ordered a mixed green salad with grilled salmon on the side and a vinaigrette dressing. Angela ordered a cheeseburger, which was out of character for her, but Catherine let it slide.

They arrived at the salon earlier than scheduled for their hair and nails which made Catherine's heart beat a little quicker. They were ahead of schedule and nothing thrilled an organizer more than being ahead of schedule.

Sitting side by side in the salon chairs with their feet in the warm, soothing water, Catherine knew that the moment was right to broach an intimate subject. "So,

Angie, Russell tells me that you have been distant lately. What's that about? Are you mad at him? Because he thinks that he's done something wrong and now you're mad at him."

Angela looked over at her friend with a sheepish grin and shook her head. Swallowing hard, she said, "Are you asking as my friend or as his campaign manager?"

"As your friend, Angie. Always as your friend and his."

"Good, because there's something that I've been wanting to tell someone, but it's a secret. It has to stay just between us. Promise me, Catherine. Swear it."

Knowing that Angela was serious about her pacts, Catherine crossed her heart.

"I swear it, Angie. Whatever you tell me will strictly stay between us and never cross my lips."

"I'm pregnant but I don't want Russell to know."

"Why not, Angie? He's your husband. Don't you think he has the right to know what's up?" Catherine said.

"Yes, of course he has the right to know. It's just after the last three miscarriages, I was afraid to say anything in case something happens to this one."

"But do you think it's right that you should go through this alone? Isn't that what being married is all about? Sharing your deepest, darkest secrets along with all of your pains?"

"No, silly, and that is why I'm telling you," Angela said, "so I don't have to go through this alone. What if I lose the baby again and he got his hopes up? He will be devastated."

"Oh, Angie. You have to let him in. He thinks you're mad at him about something and doesn't know how to talk to you about it. He said that you asked him to sleep in the other room."

"Because he will notice that I have a baby bump and then start asking me questions," Angela said with a childish whine. "I need to protect him from the fallout."

"You say fallout and I say honesty. Besides Angie, this entire situation puts me in a compromising position. Don't you think? Given that he and I are working closely together on this campaign."

"I know and you're right, Catherine, but I need to protect him. You remember last time—"

"How could I forget? It was a nightmare for both of you," Catherine said, taking a deep breath. "Nevertheless, you have to talk to him. He's your husband and as such, like it or not, he has to be involved in this process. I mean it, Angie, you have to tell him."

"I know, I know," she answered, holding up a hand as a sign that she gave in. "I will tell him."

"You swear?"

"I swear," Angela said, crossing her heart.

"When?"

"When what?"

"When will you talk to him?"

Taking another deep breath and blowing it out slowly, Angela replied, "Friday, after I see the doctor and he assures me that all is well."

"Oh, Angie, I'm so happy for you both. You do realize that I am going to have a hard time hiding my exuberance when I'm around the two of you."

"Save your happiness until I see the doctor on Friday."

"How far along?"

"Friday will be ten weeks. I've never made it this long before and don't want to jinx it by telling Russell or anyone else about the good news too soon."

They continued to talk about everything but Catherine deliberately avoided the subject of Jake. She didn't dare bring him up because it would force her to admit her growing attraction to him.

Avoiding commitment was her specialty. Catherine shied away from entanglements that would derail her career in any way. Life was less messy that way—or so Catherine told herself. Besides, when you involved yourself in someone else's life, things tended to become messy very quickly, and if there was one thing Catherine Lawrence liked, it was her life being neat and organized.

"So, tell me more about this new neighbor of yours," Angela broached the subject, for the third time that day.

"I told you, Angie, we aren't talking about this. He's handsome, surfs all day, and nearly got eaten by a bull shark last night. End of story!"

"But I can always tell when you're holding something back, Catherine, and right now you are not telling me everything."

"Fine," she relented, not daring to look at her friend as she blurted out, "He kissed me last night."

"What? Jake kissed you?" Angela gasped out loud. "Why would you withhold that tasty little morsel from me, Catherine Marie Lawrence? You are not a very good friend."

"How can you say that, Angela Jean? And how could you even think such a thing? I'm a great friend. Certainly, the best friend you've ever had."

"We have been together almost the entire day and this is the first I'm hearing about a kiss between you and this handsome Aussie." Angela wagged her finger at Catherine. "You are the worst friend ever."

Catherine's face turned bright red.

"We kissed. It was nice. End of story. He went home, and I went to bed. Alone!" she added for clarification. "Nothing more to talk about. Really, end of story. I swear!"

"I beg to differ—"

"You can beg to differ all you like, Angela Tillman," Catherine snapped, "but I'm telling you that until there is any real news to share with you, the subject is closed."

Angela let out a huff of air to show her exasperation. She was about to protest again before the expression on her friend's face made her decide against it. Dropping the matter altogether, Angela switched to a more neutral subject.

When their hair, toes, and fingernails were perfect, the girls said their goodbyes to one another and went their separate ways. Angela headed for home to finish getting ready for the evening's event, and Catherine stopped by the office to tie up a few loose ends before making her way over to the aquarium.

Her staff had arrived early, and they were overseeing the table settings, lighting, and decorations, as well as the setting up of the podium and white linen chair covers being placed on every chair in the room. Several staff members were currently tying blue satin ribbons into bows on the chairs. Things were going smoothly. Catherine had nothing to worry about.

Patricia was nowhere to be found even though her assistant assured Catherine that she had been there earlier and had already done her part. Catherine glared at the assistant and she faltered, looking away. Quickly checking the assistant's story, Catherine found that everything seemed to be in order so she let it slide this time.

At four-thirty, Catherine insisted that everyone leave, giving them plenty of time to get ready for the evening's event so that they could be back at the aquarium by 6:30.

She wanted everyone fresh and ready for a full night of campaigning.

Glancing at her phone, Catherine wondered why Tillman had not returned her phone calls. It was as if he was avoiding her for some reason. It was hard being a proper campaign manager to a ghost of a candidate.

Nearly everyone had left, except for a few stragglers who were seeing to the last-minute table arrangements that had just arrived. Catherine checked and double-checked her list, examining the place settings at the head table, when Russell Tillman's smooth, melodic campaign voice rang out loud and clear through the entire venue.

"There's my girl!" he practically sang the words as if he had been searching everywhere for her and not the other way around. Casually strolling up to her, Russell gave her shoulders a friendly squeeze. "You have outdone yourself, my dear, but then I knew you would."

"There he is," Catherine announced loudly, trying to look pleased to see him as staff members glanced their way.

She pulled Russell aside.

"Where have you been all day, Russell? You haven't been picking up your phone," Catherine said, unable to control her frustration.

She quickly broke eye contact with him, giving the few staff members another large smile before leaning in to continue their conversation.

"Is that a tan you are sporting, Russell Tillman? Do you have a tan?" she badgered, repeating herself and feeling as if her head would explode at the same time.

Russell gave a laugh that made Catherine sigh loudly.

"I was playing golf with a few bigwigs. You can relax. I haven't been doing anything nefarious, if that's what you were thinking. It's all on the up and up." He forced a smile to his lips as someone walked past them. "Walk with me," he insisted, making his way towards the corner of the room, away from eavesdropping ears.

"Keep it together, Lawrence. You've got this. I knew you were the woman for the job," Tillman said, squeezing her arm as if he were a football coach giving a reluctant player a pep talk.

Ignoring her irritation, he turned and lifted up his arm in greeting to the rest of the staff members who were still meandering around.

"Great job, everyone. Now, go home and get ready for tonight. It's going to be a long one," he said, making a big show of it. "Meet you back here by seven."

"Six-thirty!" Catherine corrected as he walked away, waving halfheartedly over his shoulder at her as an acknowledgment that she had said something.

It was the first time since the campaign started that Catherine was worried, and not just about the numbers. She had a secret that she was withholding from him, and it bothered her that he might have a secret of his own.

Well, if he is hiding something, it will come out in the light of day, she told herself.

She glanced at her watch. It was four-thirty-five and she had just enough time to drive home, finalize her hair and makeup, get dressed, and make it back here on time.

Her mind was ticking off her list when she suddenly thought of Jake. She wondered what he was doing right now. She felt goosebumps travel up her arms remembering how the stars had sparkled in his eyes the night before and how her skin warmed under his touch.

"Stop it!" Catherine reprimanded herself. "Jake Ryan is definitely not a priority at this moment...". She exhaled as she remembered how he smiled at her the last time they were together, how he held her in his arms, how they kissed.

Oh, who am I kidding?, she thought to herself, *He's dreamy, and if I'm going to indulge in a few harmless thoughts of any man, it might as well be one as cute as Jake Ryan. Besides, what's the harm?*

CHAPTER 9

*C*atherine arrived home to loud reggae music booming from the common area at the back of her condo, and about thirty of Jake's closest friends mingling around outside. Catherine couldn't help noticing that nearly all of his friends were incredibly good looking, tan, and fit. She would've given anything at that moment to attend a simple barbecue with Jake instead of a fancy fundraiser for a candidate who was being somewhat evasive about what he was up to.

Spying on everyone out of her bathroom window while she touched up her makeup, Catherine saw Jake standing by the grill, flipping hamburgers and turning the hot dogs with a drink in his free hand. He was chatting up a pretty, young woman in a gingham bikini. A slight ache formed in Catherine's throat as her jealousy caught her by surprise. She couldn't remember a time when she had been jealous of a guy. It didn't feel good to her.

Maybe I'm getting sick, she worried.

The woman at Jake's side had lush, brown hair that was pulled back into a cute pony-tail, high atop her head. She appeared to be in her early twenties.

And would you look at that perfectly tanned, hourglass figure of hers, Catherine thought.

Her petite stature made her look much younger than Catherine, like a little doll.

Catherine let the window shade fall back into place and took a deep breath. She simply wouldn't spy on Jake's party anymore, she told herself as she applied some lip gloss, pressing her lips together to ensure even coverage.

Then, as if drawn to the window like a moth to the flame, Catherine was pulling the shade back once again. The cute girl was leaning in towards Jake and placing her long, delicate fingers on his arm, giving him a friendly, familiar squeeze and laughing.

Catherine turned from the window.

"You would think that he was the popular host of the Tonight Show, for goodness sake, the way that young woman is carrying on," Catherine said out loud to herself, unable to explain the sudden nausea she was feeling as a severe pang of jealousy hit her.

Returning to the mirror, she checked her reflection one last time. Her elegant, form-fitting gown was black on white organza. The top portion was black, form fitted with a V-neck wedge in the front and back, and cinched in the waist with a bow in the front. The skirt was full, black over white, with delicate black roses encircling white crystal centers dispersed here and there over the skirt. Catherine wore her hair swept up, with soft, long curls reaching to the back of her head, culminating into an elegant, full knot with crystal studded hair pins throughout to catch the light. Simple crystal drop earrings and matching choker completed her outfit.

"I am a campaign manager with lots of people depending on me to make good decisions tonight. Focus, Catherine Lawrence! Your plate is full. This is no time to lose focus of your plan," she whispered to her reflection in the mirror as she finished her hair and gave a nod of approval. "There is no time for sore throats, stomach aches, hypochondria or men—"

Catherine took one last look out the window, despite herself, pulling back the shade to check the weather and determine how heavy of a wrap she would need for the evening, she told herself. That's when she saw that the attractive young woman was still draped all over Jake's arm. She felt her cheeks color and was utterly mortified when Jake's eyes connected with hers.

Getting caught spying out the window by Jake, she thought with humiliation. A moan escaped her lips, but she smiled back and waved.

Jake gave her one of his big grins which made Catherine feel even more foolish as she let the shade slip out of her hand.

Quickly grabbing her handbag from the bed, she began turning off lights, making sure to leave the living room light on so that the condo wouldn't be completely dark when she returned later. Walking to the back door, she waved politely to Jake and his guests. A few people looked her way before she closed the blinds and left through the garage.

She didn't want to think about anything but the dinner ahead of her. All of her focus needed to be on the campaign.

Immediately, one of Jake's good friends elbowed him in the side and asked, "Hey Jake, who's the pretty sheila next door?"

Then another stepped up to the barbecue.

"Yeah, Jake, tell us about this one. Have you two gotten close?"

The young woman in the gingham bikini stepped away, putting a shirt over herself and muttered to no one in particular, "Isn't it getting chilly?"

Another gentleman knocked the neck of his glass bottle against Jake's.

"Is she single?" he asked with a sly wink.

Jake took a deep breath and smiled, saying very little about his lovely next-door neighbor, and continued to be very tight-lipped about Catherine for the rest of the evening.

The aquarium was lit up with twinkling lights and rented chandeliers in the room that had the majestic orcas swimming on one side of the hall to the left, and the playful and graceful dolphins on the right. A colorful coral reef, which included tropical fish, accented the stage area where the speeches would be made. The animals on display signified beauty, elegance, and strength.

There were multi-colored lights rotating throughout the jellyfish tank from red, blue, green, and purple to accentuate the beauty of their form and tentacles as they swam around the tank in an exotic dance.

Catherine wanted Tillman's constituents to see him and his campaign as ever-changing and evolving like the beautiful fish that were on display before them.

Out with the old candidate and in with the new candidate, Russell Tillman.

As an extra bonus, Catherine hired the band, Hootie and the Blowfish, for the evening's musical entertainment, which was sure to be a huge hit. The name of the band and the style of music perfectly fit the theme of the evening. Many of their songs had double meanings and allegorical verses, the ideal match for their political campaign.

Tillman and Angela arrived exactly at 6:30, leaving enough time for Catherine to go over Tillman's speech with him.

Catherine hugged her best friend and couldn't help but marvel at Angela's poise, beauty, and grace.

"You're a lucky man, Russell Tillman," she said.

Angela had a law degree from Stetson, which was where she had met Russell. "I know. She tells me the same thing every day," he replied, looking down at his wife adoringly.

His statement earned him a discrete but playful elbow to the side from his wife. The three of them moved off to the side as Catherine directed them to where they would stand when guests entered. Catherine and three of her top office managers would be waiting at the end of the line to help guests find their seats.

Catherine was just about to give Patricia a call when she noticed a shift in the atmosphere of the room.

"What are—" Catherine was saying when she noticed a strange look cross Angela's face. Then Russell looked up and stared at someone across the room. Catherine turned to see what the commotion was all about and that's when she saw Patricia, who had just paused for dramatic effect before making her way across the room towards them.

Outwardly, Catherine worked hard to maintain her calm composure as Patricia walked up and stopped directly in front of the three of them. She posed, sticking her left leg out to the side to accentuate the high slit running up the side of her gown. A few flashes went off in front of Catherine and Angela, blinding them for a moment while Patricia smiled provocatively for the cameras.

Her luscious blond hair had been swept up on the sides, held in place by a small antique looking tiara, while the back flowed down in a cascade of ringlets. Her dress was a strapless, form-fitting gown, meant to outline every curve. The red, floor length gown sported a bustier that pushed her ample breasts to the forethought of any man's mind and the long slit up the left side of her dress swung open as she walked or stood. Sliding her left leg forward to emphasize the slit, Patricia showed off a lovely expanse of thigh. The back of the dress was equally alluring as it laced up her lower spine leaving the rest of her back very exposed. Turning to greet them, Patricia pretended not to notice Angela's and Catherine's disapproving looks.

Angela leaned over to Catherine and whispered, "Who does she think she is?"

Catherine responded, with a shake of her head.

"I'm not sure but I have to hand it to her, the woman can make an entrance."

"Simply despicable if you ask me."

"Now, Angie, don't be peevish. The woman has a lovely shape and knows how to show it off. It isn't her fault that she doesn't possess any sense of decorum."

Angela chuckled and straightened up a little taller, smiling for the cameras. "Touché."

"Patricia, you look absolutely stunning in that gown," Tillman complimented her, taking a hold of her hand when she reached out to him. He patted the back of it courteously before letting go.

Catherine thought that she noticed Russell's hand holding onto Patricia's a bit longer than necessary.

"Yes, Patricia, that shade of red really brings out your complexion," she admitted.

"I believe you have met Mrs. Tillman, my wife," Russell said as Angela moved in closer to him, nudging him in the ribs and clearing her throat.

"Angela, this is Patricia Grant, who is one of our top lobbyists in the office," Catherine added, smiling as sweetly as she possibly could.

"Well, aren't you sweet, Catherine," Patricia quipped before turning to face Angela. "Angela, it is such a pleasure to meet you." She held out her hand.

"You may call me Mrs. Tillman, Ms. Grant. I don't believe that you and I know one another well enough to be on a first name basis since you work for my husband and we've only just met," Angela pointed out.

Catherine could tell that Patricia was taken aback by Angela's words as well as taken down a notch or two. She seemed to deflate slightly. By the look on her face, you would have thought Angela had slapped her.

Patricia quickly regained her composure.

"Yes, of course, Mrs. Tillman. Please forgive me."

Catherine stepped in, taking pity on Patricia as she seemed to turn the same color as her dress.

"Will you please greet the guests after they come through the line and show them to their table," Catherine said with a sympathetic nod. "Thank you, Patricia."

"Of course, Miss Lawrence. And it was a pleasure to meet you, Mrs. Tillman," she replied, before turning to leave.

As Catherine turned around, she heard Russell begin to chastise Angela.

"I will not hear any more of your excuses regarding that *woman*," Angela said. Her tone carried the desired effect. "I am putting an end to this before it has a chance to start, Russell."

"There is nothing going on, Angie," Russell replied angrily under his breath.

Catherine gritted her teeth.

"I will take care of that situation," she assured Angela as her eyes met Russell's.

"If the two of you will excuse me," he said, "I need to use the restroom and tidy up before guests arrive."

"Of course," Catherine said with a smile as he walked away.

Then, pulling out her phone, she sent out a group text, announcing to the entire crew that it was showtime.

Taking a deep cleansing breath, Catherine turned back towards Angela.

"I really have to apologize, Angela. Patricia can be a thorn in my side from time to time, but she is really good at what she does."

Catherine gave Angela's hand a squeeze.

"I'm certain that she is," Angela said, squeezing Catherine's hand. "I'm just glad that I have you working alongside Russell because I know you have my back. And I hate to admit it but I know that if something happened between those two you would tell me about it first, right?"

Pulling Angela into a hug, Catherine whispered, "I have your back, Angie. The truth is, I don't trust that woman."

As the evening wore on Catherine felt that everything was going according to plan. Well-wishers stopped her throughout the evening to tell her what a wonderful time they were having and to shake her hand. The room was packed with supporters who applauded Russell's speech with great enthusiasm. Catherine felt sure that Tillman's approval rating was going up and with the revenue gained from the proceeds, he would be able to afford more advertisement and another trip through the state to visit a few lagging counties.

Catherine began to go over her list of things to do. Speech, check. Dinner, three courses, check. Band playing in the background, double check. Dessert, not served yet.

Looking around the room, Catherine didn't see Patricia. She glanced down at her watch and realized that it was taking the dessert course an unusual amount of time to be served.

Looking around for the maître d', Catherine didn't see him in the sea of people. She made her way to the kitchen and peeked inside to see total chaos. Two of the cooks were shouting at one another and the waitresses were attempting to stack dishes up on trays, dropping utensils on the floor. The dishwasher came through a door to collect another tray of dishes when he slipped and dropped the entire mess onto the floor with a loud clatter. Dishes, silverware, and glasses fell to the ground, breaking into pieces. One of the servers screamed as a shard of glass cut her leg. Two more people came running to assist and another person yelled for a broom.

Catherine caught sight of the maître d' and made her way over to him. "What is going on here? The dessert should have been out twenty-five minutes ago."

"The torch gun used to caramelize the flan isn't working. I have sent someone to retrieve a couple of torch guns from my restaurant," he said.

It was fortunate Catherine never left anything to chance and had picked up two small torches earlier in the week. They were in the back seat of her car. Handing over her keys to a young man, she gave him detailed instructions where he could find her car. A few minutes later the desserts had been caramelized and fresh fruit was being placed on top of them. Soon, the first tray left the kitchen. Then the young man returned with two more torches, and the kitchen was once again humming along.

Tillman definitely doesn't appreciate me enough, Catherine giggled to herself as she pushed open the door that she thought led back out to the main hallway. Instead, the door led into an employee stairwell. As she turned around to go back, Catherine heard two voices coming from the top of the stairwell and stopped.

Recognizing the voices, Catherine peered around the corner and up the stairwell and saw exactly what she didn't want to see, Russell standing too close to a female body in a full-length red dress. Her stomach dropped.

Catherine cleared her throat loudly.

"Now that I have your attention, I would suggest that the two of you vacate the stairwell immediately. And for heaven's sake, take separate entrances back to the party!"

There was a yelp and a curse from the woman.

"I'm going to give you both until the count of three," she advised in a clear, crisp tone, "and if I don't hear your feet scurrying like the rats that you are, I will come up there myself!"

Silence.

"One!" She paused. "Two..."

She heard rapid footsteps quickly running up to the next flight of steps. Then, the sound of a door slamming shut echoed through the entire stairwell before a second door quietly closed a minute later.

"And that, ladies and gentlemen, is how it is done," she murmured to herself before returning to the ballroom.

Her needling suspicions had only been that until now. To have those suspicions confirmed made Catherine sick to her stomach. This was going to ruin the campaign, a marriage, and possibly a friendship. How could the two of them be so stupid?

Catherine stopped at the dolphin tank and watched them swim and play. She pondered what to do about the situation.

She scanned the dining hall and found Russell standing near a table talking nonchalantly with a couple of patrons. He looked anxious. His eyes caught hers for a full moment before they moved on to someone else across the room. Catherine followed his gaze and caught sight of Patricia touching up her lipstick before she hastily made her way to her post near the stage.

Catherine wondered if Angela had noticed their absence and found her best friend chatting with a group of women at the other side of the room.

A few minutes later Russell joined Angela, putting his arm around her. Catherine watched Angela's face and realized that the lapse in time had definitely not gone unnoticed by her.

Was keeping affairs out of the limelight going to be one of my new job responsibilities? Catherine wondered. She looked at her watch and realized that she was now behind schedule.

Several hours later, Catherine was saying goodbye to a few more guests when she pulled Russell aside.

"You and I need to talk first thing tomorrow about your personal relations with staffers."

"It was an isolated incident, and nothing—"

"Save it Tillman," Catherine said, cutting him off. "You have put me in a very compromising position, and I'm rather displeased about it."

"I can explain."

"Yeah, yeah, sure. That's what they all say when they get caught," Catherine added. "How long?"

"How long, what?"

"How long has it been going on?" she demanded.

"I assure you that nothing has happened."

"Of course, it has. Who do you think you are talking to?" Catherine glared at him before throwing out smiles to everyone else who passed by. "Oh, and by the way, I just thought you should know that Angela noticed your absence as well. The reason I know that is that I saw it written all over her face when you sat back down."

"I'll handle her," Russell said, sounding very self-assured. "You just take care of the campaign."

"I would love to do just that, Russell. And you just clean up this mess before your wife or any reporters sniff this little fiasco out or you can kiss that Governor's office and your wife goodbye."

"What are we discussing?" Angela inquired, stepping up behind her husband to take his arm.

"The fact that I am exhausted and will be calling it a night," Catherine answered quickly, giving her friend a reassuring smile, squeezing her arm. Lying to her best friend's face made her feel more sick than Catherine had ever imagined. But the fact was, she had no real hard evidence that anything was actually going on. So why would she hurt her friend on a mere hunch?

"My feet are killing me, and I can barely keep my eyes open," Catherine continued as she pulled out her phone, sending out a text to the clean-up crew to tell them she was leaving.

"Do you want our driver to give you a ride home?" Angela asked, looking concerned.

"No. I'll be alright. I just need to get some sleep," Catherine insisted, leaning over to kiss Angela on the cheek. "This will wrap up here in the next few minutes and the two of you are free to retire for the night. I just need to talk with one more person before I leave," she said, looking around until she spotted Patricia near a table, talking with a very distinguished looking gentleman. "I'll talk with the two of you tomorrow."

"Be safe," Angela said as Catherine walked away. "Oh, and Catherine?" she called out.

Turning around, Catherine paused.

"Yes?"

"Great party, love. I'll call you soon."

With a nod, Catherine turned back around and walked over to Patricia.

"Can I talk to you for a moment?" she asked before turning to the man Patricia had been talking to. "Please, excuse us a moment."

"What is your problem, Catherine?" Patricia protested. "Can't you see that I am having a conversation with a wealthy constituent?"

"Oh, I can see that a lot more than that has been going on, Miss Grant, and I want it to stop. Now!"

"You're crazy, Lawrence," Patricia retorted, turning her back to Catherine as if she were going to leave.

"Where do you think you're going?" Catherine asked, taking a hold of Patricia's arm.

"I'm tired and I plan on going home now," Patricia exclaimed haughtily. "If you don't mind?"

"Think again," Catherine said, taking a large calming breath to keep from losing her temper. "You came late, remember? You're in charge of supervising the clean-up crew and collecting the funds for the evening," she said coolly. "Oh, and I want a full report of the revenues on my desk tomorrow morning when I come in. And Miss Grant?"

"Was there something else?" Patricia replied, stiffly. "Can I rub your feet, draw you a bath?"

"Funny," Catherine replied dryly. "I know how much money we actually collected tonight, so, there better not be so much as a penny missing."

"Says who? And with what authority?"

"Says me—the campaign manager and your boss, that's who," Catherine fired back. "And if you don't start taking this job more seriously, Miss Grant, your days with this campaign will be numbered."

Patricia Grant was still seething forty minutes after Catherine had left. If anyone had looked closely, they would have noticed the little muscles in her jaw line flexing. But Patricia was wearing her game face. The smile she placed there was too forced to be real. She worked halfheartedly alongside the few straggling staffers cleaning up the aquarium after the gala. The last hour or so had given her time to think.

"Who does that do-gooder think she is?" Patricia exclaimed under her breath. "The gala was a success due to the efforts of the entire team and not just Miss Lawrence. The way she lords herself over me, one would think that she pulled the entire event off single-handedly," Patricia scoffed angrily.

Pulling out her phone and pushing the record button, Patricia began to talk into it in a low whisper. "Russell will get an earful from me regarding Miss Catherine Lawrence come Monday morning. I bet he had to smooth things over with the Missus. Note to self, the plan is going well. Miss Catherine Lawrence better watch her back," Patricia said, before noticing two staffers looking in her direction.

Patricia turned her back to them so that she could finish recording. "She doesn't know who she is messing with! We are well matched in so many ways, Miss Lawrence and I. But I don't play to lose," she concluded, turning off the recorder before looking around.

With a smile, she threw some trash away, scanning the room to see if anyone was still looking in her direction.

"I am willing to climb that political ladder regardless of the hurdles and in spite of the men I have to step over to get there," Patricia murmured to herself. She stopped to admire her reflection in the glass of the nearest fish tank, adjusting her tiara and smoothing a stray hair back into place, she gave herself a self-assured smile before winking at her reflection.

Then, gathering up the night's receipts and funds and making sure that the box was locked, Patricia sashayed from the room through the side door and to her car.

"You can kiss my tasty little biscuits, Miss Catherine Lawrence. I'm out of here," Patricia murmured as she started up her sports car and drove home.

CHAPTER 10

*C*atherine kicked off her shoes when she reached the car and looked forward to getting out of her evening gown. It had become more uncomfortable as the night wore on. She put the roof top down and turned the music up before speeding out of the parking lot singing along to the words of Journey's, *Any Way You Want It*. Music always made her feel better.

After everything she'd witnessed during the evening, she was in desperate need of some unwinding. A hot shower, a glass of wine, and her warm, comfy bed were just what the doctor would have ordered.

When Catherine pulled into the garage, she could hear music. She entered the house and looked out of her sliding glass door. The party was still going strong. Music blared from someone's radio while a boisterous game of volleyball was taking place.

"Take that, you dag," Jake yelled as he spiked the ball, hitting it over the net hard and down the center of the hastily drawn lines of the volleyball court.

"You're such a cocky bloke," someone yelled back.

Catherine opened her window and watched the party, snorting with laughter at the group's antics.

Dusting the sand off of his shorts, Jake laughed the insult off.

"You're such a dandy, Pete," he yelled back, causing his friends to laugh even harder.

Catherine went to her bedroom, changed into a pair of comfy sweats and a t-shirt, and let her hair down. Then, she poured herself a glass of wine and headed outside.

The last thing I need is a rowdy party going on just outside my condo, Catherine thought to herself,

Opening the sliding glass doors, glass of wine in hand, she stepped outside and moaned with ecstasy as the cool sand soothed her aching feet. It was like a healing balm relaxing every tight muscle in her body. Sipping the wine, Catherine savored the way it slid down her throat, soothing her.

Catherine pushed back a stray curl behind her ear and made her way over to Jake. He was jumping up to spike another ball over the net. His shirt was off and despite the cool breeze his chest was glistening with perspiration.

When he saw her, all interest in the game seemed to disappear, as he let the ball drop to the ground.

"There you are," Jake said. "Look fellas, it's my beautiful next-door neighbor. All my friends have been asking about you. Catherine, these are my best mates."

The game broke up and some of the group grabbed a new drink from out of the cooler, twisting the lid off their beer while others retrieved their drinks from the makeshift table near the fire.

"Cheers," they called out, raising their beers and glasses to her.

Nodding her head, Catherine smiled.

"G'day. That is right, isn't it?" she asked Jake out of the side of her mouth. "You do say G'day even at night? Did I say that right?"

"Perfectly. I might have mistaken you for a local Aussie if I didn't know any better," he teased, throwing a smile to his friends over her shoulder. "I see you brought your own refreshments. That must mean that you've decided to join us."

"I'm really beat," Catherine said, a bit embarrassed by the attention she was receiving. "I thought I would just go to bed, but the music was too loud."

Jake turned to one of the guys and yelled, "Hey, Mick, let's get out the guitars and make our own music. Turn off that stereo while I fetch Catie a lounger."

"No, really—" Catherine protested, but it was too late. Jake ran back to his place to fetch her something to sit on. "I mean, of course I would be delighted to join the party!" she called out, holding up her glass of wine as Jake came running back with a lounge chair and a blanket.

Another round of cheers immediately went up as Jake presented Catherine with her chair, setting it close to him and the fire, as well as a green blanket to keep her warm.

"In case you get chilled, Catie," he said gallantly.

"Thank you, Jake," Catherine said, shaking her head and turning toward him. "You are such a gentleman and you can read my mind. I was getting a bit chilled."

"That's what I do," he teased. "It's sort of my superpower."

"What else can you do with your superpowers?" Catherine teased back, surprised by her own boldness.

Jake grinned, his rugged, chiseled jaw showing a day's growth of stubble. The firelight was reflected in his eyes. The mischievous glint in his glance hinted at Jake's playful nature. She couldn't help but smile as he gently draped the blanket over her lap when she sat down.

He rested his hand upon her stomach.

"I would be happy to show you later," Jake winked, causing Catherine to flush all over.

"Oh, my! But don't you think your girlfriend will be jealous?" Catherine said, pointing towards the young lady she'd seen draped all over Jake's arm earlier.

Turning his head to see who Catherine was talking about, Jake began to chuckle.

"That's just Tilly, my best mate's sister. I promised to keep an eye on her while he was out of town, to make sure that she didn't get into any trouble." Jake smiled, suddenly understanding what she was getting at. "Did you think that she and I were a thing?"

"No." Catherine blushed. "Anyone with eyes could see that she is just a kid."

"Well, I would hope so. She's nineteen years old," Jake asserted. "She's just a baby. But a deal is a deal, my Pops always said. So, I thought it best to keep her close."

"Then you were just being a good friend?"

Making a noise deep in his throat, Jake chuckled again.

"Were you jealous?"

"Of who?" Catherine asked with a scoff. "Her? Besides, how could I be jealous when you and I are merely neighbors? I'm not even your girlfriend. What right would I have for being jealous?" She tipped her glass of wine to her lips.

"Would you like to be? My girlfriend, I mean," he asked with a playful wink. For the first time ever, Catherine found herself speechless.

"Hey you bunch of bludgers, what would you say if we kick this thing off with a slow ballad from home?" Jake said to his friends, still maintaining eye contact with Catherine.

Swallowing hard, Catherine took another sip from her glass of wine. She felt the heat return to her cheeks. She was thankful that Jake chose that moment to turn around and address his friends. It had been a long time since anyone had caused her to be speechless.

The party continued until two in the morning, at which time Jake said goodbye to the last of his friends. When he headed back to check on the fire and put it out, he found Catherine, still lying in the lounger, curled up and sound asleep. The soft green blanket was pulled up to her chin and her empty wine glass pressed to her chest, held there by one hand.

She looked so peaceful. Jake removed the glass from her hand, setting it down next to his guitar. Then, picking her up, he smiled to himself when Catherine made some cute sleepy noises. She wrapped her arm around his neck and rolled her head forward, nuzzling into him. Jake adjusted her weight and gently cradled her in his arms, trying hard not to wake her.

Catherine moaned again and made a few more sounds as if she were talking to someone in her sleep. Her head lolled as her hair tickled his nose.

Carefully sliding her back door open, Jake stepped inside her apartment, wiping the sand off of his feet before progressing into the bedroom to lay her down on the bed. He straightened the green throw over her before standing back to observe his handiwork.

When he looked down at her in the soft glow of moonlight coming through the sheer curtains, something tightened in his chest.

He walked over to the window and closed the curtains, making sure that there would be no more late-night peepers gawking at Catherine through the window. Then he walked back to the bed to tuck in the blanket around her as his mother used to do for him.

Then he leaned down and gently touched his lips to her forehead.

"Sleep tight, beautiful," he murmured in her ear before walking from the room and locking the back-sliding glass door. He would leave through the front door, making sure that it was locked tightly behind him.

He ran back to the fire pit and doused it with water, retrieved his guitar and Catherine's wine glass, and headed back to his condo. He double checked Catherine's door to make sure that he had actually locked it before stepping over to his own condo door.

Stepping inside, Jake turned on the light, leaned the guitar against the couch and placed the wine glass on the kitchen counter before turning out the lights.

CHAPTER 11

*C*atherine spent the next two weeks averaging the revenue, counting the numbers, and getting ready for early voting numbers to start rolling in at the end of October. Today was only Friday, October sixth. As it stood right now, the numbers showed Tillman well ahead of the other two candidates.

Tillman called Catherine on her phone and asked her to his office.

"Close the door and have a seat," Russell said in his friendly campaign tone.

This meant one of two things to Catherine. He either wanted something or he was up to something. Things had been strained since the night of the ball. They really hadn't had time to sit down and have that heart to heart talk Catherine had wanted to have. He always had one excuse or another, and she assumed Angela had not told Russell her good news either or he would have said something to her.

"I wanted to tell you that the amazing job that you have been doing has not gone unnoticed by me, and I haven't forgotten about our celebratory dinner—"

"That's okay, Russell, I don't expect dinner," Catherine smiled pleasantly, "and we've worked hard on the campaign trail the past few weeks together—"

"Exactly!" he boomed, cutting her off. "We have worked hard, and the road ahead is about to get a lot harder. Especially when I win this thing, for the both of us, because this is as much my fight as it is yours." He cleared his throat. "So, with that being said, I've decided that I, I mean we…we both…in fact most of the primary staff…need to take a well-deserved three-day holiday…" he stammered, clearly searching for just the right words.

"What are you talking about, Russell? Are you crazy? Now?" Catherine exclaimed, already shaking her head emphatically.

"Listen, Catherine, I've thought this thing out," Russell said smoothly, committed to his point. "I need you to put twenty well-informed staff members on as a skeleton crew, to answer the phone and handle small problems until Tuesday. They will be paid, of course. Then put one person you trust in charge who has your number in case of any real emergency, should one arise."

"But—"

"No buts. Then you and I, along with the senior staff, will take a well-deserved three days off. Call it a paid gratuity, for all the hard work they've put in. The twenty who stay behind to work should get a day or two off during the week next week. Our team deserves this bonus," he insisted, giving her a stern look she'd come to know all too well. The one that said that this discussion was over because his mind was already made up.

"But Russel, what is this really about?"

"I don't wish to discuss it further, Catherine! I told you what I need, and the matter is final!"

Pondering his words for a moment, Catherine watched as Russell strolled over to his desk and sat back down. They had all been working long hours, weekends, and late nights for the past six months straight without a break. Although she was fuming over the change of plans, Catherine decided that it was best to acquiesce to Russell's wishes.

"All right. I'll have twenty people's names for you by the end of day."

"Why don't I make the official announcement and you let it be on a volunteer basis. You might get better results. Then, worst-case scenario, you pick out the last few to fill the slots, if need be," Russell said.

Always the politician, Catherine thought to herself, and yet, his plan made more sense than hers, so she nodded her head in agreement.

Russell stepped out into the middle of the office to get everyone's attention and made his grand announcement.

The entire office erupted into a loud, boisterous celebration of clapping and cheers. They even had more than enough volunteers who wanted the overtime, now that money was involved.

The only thing left for Catherine to do was figure out what she was going to do with three entire days off.

Most of the staff had left by three o'clock, including the senior staffers and Tillman. Catherine was the last to leave, placing important paperwork on Marge's desk. She would be in charge while Catherine was off. This would be the first Friday that she would be home before rush hour. For some reason she felt a little giddy over the prospect of having three days to herself.

The sun was shining and the thermometer read eighty-four degrees. This was the kind of weather convertibles were made for. Slipping on her favorite sunglasses, Catherine put the top down and turned up the music as she drove home. The late afternoon sun was shining on her face and her hair was flying in the wind. She could smell salty sea air mixed with the fragrance of flowers from the corner stand when she stopped at the light. A well-dressed businessman eyed Catherine, admiring her beautiful auburn hair glistening in the sunlight.

"How are you doing today?" the man said, leaning over his passenger seat to speak to her.

"It's a glorious day, don't you think?"

"That it is," he said. "Made even more so by seeing someone as beautiful as you sitting at my stoplight."

Smiling broadly, Catherine knew exactly what the man was about. It wasn't the first time someone tried to pick her up at a stoplight or standing in line at the grocery store.

"Thank you for the compliment, sir. You are most kind," she said, deciding that she would take the next right as soon as the light changed.

"Hey, how about you and I get a drink together?"

"Thank you very much for the kind offer but I have an appointment to get to," she said, waving goodbye to the man still sitting at the light as it turned green.

CHAPTER 12

*P*ulling the car into the garage, Catherine put the top back up and turned off the engine as the garage door came down. The drive home had been glorious.

Catherine automatically checked her phone before putting it back into her pocket. She needed to relax for a few minutes. She actually felt excited about the next few days and there was a bounce in her step as she came through the door from the garage. Catherine was intent on enjoying her time off. But first, she would put on her bathing suit and go for a walk on the beach to look for some seashells.

On her way to the bedroom, she stopped to take a steak out of the freezer. Tonight, she would treat herself to a steak barbecued on her little grill.

Ten minutes later she was out the door wearing her favorite black bikini and white shorts. She grabbed a little white tunic for later and tucked a beach towel under her arm.

It was just a short walk to her favorite inlet, a secluded spot behind a mound of sand with some tall sea grass to hide her from view. Catherine spread out her towel and took off her shorts. She began to comb the beach for some seashells in pristine condition. Catherine collected the shells and kept them in a large glass jar that stood on her end table. It was filled with only the best shells she had collected over the years.

The area was nearly vacant at this time of day, which added to her sense of calm and peacefulness. Catherine lifted her face towards the sun and closed her eyes, breathing deeply. The ocean breeze was heaven to her.

Looking down, she began to hunt for seashells once more when she came across a sand dollar in perfect condition. Turning the shell over to ensure that it was no longer occupied, Catherine slipped it into her pocket. Further down the beach, she came across another rare find, a shark tooth. While she was wandering the beach, her mind jumped from one subject to another, finally settling on her handsome neighbor, Jake. She hadn't seen or spoken to him since the night of his party, two weeks ago, and she wondered why. She didn't want to obsess over him, but all her attempts to push him away from her thoughts only made her think of him more.

Sighing, she bent over to pick up a large orange shell that was perfectly shaped and vibrant in color. She loved these because of their name, Cat's paw. Her grandmother would tell her that they were named after her rather than being named for their obvious shape and coloring.

She wondered what Jake would think of her shell collection.

"Why? Why am I thinking of him? He would probably laugh and think I'm being silly and nostalgic," she said to herself.

Where was he? Why wasn't he surfing? This was her first day to come home from work early, and he wasn't home.

"I'm being ridiculous," she groaned, bending over to pick up a large purple and coral colored shell as her mind continued to push her thoughts towards Jake Ryan.

The man was forever shirtless, tan, and fit. His smile had a way of making her feel as if it was created especially for her. But recently, he seemed to have dropped off the face of the Earth. Catherine felt as if he was giving her the cold shoulder. He hadn't called or stopped by. To her, it was a childish way for a grown man to handle whatever was on his mind. In business and politics, one would address any situation with communication, guidance if needed, and occasionally a lot of finesse.

"Australian!" she said out loud. He'd deserted her when they were just getting to know one another. She was mad at herself for even caring for him in the first place.

She continued her walk down the beach for about half a mile, picking up a few more shells as the sun began to descend lower in the sky. The air was getting colder, and she decided that it was time to turn back. When she'd reached her spot, she discovered that it was occupied.

Jake was reclined upon her towel, looking completely relaxed, as if by magic her mind had conjured him up. Catherine stopped abruptly as she stared at him.

"Hey, what are you doing here? I mean, how are you?" she said, trying to act casual, willing her heart to stop beating so hard. She shivered and he handed her the coverup he'd stashed under his head as a pillow.

Catherine slid on her coverup and sat down next to Jake, maintaining enough distance to be proper. He hadn't answered her yet.

"What are you doing here?" she repeated.

"I heard you the first time. I was thinking about how to respond," Jake said, sounding absolutely miserable.

"All right, so respond. Where have you been for two weeks?"

"I've been away at a surfing contest."

"Oh," was all Catherine could say as her disappointed tone rang in her ears. She wondered if he could hear it too.

"So, you missed me."

Her cheeks turned red.

"What would make you say that?"

"Just by the look on your face when you came around the sand dune. That was the look of a woman who had missed someone, rather than the look of a woman who was simply saying hello to her neighbor."

"Don't be silly. We don't even know each other," she protested.

"And whose fault is that?"

"You certainly wouldn't be talking about me, since I'm certainly not the one who just up and vanished without a word of goodbye!"

"So, you did miss me?" Jake said.

"Don't be ridiculous," Catherine protested. "How can you miss someone you don't even know? One moment I feel we are getting closer, then the next minute you are gone for two weeks without a word."

"So, you are saying that you'd like to get to know me better," Jake said, looking out at the ocean.

"Jake, I don't want to fight. I don't want to play games either. I'm just a girl, with a crazy, busy career that gets in the way of my social life. I don't know anyone who wants to take a back seat to my career—"

"So, do you want to get to know me better, or don't you?" he asked, turning back to look into her eyes.

"Yes, but only if you understand that my career comes first," Catherine answered, shocked to realize that she had said that out loud.

There was a certain pleading look in Catherine's eyes that caught Jake off guard and his heart constricted.

"So, you did miss me," Jake said, to make light of the moment.

"Yes," she whispered, staring up at him. "I missed you very much."

She looked so adorable to him that his heart melted.

"Now that wasn't so hard to admit, was it?"

"Oh, but it was," Catherine replied. "Now, your turn. Where have you been for two weeks and why did you leave me alone so abruptly? Keep in mind, I'm a lawyer and I've been trained to recognize a lie. I can practically smell it coming out of someone's mouth."

With a smile, Jake touched her arm, and she felt a shiver.

"Good to know that while I was risking my life at my tournament, you missed me as much as I missed you. The truth is, I needed to clear my head. There was a particular redhead I couldn't get out of my thoughts, so I needed to figure out a few things."

"And, did you?" Catherine asked. "Figure out a few things, that is?"

With a serious look, Jake replied, "Yes I did, Miss Catherine Lawrence."

Silence followed. Catherine was the first to break it.

"Well? What exactly did you figure out?"

He stroked her cheek, ever so gently.

"I discovered that I enjoy everything about you, Catie, and I want to know everything there is to know about you. Can you live with that?"

Catherine smiled back, grateful to have an honest conversation.

"And you understand the terms? Career first, relationship second?"

"If that is the way it has to be, I can live with it until I can't," Jake said. "Deal?"

"Deal!" she replied, smiling from ear to ear. Then, she stuck her hand out to shake on it.

Cupping her chin in his hand instead, Jake leaned down and gently kissed her lips.

"That's the way I like to seal the deal," he said with a rueful smile. "Any objections?"

"None, whatsoever," she said. She rose onto her knees to kiss him back and took his face between her hands, kissing his lips.

"You're cold and it's getting dark. Why don't we go in? I'm definitely getting hungry," Jake said, standing up and extending his hand out to help Catherine to her feet.

"I took a steak out of the freezer and left it sitting on the counter. I'll split it with you," Catherine offered. "I even have stuff for a salad, and I think there is some broccoli in my vegetable bin."

"It all sounds perfect. I have a couple of potatoes," Jake said, picking up her towel and shaking it out. "Lead the way."

Feeling excited, Catherine began to walk back towards the condo. When Jake reached out and took ahold of her hand, she smiled up at him. To her surprise, she felt like a teenager again.

"Did I tell you that I have the next three days off?" Catherine blurted out.

"No, you did not. How fortunate for me that I came back just in time."

"I'm really glad you did."

"I really was away at a surfing contest," Jake said as they neared the condos. "I placed third, just in case you were curious."

"We should celebrate?"

"I should have taken first but alas, it was not to be," Jake said, bringing her hand to his lips before continuing. "My last two waves fell a little flat."

"Oh, I'm sorry Jake. You'll take first place next time," she assured him, squeezing his hand.

"Just give me a minute to get out of this suit," Catherine called over her shoulder as they entered the condo.

She quickly scampered off to her closet. First, she slipped on matching black lace bra and panties. They clung to her like a second skin. Then, she picked out a fitted cotton dress that came just above her knees. It was blue with a pretty floral pattern.

Spritzing herself with a light floral perfume, Catherine combed her hair and pulled it back with a large clip. With a last look in the mirror, Catherine dabbed on some light pink lip gloss, took a deep breath and left the bathroom.

Walking into the kitchen, she took a bottle of Halpin Cabernet Sauvignon wine from the wine cooler. It was a Napa Valley wine that she had been saving for a special occasion. This definitely felt like a special occasion. Catherine opened the bottle to breathe, while Jake went next door to change his clothes and grab a couple of potatoes.

Returning fifteen minutes later, he smelled of fresh aftershave and the stubbly whiskers were gone from his face. He wore khaki shorts and a button-down dress shirt with a Hawaiian flower pattern.

"Oh, you smell good," Catherine said. "I hope you like red wine. I've been saving this bottle."

Examining the bottle, Jake swirled his glass and sniffed it.

"Good fingers," he said before taking a sip. "And for the record, I love red wine. How did you know?"

"You looked like a red wine kind of a guy."

"I don't think I've seen you wear that dress before. It's very lovely on you," he said while popping the potatoes into the microwave oven.

"Why, thank you. It's new," Catherine said, twirling around and giving Jake the full view.

They talked about different things as Jake started up the grill and Catherine tossed together a salad.

It had been a long time since Catherine had felt so giddy. Taking another sip of wine, she set the table and lit a few candles around the table and deck to create an intimate, cozy atmosphere.

When Jake called Catherine over to check the steak, his large, strong fingers brushed against her hand making her dizzy with anticipation as the aroma of cooked steak rose in the air.

"It's perfect," she announced, looking up at him.

They sat down and began to eat.

"More wine?" she offered, seeing that his glass was nearly empty.

"Yes, please. It's very good."

"So, you were raised by your grandmother when your mother deserted you?" Jake asked, bringing the glass to his lips and taking another sip.

"I guess some people just aren't cut out to be parents even if they can bring life into the world," Catherine stated matter-of-factly, taking the last bite of food on her plate. "I must have been hungrier than I thought."

"You told me that your grandmother and father had passed away but you didn't tell me where they reside now?"

"They both reside at the Sea Pines Memorial Gardens Cemetery," she said quietly, lifting her glass only to realize that it was empty.

Reaching over, she picked up the bottle and poured herself more wine.

"Would you tell me about them? What exactly happened?" Jake asked.

"Grandma Alice, her real name was Alison but everyone just called her Alice," Catherine explained, trying to sound cheerier than she felt, "died from cancer just after I graduated high school. And if that wasn't tragic enough, two months later my father had a head-on collision with a drunk driver. He was killed on impact."

"That's awful." Jake reached out to console her, taking a hold of her hand. "Did you have any brothers or sisters?"

Feeling vulnerable, she pulled her hand back.

"I'm afraid not. I was an only child," Catherine replied, trying to sound unaffected while quickly putting up an invisible wall between them. "Dessert?" she asked, sounding nonchalant.

"Why did you do that?" Jake asked.

"Do what?" she asked.

"Shut down as if you are trying to cut me out. The room just got chillier—it dropped ten degrees in here."

She felt her chest tighten as unshed tears stung the back of her eyes.

"I'm sorry, Jake. I didn't mean to do that. The therapist I used to see in college said that it's my coping mechanism. I do it unconsciously and I want to thank you for calling me out on it," Catherine said, stacking their plates and silverware together.

"Here, let me do that," Jake insisted, taking the plates from her hands.

"But we both cooked dinner, so we both should do the clean-up," she pointed out.

"I really want to score points with the lovely woman of the house. So, I tell you what, you seat yourself right down here," he said, pointing to a spot on the counter, "and supervise while I do the dishes. Then you can let me know if I miss any spots."

Catherine smiled, jumping up onto the counter before reaching to pick up her glass of wine.

"You do realize that you are setting a precedent, right? It could determine the entire hierarchy of our relationship."

"I'm willing to take that risk," he replied with a grin.

Catherine enjoyed the fact that Jake was willing to get his hands dirty just to impress her, rather than sit around waiting for her to serve his every need.

"Your plan is working. I am swayed in your favor already and I am adding a lot of points to your plus column," Catherine teased, admiring him as he worked.

Jake flicked water at Catherine while she sat finishing her glass of wine. She squealed in surprise.

When Jake had dried the last of the dishes, Catherine handed him her glass and he set it down on the counter next to her.

"You may want more later," he said, looking deep into her eyes. "I believe there was some mention of dessert." Jake stepped in between her legs.

Wrapping her legs around his waist, Catherine felt butterflies in her stomach when Jake pulled her towards him.

"Alas, I don't have any sweets in the house. They're too tempting for me and I would eat them all and grow very fat," she explained.

He grinned as she leaned forward and wrapped her hands around the back of his neck, pulling him in for a long, slow kiss without hesitation. When their lips parted, Jake pulled back, searching her face for any sign of reluctance.

Catherine felt his heart beating wildly in tandem with hers. His scent filled her nostrils, robbing her of any willpower she had left. She wanted him to take her there and then, but thought it best to slow things down.

"Your lips are all the dessert I need," Jake said.

Reaching a hand beneath his shirt, Catherine felt the heat coming off of his bare flesh, and it made her pulse race and time stand still.

"Do you always talk this much before you make love to a woman?" she boldly asked in a low, husky voice. "Or are you one of those men who wants to hear a woman beg you?"

She saw her words light a spark, and it began to burn in his eyes as he gave her a questioning look.

"Do you always seduce men straight off of the beach by feeding them dinner and getting them drunk before taking advantage of them?"

Catherine giggled.

"My revolving door of men and busy social calendar should be evidence enough for you. You're very lucky that I had a cancellation tonight, or you might have been forced to wait another three months for a reservation," she teased. "Are my seductive powers of persuasion working on you?"

"Oh, yes. Your powers of persuasion are definitely working their magic on me—"

She covered his lips with a finger.

"Has anyone ever told you that you talk too much?" Catherine interrupted.

"I've only had one complaint, thus far," he admitted with a chuckle before leaning down and passionately kissing her lips. He brought a hand around the back of her neck to pull her even closer as he deepened the kiss.

Catherine felt his heart pounding beneath her hand. It stirred something in her that had been buried for far too long. The tension tightened somewhere deep inside of her every time he shifted his weight between her legs, and she wrapped her legs even tighter, pulling him closer.

His hand found its way beneath her dress, sliding along the sensitive, silky skin of her thigh to tease the elastic at the leg of her panties. Catherine dropped her hand down to his with the intention of objecting but stilled when his finger slipped inside of her, touching a sensitive and very swollen part, causing her to moan with pleasure.

"Please..."

"Please, what?" Jake murmured. "Say it."

"Please, don't stop," her voice quivered as his fingers found her core.

"Yes! Oh yes!" she cried out as one and then two fingers slid home. Catherine panted heavily, feeling the need for more of him.

She felt almost frantic, helping him as he pulled her dress up over her head. She locked her legs around him once again. Jake's hand slid up her back, unfastening the strap of her bra and letting it slide off to land somewhere on the floor at his feet. She shifted to pull his shirt off over his head, and moved with frenzy as their lips met again, wildly searching and exploring one another.

Catherine moaned when his lips traveled down her neck, cupping her breast in one hand, licking, suckling and kissing her, which made her shudder with sheer desire.

Looking around and seeing the dining room table, Jake slipped his hands beneath her, intent on transporting her to the spot but was waved off as Catherine pointed to the bedroom. All the while he was kissing her with wild abandon.

In the darkened room, the only light that shone was from the candles still lit in the kitchen and the moonlight that shone through the sheer curtains lining the bay windows. Jake laid her gently down on the bed and took a step back to admire the view. She was the most beautiful woman he'd ever seen. The sight of her laying there, wanting him, nearly drove him to the edge.

"You're killing me, woman," he said, turning his back to her as he raked his fingers through his hair, taking a deep breath to regain some semblance of self-control. "I feel like a schoolboy who can't control himself."

"Hurry," she whispered.

"Are you certain about this?" he asked. "Because we are entering the point of no return for me."

Coming up onto her knees, Catherine reached for him. "Jake Ryan, I want you. I need you desperately," she whispered.

He could see the pleading in her eyes. The fuse that burned inside of him exploded.

Their hands searched frantically for a hold as they both spiraled out of control. The pent-up desire they both had been denying for too long was suddenly unbound.

Catherine sighed as he moved into her arms, crushing her to him, their bodies melding perfectly together. Catherine deepened the kiss and opened her mouth to the silky feel of his probing tongue. Pushing his shorts off of his hips, Catherine ran her hands along the smooth, muscular skin of his tight thighs and buttocks.

Jake inhaled sharply, and she moved her hands over his taut stomach muscles while he kicked off his shorts, freeing himself from the confines of any clothing.

The sheer frenzy she created when she took him even closer to the edge.

"Hold on, love," he said, putting a shaky hand upon her hand that had just wrapped itself around his swollen member. "We have to slow this down or the party will be over before it begins."

It had never felt like this for Catherine. No one had ever made her feel so out of control before. This overwhelming desire for another person was just something she had read about in sappy romance novels. This stuff wasn't real, it couldn't be.

She was always so bound up by her fears, anxiety, and self-control that this strange emotion was completely foreign to her. Why was she so drawn to Jake? She had no answer, except to say that at that moment she wanted this man with all her body and all her heart.

Wrapping his large hand beneath her chin, Jake pulled her closer, kissing her already swollen lips slowly, exploring the taste of her before slipping inside of her. He groaned, and feeling himself approaching the edge, his fingers dug into the soft flesh of her rump. Time slowed down as he moved.

Catherine explored every inch of his skin, tangling her fingers through his hair when his lips met hers once again. Their bodies melded together as their need to possess the other overpowered them both.

She pushed Jake onto his back and straddled him. He reached up, cupping her chin and forcing her eyes to his. At that moment, they became one. There was something so intense about his gaze, it emboldened her, and she began to ride him harder.

Suddenly Jake flipped her back over, slowing the pace down to an almost agonizing crawl. Catherine raked her nails down his spine in frustration, and Jake sucked in a breath.

"Yes, yes, more," Catherine panted as her passion began to crest. Their hands intertwined and she savored the strength she felt in Jake's arms.

Throwing her head back and arching into him, Catherine cried out as the warmth of sweet release broke, spilling from her body in a rush. Then Jake shuddered, losing the last shred of his self-control as his body sought its own release and he groaned, pulling Catherine with him.

They lay spent and trembling in one another's arms while they both regained their breath.

"Who would have known?" Jake said.

"Known what?

"That you would be the one to ruin me for anyone else."

She smiled and kissed his chin and then his lips, softly.

"I don't quite know what came over me."

"Never worry about being yourself with me. The fact is, I am fascinated by you and every one of your moods. But I will admit, this one is by far my favorite."

CHAPTER 13

*C*atherine awoke to the aroma of eggs, toast, and coffee. She sat up as Jake strolled into the room, carrying a tray.

"What's all this?" Catherine laughed in surprise.

"I figured that I would feed you well, then perhaps you might give me another go," he said, setting the tray down on her lap.

"You feed me this well every morning, and I will grow too fat to move."

"With all of the cardio exercise you will be getting with me around, I'm afraid that will be impossible," Jake teased, which made Catherine roll her eyes. "Have you decided what you'd like to do with three days off?"

"I haven't had three days off in a row for so long, I couldn't really say what I would want to do with them," she said, wistfully.

"Well," Jake replied, "if you're up for a drive, we could always go to Savannah. It's only a couple of hours away and I've never been there. I hear there's a lot to do, and we would never get bored. What do you say? Are you up for a little walkabout with me?"

"I sure am," Catherine smiled. "And I doubt that you'd ever be boring, Jake Ryan," she continued. "Let's see, if you start packing now while I get a shower then pack, we could be on the road by 10:30, so that puts us in—"

Jake placed a finger over Catherine's mouth, and she blinked.

"We will make this as stress free and easy as we can. We will get there when we get there and it will be perfect. Deal?"

"Deal!" Catherine agreed, biting down on her buttered toast.

"Now when we get to the Georgia border, I'll let you get a Savannah brochure so you can pick out three places you want to visit. Other than that, we are free spirits and we will explore the great unknown together, because that's the way I like to travel."

She raised an eyebrow at him.

'There must be organization!' a small voice in her head screamed, but she pushed it aside.

"This is going to be fun."

While Jake drove to Savannah, Catherine chose her three points of interest. "I've decided on the stroll down Bay Street for shopping. Then a walk through the infamous Bonaventure Cemetery. And for my final choice, I want to take a guided tour of the downtown area and Oglethorpe's square."

Catherine was eager to learn about the history of one of the oldest Southern colonial cities in America, as well as the spirits that still resided there.

" 'Some would say,' " she began to read from her phone, " 'that to understand the South one must stroll through the Oglethorpe's three east coastal cities, and walk among the oak trees covered in Spanish moss as they sway in the evening breeze to understand the spirits that remain in the shadows. The mixture of sea air mingle with the sounds of the cicadas and crickets as they send their secret messages across the night breeze. When you walk among all of that, your soul is filled with a sense of nostalgia and everything it means to be Southern.' Doesn't that just sound wonderful?" Catherine sighed.

"What are you reading?" Jake asked, glancing over at Catherine as she studied her phone intently. "One might think that you are studying for a final's exam. Besides, I thought we agreed that we were going to get away from everything, but you keep looking at that phone as if you are waiting for something."

Catherine blushed, and quickly put her phone back into her pocket.

"I know," she said. "It's just, well, I am having so much fun, and that usually means that something bad is going to happen."

"You can't think like that," Jake said, "Why are you scrunching up your face at me?"

They picked up a few pamphlets and drinks as they stopped at a gas station for a break.

"There are so many cool things to do and you've told me I can only choose three of them. There is this historical square, and, oh, this one," she said, pointing at a particular pamphlet, holding it out for him to examine as he drove.

"You realize I can't read that thing while I'm driving, right?"

"I know, but it's just so hard to pick one or make a decision."

Catherine gave Jake her best sad face in hopes that he would be persuaded to see things her way.

"Are you sure you wouldn't want to make it four things?"

"Absolutely not," Jake chuckled as he pulled up to a red light, plucking the brochures out of her hand. "I give you four and you ask me for five. Where does it end?"

"All right, all right. Point taken. You got me there."

She sighed and rolled her eyes as she began to pull her phone from her pocket. She realized that she had a habit of looking at her phone when she noticed Jake was studying her.

She gave him an apologetic smile and immediately put the phone away.

Leaning over, Jake pulled her to him for a quick kiss as the light changed, and someone began impatiently beeping their horn.

"Sorry Mate," Jake said, waving at the person over his shoulder as he stepped on the gas.

"So, you want to find a way to tour the historical square area? I'll tell you what I'll do for you. If you leave that to me, I will make something happen," Jake said, giving Catherine a brilliant smile. "Now I want you to stop stressing so much and learn to relax a little more."

"Is that an order?"

"No, beautiful, just good old-fashioned advice."

"Then I think I will take it."

Catherine tipped her seat back a couple of notches to let the sunshine warm her face. She propped her bare feet up on the dash.

"You will not find anyone more relaxed than me this weekend."

"Now that's more like it!" Jake gave her hand a squeeze.

"Just keep your eyes on the road or we'll end up in a ditch somewhere."

Their playful banter continued as they drove on, arriving in Savannah a little after one in the afternoon, just in time for lunch. They stopped at the riverfront to eat at the Pirate House. They learned all about the history of the pirate smugglers over their signature sandwich of roast beef, honey mustard, tomatoes, lettuce and dill pickle on soft, white bread, that was paired with a sampling of three hand crafted beers. Afterwards, they bought matching pirate hats in the restaurant's store before continuing on to Bay Street to do some more shopping.

Walking hand in hand, they laughed and talked as if they didn't have a care in the world. Catherine heard a familiar laugh coming from across the street. Craning her neck, she spotted the couple walking hand in hand on the other side of the street. She couldn't believe her eyes. Did she just see Russell and Patricia walking down the street?

"Are you all right, love?" Jake asked, concerned by her sudden mood shift.

Catherine took another look over her shoulder.

"Did you see that couple across the street?"

"Where?" he asked, looking back.

Catherine looked again and saw the striking couple who were wearing matching ball caps.

"There," she pointed. "I think that's my boss, Russell Tillman, and his speech writer, Patricia Grant."

"That would be too much of a coincidence, Catie."

"But her laugh..." Catherine said.

"I think someone has work on the brain," Jake said, giving her a stern but playful look.

Catherine shook her head and looked again.

"I'm sure you're right. What was I thinking? Russell would never be caught dead in jeans, a Nirvana t-shirt, and a baseball cap," she admitted, realizing that she must be mistaken.

"We are in a safe zone here," he said. "There is no work when we are on vacation."

"That's easier said than done."

Jake linked his arm with hers.

"No work for my Catie! Only fun, sun, and play."

She laughed.

"That sounds like heaven to me."

Chase Stoneman's heart stopped for a moment when Catherine suddenly turned around, but of course he was unrecognizable to her by now. He had grown out his short, cropped hair nearly to his shoulders. A beard of two weeks covered his face. Not even his own mother would recognize him at this point if she walked past him on the street.

He'd been following Catherine and her new boyfriend down to Savannah to see if he could get any dirt that could be useful to Patricia. Then he saw Catherine pointing across the street at someone.

There was a couple walking on the other side of the road that caught his attention as well. They were dressed like any other tourists, in jeans, t-shirts, and matching baseball caps, except that there was something so familiar about the woman. Of course, the couple only looked like Patricia and Russell Tillman—but if he edited the pictures just right and left them a bit grainy, he could pass it off as the real thing.

Chase changed directions, stopping at the corner to wait for the light to change before crossing the street. He may have come down to Savannah to dig up dirt on Catherine Lawrence, but now he found a new mission.

He followed the new couple into the restaurant with a devious smile on his face. If he lost Catherine and Jake at this point, it didn't matter to him. He knew where they were staying and would catch up with them later. For now, Chase had a new target to pursue.

CHAPTER 14

*C*atherine and Jake continued to stroll arm in arm, carefree and happy as they made their way up the cobblestone avenue.

At four o'clock, Jake surprised Catherine with a tour of the city. He'd rented a private horse and carriage which also came with its own private tour guide.

The jet-black mare had a silver bridle adorned with silk flowers and the gleaming white carriage contrasted beautifully with its red velvet seats. The driver wore coat tails and a coal black top hat.

"Oh, Jake this is so much better than anything I had in mind," Catherine said, overjoyed by his thoughtful surprise. Once seated in the carriage, their personal guide placed a blanket over their laps. Catherine snuggled in close to Jake as they set off on their adventure.

The late September air was cool and crisp as the tour guide told them facts about the different landmarks of the city.

"Who was the family that built that house?" Catherine asked, interrupting the tour guide for the third time since they'd set off.

"I'm sorry, Miss. I don't know the answer to that," he said, before continuing on with his well-rehearsed talk. "Over the years, many notable residents have called Savannah home, including composer Johnny Mercer, inventor Eli Whitney, and Juliette Gordon Low, who founded The Girl Scouts of America."

"I heard that Savannah has several sister cities. Is that true and if so, how many exactly?" Catherine asked.

Taking a deep breath, the tour guide looked over his shoulder and smiled patiently at her, while pulling the carriage to the side of the road.

"Well, let me see, I believe there are five." He began to count on his fingers. "Yes. There are definitely five. Batumi, Georgia. Patras, Greece. Jinjiang, China. Halle, Germany. And last but not least, Kaya, Burkina Faso," he said with a smile, looking very pleased with himself for remembering all five of them.

"That is very impressive," Catherine said. "I don't think that I could have remembered all of those, let alone pronounce them right. What about you, Jake? Could you have remembered those cities and countries?"

Grinning broadly, Jake was amused by her curious mind.

"No. I'm certain that I would not have been able to remember all of those cities and countries," he laughed.

The tour guide pulled his carriage back out into the lane, and resumed his speech where he had left off.

"Designated by the U.S. government in 1966, the city is one of the largest National Historic Landmark Districts in the country."

As the carriage turned in front of Forsyth Park, Catherine heard a familiar cackle and turned quickly to see two city trolleys stopped at a light. She got a glimpse of the same man and woman she had seen earlier that day, seated at the back of the bus.

Quickly reaching for her phone, Catherine punched in a few numbers before catching sight of Jake staring at her.

"What are you doing?" he asked.

Opening her mouth to answer, she quickly closed it again and immediately put her phone away.

"Nothing," Catherine assured him while trying to get a better look at the couple on the trolley, "except having some fun in the sun, and relaxing."

As their carriage came around the corner, they stopped behind the trolley as their tour guide finished explaining the significance of the landmark in front of them. Catherine tried to be subtle as she observed the trolley that had started to pass them, but her actions didn't go unnoticed.

Giving her a gentle nudge, Jake motioned with his head toward the tour guide.

"He's going to think you're no longer interested in his explanations if you don't pay attention."

"I'm certain I just saw Russell and Patricia on that trolley. Call me crazy, but it's my spidey senses. They're tingling."

"No work, just fun, sun, and play," Jake reminded her.

"You're right," Catherine conceded, annoyed with herself for ruining this perfect moment.

"Please, go on. Could you repeat that last part again? And I promise this time I will pay better attention," Catherine said, crossing her heart.

Giving her a patient smile, the tolerant tour guide repeated his last statement, pulling the carriage over to the side of the street again so he could explain the significance of the monument he was pointing out.

As she listened, Catherine tried to forget what she was certain she'd seen. Yet, suspicion swirled around in her mind.

I knew that Patricia was a political climber, but even I'm not that limber. How could I have been fooled by Russell all of these years? I don't want to think about the fact that I work for a liar and a cheat. How can someone lie to my face so convincingly and cheat on his wife, who happens to be my best friend?

Chase Stoneman followed his targets on a rented scooter bike, snapping pictures everywhere they stopped. It was by sheer luck that they all ended up falling right into his lap at the same time. He knew that it wasn't Patricia and Russell, and yet the couple looked so like them it was uncanny.

Chase was giddy with delight when he realized his good fortune.

Later, he would edit the pictures and use them to discredit Russell, Patricia, and Catherine at a time of his choosing.

When Patricia hired him, she didn't expect him to betray her. He counted on her naiveté.

He had known exactly what Patricia had in mind that fateful night at The Blue Martini. He was supposed to humiliate Catherine Lawrence and Russell Tillman. But Chase had become suspicious of Patricia's motives when she didn't stick around for breakfast the night after they sealed the deal. He was no fool, and quickly figured out that Patricia hadn't been exactly forthcoming about her plans.

Chase became even more suspicious when Patricia began staying late at the office every night, resulting in not having time for him, not even to *discuss* things.

And whenever Chase did phone Patricia, she wouldn't pick up even if she was free. When he called Patricia's office, her secretary told him that she was too busy to speak with him. The memory still made Chase burn with fury. He was getting bolder with each passing day.

An evil, sardonic grin stretched across his lips.

"Play me for a sucker at your own peril, Patricia Grant," Chase said under his breath, snapping another intimate picture of her and Russell's look-alikes kissing at the back of the bus. "You think you're untouchable? Think again." He relished the thought of Patricia's life being laid open for the world to see.

Sunday morning dawned, and Catherine awoke with a start as the telephone rang. Half asleep, she felt Jake's side of the bed and found it empty. Rolling over to answer the phone, she heard a cheery voice informing her that this was her wake-up call.

"Thank you, but I didn't make a request for a wakeup call."

"Your husband did," the woman told her.

"My what? Oh, that's right," she said as she noticed a note taped to the telephone itself. "Thank you."

The note read:

> Good morning, beautiful. I have a special surprise for you. I need you to dress in something comfortable and bring your hat and sunglasses.

We're going on an adventure, and we will be out all day.

I also need you to meet me in the courtyard in forty minutes from the time of your wake-up call.

-XOXO Jake

Catherine jumped out of bed with a happy grin and headed straight into the shower. Forty minutes wasn't very long to get ready.

After her shower, she dabbed on a little lip gloss, grabbed her bag, room key, sunglasses, and the big floppy hat she had bought yesterday before heading out the door.

She nearly skipped all the way down to the lobby. Catherine usually didn't like surprises, but she couldn't wait to see what Jake had for her.

As she opened the lobby's French doors and stepped out into the courtyard, Catherine saw Jake had set up a romantic brunch for the two of them. The menu included an assortment of quiches, powdery beignets, fluffy buttermilk biscuits, sliced ham, crispy bacon, savory sausage, fresh fruit, several juices, coffee, and tea.

"There is enough food to feed an army!" Catherine said, kissing Jake good morning and taking the seat that he held out for her.

She noticed everything about him from his khaki shorts to his black, Gold Coast t-shirt from Australia.

"Nothing but the best for my girl," he replied.

"This is all too much, Jake. How are we ever going to eat all of this?"

"I figure that what we don't eat, we can take with us," he answered, retaking the seat next to her. "Besides, after last night," Jake said, with a wicked grin, "I figured you might be ravenous."

"I am rather famished," she said, leaning over to kiss him passionately. "But not necessarily for food, if you know what I mean. I'm so glad you suggested that we get away from it all. I'm especially grateful that you insisted I leave work behind. It's been good for me."

"You must know that it isn't over yet," Jake said, "We haven't finished our tours."

"Oh?"

She plucked a tasty looking spinach quiche from the tray as Jake helped himself to some ham. The waitress poured Jake a cup of coffee and some herbal tea for Catherine.

While they ate and talked, Catherine admired the beautifully landscaped courtyard. There was a fountain, statues set back in the alcoves, and a small pond. It wasn't a large area, but it had the illusion of spaciousness due to the way it was laid out. The flowering jacaranda, bougainvillea, azalea, magnolia, hibiscus trees, and shrubs mixed among the other features of the courtyard made it seem as if they were in a Southern garden.

The atmosphere made her feel as if she were sitting in the garden of one of the large, post-Civil War homes scattered across the south.

"So, besides the Bonaventure cemetery, what else will we be seeing today?" Catherine asked, causing Jake to pause in the middle of buttering his biscuit to consider her question.

"Well, sitting here admiring your beauty has made me rethink our plans," Jake said, then took a bite of his biscuit, "but a plan is a plan only if you carry through with it. So, I am open to visiting any sites you desire."

"You're on." She smiled widely and took another beignet from the tray, moaning in pleasure as she bit into it.

"But if you keep that up, I may have to take you back to our suite for an hour or two," Jake warned her.

"Only if I can take another beignet with me," Catherine insisted, wrapping it up in her napkin.

"Deal," he said, signaling the waitress over. "Could we please get the rest of this boxed up in a picnic basket? We will pick it up on our way out, a little later on."

"Right away, Mr. Ryan. It would be my pleasure," the waitress said.

Taking Catherine by the hand, Jake wore a large smile as the two of them walked through the doors of the hotel.

Catherine looked at Jake from the corner of her eye. She wondered what he was thinking while they rode the elevator back up. The expression on his face was happy. It felt good to have someone who looked at her that way.

It was like a dream, a wonderful fairytale, a whirlwind romance, but it could all end suddenly, so she cautioned herself to be careful. The delirious happiness she felt at that moment could all be gone in a blink of an eye.

The wise words of her grandmother came flooding back to her.

"There are no mistakes, dear child, just good and bad decisions, and the only thing holding you back is your own fear."

Fear is such a dreadful word, Catherine mused as she sucked the powdered sugar from her fingertips while giving Jake a seductive grin. She leaned in and kissed him passionately. The elevator doors opened and a parent covered the eyes of her small child.

"Get a room," the disgruntled mother said, as the two of them jumped off the elevator before the doors closed.

Looking into Catherine's eyes, Jake replied with a saucy grin.

"Thank you for the advice, ma'am."

An hour later, Catherine stretched before climbing back into bed and snuggling up next to Jake's warm body.

She felt satisfied by their love making. They lay together, safe and secluded in their plush hotel suite.

He jumped as she shifted, which made more of her skin touch his.

"Good heavens, woman! You're cold. Come here, I must save you from freezing."

He gathered her in his arms. Catherine giggled at his life saving efforts. She was grateful for his warmth and thrilled by his loving touch.

CHAPTER 15

By Tuesday morning, Catherine was back at work in her pristine business suit with a large box of beignets for the upper management team meeting. She couldn't hold back her smile. To everyone's surprise, it had taken the usual place of her professional facade.

There was three weeks left until the primary and there was no room for mistakes. The goal was in sight and the plan was set, which would give Catherine a tight opportunity to bring this campaign home. It was something she had been preparing for her entire life.

The plan was laid out to the last detail as she had explained to Jake during the car ride home from Savannah. He had been somewhat disappointed by the news, but at the same time he seemed to understand what it meant to her. She couldn't afford to be distracted, which was exactly what happened when he texted her a picture of himself, sleeping in her silk pajamas.

Catherine sent back an emoji of a smiley face with a heart-shaped kiss on its lips and closed her phone.

She began the morning meeting by laying out her game plan for the final stretch of the campaign in great detail, which included Russell's strategic plan for the remainder of the race. Catherine handed the plan documents to him as he rushed into the room, an apologetic smile plastered across his face.

She had been unable to reach Russell for three days before he reappeared this morning. She thought it was strange, but decided to let the matter slide for the moment. Their eyes met, and she conveyed her message without words.

They would speak soon.

In the back of her mind, Catherine was already putting on her tool-belt and preparing to fix the new mess Russell had created if he and Patricia really were having an affair. She didn't want to believe it, but she would face that matter when she came to it. For now, she put on her game face and continued the meeting.

Besides, Catherine figured that Russell would have something to say about the fact that she had scheduled his tasks so tightly every day from now until election day. He could argue the matter over with her later, then suck it up. If he wanted to win, this is what it would take to achieve victory.

She was also counting on the fact that Russell would never let on to the staff that he was completely in the dark about her plans for his campaign. Catherine watched him as he smiled and nodded throughout the entire meeting. It wasn't long before she began delegating the various weekly tasks to key staff members before turning the meeting back over to Russell. He quickly ended the meeting and dismissed everyone except for her.

"I thought I told you to take the weekend off, Catherine, and yet, I must commend you on your thoroughly thought-out planning. We can discuss some fine tuning of my schedule later," he said with a politician's smile.

Catherine recognized this as one of Russell's typical avoidance tactics. A red flag immediately went up.

"Yes, we will do some fine-tuning later," she assured him, smiling pleasantly.

"You should've gotten away this weekend. The weather was beautiful."

"Were you by any chance in Savannah this weekend, Russell?" Catherine asked, nonchalantly.

"No," he said, looking down at some papers on his desk that were left there by Marge for him to sign. Russell straightened up in his chair and looked up at Catherine. "Angie had a work thing out of town, so I stayed around here and played golf with some friends."

She narrowed her eyes at him, a tactic used to break suspects during cross examinations.

"Are you certain that you weren't in Savannah this weekend?"

"No. Of course not. I would have told you. Why are you asking me that again? Why are you looking at me like that?"

"I could have sworn I saw a man that looked just like you walking down the street with a woman that looked exactly like Patricia Grant—"

"Let me just stop you there, Catherine. I have never cheated on Angie and I certainly wasn't in Savannah this weekend."

"Really? What about you and Miss Grant in the stairwell at the dinner not too long ago?"

Russell looked suddenly flustered by the question. His face flushed red. "That was a misunderstanding—" he began to say as Catherine cut him off.

"A misunderstanding is something you apologize to a friend over. I'm talking about the two of you hiding out in the stairwell at your fundraising dinner." She raised her voice to an indignant pitch.

"First of all, I was hiding out there to sneak a quick cigarette—" he began to say.

"Russell," she said, in a disappointed tone. "I thought you gave those things up three years ago. You swore to Angela—"

"I know, and don't take that judgmental tone with me. The stress of the last six months got the better of me and I picked up a pack. So, what! That's not the point. I was hiding out in the stairwell and Patricia sauntered in. What was I supposed to do? Kick her out?"

"As a matter of fact, yes. That's exactly what I would have done. The woman is trouble, Russell. With a capital T."

"So, I'm not you and I didn't kick her out. What harm was done?"

"What harm was done? Russell, you're a smarter man than that," Catherine said. "I'll tell you what harm was done. Angela noticed that the two of you were missing from the room at the same time. And furthermore—"

"Oh, here we go with one of your famous furthermore—"

"Well, you opened the door by asking the question, so you should know you are going to get the answer, Russell."

"Who are you, my mother?"

"No, I'm your campaign manager and friend. You need to hear this. Patricia Grant has been a thorn in my side since the day she began working here. She is up to something, I can feel it in my bones, even if you choose to bury your head in the sand."

"We have been over this before—"

"And we will go over it again until you see reason."

Putting his hands up as a sign of defeat, Russell conceded her point.

"Fine. Let's just say that you are right. And mind you, I'm not saying that you are. But if you were correct in your assumption, what harm has actually been done?"

"Well, I guess we'll see about that little fiasco, won't we? Because sometimes, rot is festering just beneath the floorboards, and it's not evident until the floor collapses under you."

"Point taken. But that's not going to happen in this case—"

Wagging her finger at him, Catherine grimaced.

"I beg to differ, Russell—"

"You can beg to differ all that you wish, Catherine, but until the floor collapses beneath us, we have no real evidence. Do we?"

"Your debating skills are still sharp, my friend. But they won't help you in the least when you are out of this race because you refused to listen to me," Catherine said, shaking her head.

"I don't want to argue with you, Catherine—"

"Then, don't. I'm telling you, I saw a couple in Savannah this weekend and could have sworn it was you and Patricia. You just make sure that you have receipts and golfing score cards, so you can account for your whereabouts this weekend."

"I will dig them out of my waste bin in my office at home. Do you feel better?"

"As long as you can account for your whereabouts, I'm ecstatic. My spidey senses are tingling, and I feel that you are going to need the evidence to prove your innocence."

"Good. So, moving on to a more pleasant topic, I believe I owe you a celebratory dinner for that incredible coup you pulled off at the aquarium a few weeks ago. We would not be this far ahead in the polls if it wasn't for you," Russell said.

"Really, Russell, that isn't necessary."

"I insist. We are going out tonight. I won't take no for an answer."

Taking a deep breath, Catherine nodded.

"Alright," she said, turning towards the door. "But I will meet you at the restaurant. Just text me the name and time," she called over her shoulder as she reached the door, resting her hand on the handle. "Russell, is there anything you wish to confess to me? Anything at all? As your campaign manager, I am sworn to secrecy and would be obliged to help you clean it up."

Russell looked hurt.

"I'm going to be the next Governor of Florida because of you, Catherine. I must be above reproach."

Catherine chose her next words with great diplomacy.

"Yes, Russell, you do need to be above reproach. And I don't wish to be placed in a compromising position because I didn't have a clue as to what was going on behind closed doors."

"All is well at home, Catherine. I assure you."

"Have you and Angela talked yet? Did you straighten out what was going on with her?" she asked.

"We haven't had time for a heart-to-heart talk, if that's what you're asking. But everything is fine. I would tell you if anything was wrong."

"Good to know, but I still think that you need to talk before things get too muddled," she said as she opened the door. "Text me the details for tonight."

"I will as soon as I make the reservation."

A few hours later, Russell texted Catherine to tell her that he had made a reservation for seven thirty at Bella Valentinos. She saved the information to her phone and sent back a smiley face emoji. He asked again if she needed him to pick her up or send a car. She declined both options and assured him that she would arrive at the restaurant on time.

Catherine finished her day at the office and headed home to change for dinner. Questions whirled around in her head. She completely understood his motivation for treating her to a celebratory dinner. He wanted to make sure that she wasn't upset with him. Catherine just didn't know if she could sit across the table from Russell tonight, not knowing if he was a liar. Would she be able to hide her disdain for him?

Seeing Russell and Patricia together at the gala and knowing that they were the couple in the stairwell had left a bad taste in her mouth. And even though his explanation was somewhat reasonable, Catherine couldn't help being skeptical about it. Just the thought of the two of them together in Savannah made her sick to her stomach.

Angela was her best friend for heaven's sake. What game was he playing? Catherine wondered. The moral implications of Russell's bad choices reflected poorly upon her own reputation, and it infuriated her.

What if he had been seen by someone? It would be political suicide, for the both of them.

Catherine let out her breath, unaware that she'd been holding it, and genuinely considered calling Russell to cancel.

"I could tell him that I'm sick. No, he'll never buy it," she said out loud, looking at herself in the mirror. "I haven't been sick even one day in five years."

Unable to come up with a plausible excuse, Catherine pursed her lips and reapplied a nude colored lipstick, then zipped up her makeup bag and put it back into the drawer.

Was this job really worth all of the trouble she was going through right now? Not to mention the moral dilemma?

"Who would I be, if I wasn't Russell Tillman's right-hand woman, and this job was gone tomorrow?" she asked herself out loud.

Stepping into her walk-in closet, Catherine decided to wear a classic, black Chanel sheath dress with a black jacket. She pulled a pair of black spectator pumps with stiletto heels down off the shelf. They were the perfect pair to complement her outfit. She pulled her hair back into a sleek chignon at the back of her head, which elongated her neck. Then, she added a pair of pearl earrings and a pearl choker to finish off the look. It was simple, sleek, and elegant.

She grabbed her small clutch purse and keys and headed to the garage and climbed into her car.

"Put that smile on your face, Buttercup," she said to her reflection in the rearview mirror. "This is what you trained for your entire life. Don't wimp out on me now!"

Jake came walking up the sand, exhausted after riding a few early evening waves, and placed his board upon the sawhorses under his porch. That's when a camera flash caught his eyes. It was coming from around the corner of the building. He realized that someone was sneaking around the back of Catherine's condo.

Jake quickened his pace and came around the corner, surprising the would-be-intruder standing at Catherine's bedroom window. The two of them locked eyes before the intruder pulled the hood of his jacket up higher to cover his entire face, and took off running for the street.

"Hey! Oi! Stop!" Jake yelled, hurtling himself over one of Catherine's deck chairs. He leapt over the treadmill and gave chase.

Jake raced around the corner of the condo to see the taillights of a light-colored compact making a clean getaway.

"Who would be peeping into Catherine's window?" Jake wondered.

Catherine's garage door opened and he saw her car pull out.

She lifted a hand and waved to Jake as she shifted the car into drive and pulled away. He raised a hand, trying to stop her. When her vehicle disappeared from sight, Jake decided to tell her about the incident later. For now, he would be more vigilant in his patrol of the neighborhood, more specifically, Catherine's place.

CHAPTER 16

$\mathcal{C}$atherine walked into the entrance of Bella Valentinos promptly at seven twenty five and gave the host her name. He guided Catherine over to a table near the back corner of the restaurant. As he was leading her over, Catherine spotted Russell sitting at the bar nursing a scotch with a scowl on his face.

She was just about to ask the host to let Mr. Tillman know that she was there, when Russell looked up and saw her. Catherine wondered what had changed his mood. He grabbed his drink and made his way over to her. His expression stayed sullen, until he grew nearer to the table. That's when he put his game face on.

"I see you made it. Prompt as always. Not that I had any doubt." He motioned towards the host. "Would you like a drink from the bar?"

"No, thank you. I'm driving. I'll just have sparkling water," Catherine replied.

"I will have your waiter, Anthony, bring your drinks over right away," the host said. "Enjoy your meal."

Catherine looked out the window to the view of the beach. Bella Valentinos was not directly on the beach but had a beautiful view of the Atlantic Ocean. The moonlight played across the water as the waves flowed in and out, and the foam lapped upon the sand. It felt very tranquil and hypnotic to Catherine as she stared out the window.

Russell must have noticed her dispassionate composure.

"Why do you look so sour tonight?" he asked.

"What are you talking about, Russell?" she countered, trying to change the subject.

"I've known you for four years, Catherine. You might as well spit it out," he prompted, "You really don't have a very good poker face."

Looking around to ensure that no one was close enough to hear what she had to say, Catherine decided to clear the air between them.

"Yes, we've known one another for over four years now, and I thought that made us friends. Hell, I was the maid of honor at your wedding, so this is hard for me to say..." She stopped and looked around before focusing her attention back on Russell. "I know about you and Patricia Grant, Russell," she stated adamantly, looking him straight in the eye.

At first, he attempted to deny the allegation. "What are you talking about, Catherine?"

"You and Patricia have been having an affair. Or should we simply refer to her as Malibu Barbie, for privacy purposes, of course," Catherine quipped.

"You've got it all wrong, Catherine," Russell assured her. "Miss Grant and I are merely colleagues."

"Do I?" Catherine fired back.

"Yes," he quickly replied. "We are simply professional—"

"Save it for someone who doesn't know you like I do, Russell," she chided, cutting him off. "Something was going on in that stairwell a few weeks back. The two of you were doing something more than simply playing patty-cake. The question is, what, and has anything transpired between the two of you since?"

He just shrugged.

She shook her head, furious with him but trying to keep it together.

"What were you thinking? No, forget it. You weren't thinking!" she scolded, waving their waiter away as he approached their table to take their order.

Taking a deep breath, Russell hung his head.

"I could sit here and pretend that I don't have a clue about what you have been up to," she said. "But that's just not my style and you know it. I put my personal and professional reputation on the line to be your campaign manager and you managed to piss it away in one-fell-swoop." She waved her hand around dramatically, searching for an appropriate word. "Of all the stupid, irresponsible, selfish, ignorant things you have ever done, Russell Tillman, this takes the cake!"

"Now hang on there, Annie Oakley, before you go shooting everything to hell. I told you what transpired in the stairwell—"

"But you left something out, didn't you?"

Taking a deep breath, he blew it out slowly.

"It was a mistake…"

"A mistake?" she whispered, taking a quick glance to make sure that no one had been listening to them. "A mistake is something you do unintentionally!" she snapped. "You can bet your sweet derriere that this, what you did, was no mistake. You have put me in a compromising position, to say the least."

He hung his head between his shoulders.

She paused.

"A mistake… As if you merely neglected to tell me about a meeting you set up," Catherine muttered under her breath and looked down as if she were simply straightening out the napkin in her lap. "Of all the…" she fumed, unable to finish her sentence for fear that she would say something that she couldn't take back.

"It won't ever happen again," Russell assured her, his face turning beet red.

"I need the truth, Russell, and this time don't leave anything out."

"The night of the ball, Patricia approached me in the stairwell, and we shared a cigarette. Then she kissed me, and I didn't stop it. I know it was wrong—"

"But you did it anyway—"

"Look, you asked me to explain, and I'm trying to do that. Just give me a chance."

"You're right. Please go on."

"We shared a kiss. Nothing more. I told her the next day that it was a mistake and that nothing like that could ever happen again because I truly love my wife. And it hasn't. I swear to you, Catherine."

"So that really wasn't you and Patricia in Savannah this last weekend?"

"No. Absolutely not!"

"So, you aren't having an affair?"

"How many times can I say this to you? No. I'm not having an affair."

"But you did kiss the woman?"

"And I have regretted that mistake ever since. Look, I love Angela. I would die for her. I allowed myself to be flattered by," he looked around to make sure no one was listening except Catherine before continuing, "by Malibu Barbie," he spit the words out as if they left a bad taste in his mouth. "Some people might say that thoughts are the same as action but I would disagree. Am I perfect? Hell no, but I am perfect in my love for my wife."

"You and Angela have to talk. Put it all out there. Leave nothing unsaid, Russell. This kind of secret can ruin a marriage," Catherine said. "You and Angela are my friends."

She looked down into her lap again and dabbed the moisture from her eyes before looking up at him.

"There are no words to express how deeply sorry I am, Catherine, but this kind of confession will crush her."

"But if you don't tell her and she finds out another way, your marriage will definitely be over. I know her. You can't allow this lie to stand between the two of you."

"Then, I will tell Angela the truth," Russell said, looking away as his own eyes watered.

"When?"

"What?"

"When will you tell Angela about…this mistake that was made?"

"Just as soon as the race is over."

"No. That's too late! What if this whole thing blows up in your face? And mine as well, for that matter," Catherine pointed out. "You have to tell her before the end of the race, Russell. You both need to talk, to clear the air between you. It has to be tonight. Do you hear me? This is too important to wait."

"Fine, tonight then! I'll tell her tonight," he conceded, with a moan. "But this is going to kill her."

"Better to hear this kind of news directly from you, than from the lips of the news anchor on the six o'clock news, Russell Tillman. That would be a nightmare for everyone involved. It would end Angela, for sure," she warned him, leaning in a little closer to ensure complete privacy. "Swear to me, Russell, that you will tell her tonight. Swear it!"

"I swear it," he said, quite begrudgingly, before motioning to the waiter that they were ready to order. Then he picked up his drink and downed the rest of it in one swallow.

Catherine sat back in her seat, satisfied that the matter was settled. She picked up her water glass and took a sip before placing it back down on the table.

The waiter had been watching them and immediately appeared and recited the specials for the evening in a rather dispassionate manner. Catherine settled on the salmon with rice and vegetables, and Russell ordered the Shrimp Scampi over noodles and a salad.

Their conversation was stiff and uncomfortable at first, but they soon fell back into their normal banter.

Russell took a bite of his food and suddenly began gasping for air.

"Are you choking?" Catherine cried, hitting him on the back, trying to dislodge whatever was stuck in his throat. Russell began to wheeze. He grabbed at his throat and stood up. Catherine jumped up as well, positioning herself behind him to perform the Heimlich maneuver.

It took several thrusts before she finally dislodged the piece of shrimp, sending it sailing across their table and onto the floor.

Taking several gasping breaths, Russell wiped the tears from his eyes and sat back down.

"Thank you," he said, looking up at her.

Catherine eyed him a moment longer, before turning with a big smile on her face to assure the people who hovered nearby that all was well, and that it was a simple matter of a pesky shrimp swimming in the wrong direction. She looked around to ensure that no one had been recording the incident.

The waiter came over to see if there was anything he could do for them. Catherine assured him that they were fine.

"I'm sorry that happened to you, Russell," Catherine apologized. "Are you sure that you are all right?" she asked, reaching her hand across the table to take a hold of his.

"Yes. Thanks to you," Russell answered with a smile to assure the people still staring in his direction that he was fine. "I should never try to swallow and talk at the same time," he jokingly said to the people at the next table.

"I'm fine, Lawrence," he said out of the side of his mouth. "Stop looking at me like I just died."

"I was just worried, Russell, and if it's all the same to you, I've had enough excitement for one evening. I think I'm going to call it a night."

"I'll get the bill and walk you out," Russell insisted, looking around for the waiter.

After paying the bill and leaving a generous tip, Russell and Catherine walked out of the restaurant together and waited in amiable silence for Catherine's car to be brought around.

"I'll see you at the office, bright and early, then?" Russell asked, trying to break the uncomfortable tension between them.

"Of course," she replied, giving him a smile as her car pulled up to the curb. "Goodnight, Russell. And please, don't forget your promise."

With a somber nod of his head, Russell shut her car door and watched her drive away.

CHAPTER 17

*C*atherine texted Jake before she left the restaurant, and he was sitting on the couch waiting for her with a glass of wine already poured when she arrived home.

"I hope one of those glasses of wine is for me," she said, "because I have had one heck of a day, not to mention a horrendous evening."

Patting the cushion beside him, he handed her the glass he'd poured for her. "Take a load off and put your feet up. I'm afraid your day isn't about to get any better," he warned. Jake proceeded to tell her about the man standing outside of her bedroom window taking pictures, and how he'd tried, with no success, to catch him.

She was horrified.

"What if the man had a gun or a knife Jake? You could've been killed!" she exclaimed with a shiver of fear.

"That's not the point, love," he said, while rubbing her feet. "There was a bloody creeper outside your window trying to take pictures of you. Crikey, he's not even the first bloke that I've had to chase off."

"What are you talking about, Jake?" Catherine gasped in shock.

"Remember that other bloke I chased away? It was shortly after you'd slammed the door in my face," he explained. "I was coming back from surfing and saw some slimy bloke in a hoodie, poking around your place. I yelled at him, and he took off running."

"I remember you yelling at me because my curtains were too sheer," Catherine replied.

Taking her into his arms, Jake pulled her close.

"Don't be angry," he cajoled. "Here's what I'm going to do. I'll stay here tonight and keep a watchful eye out for the dirty mongrel. And look, I even have more wine," he added, holding up a nearly full bottle of wine.

With a happy sigh, Catherine smiled.

"After the dinner I just had tonight, I could really use a double."

"Your wish is my command."

"Just take me to bed and love me," Catherine whispered, downing the contents of her wine glass before handing it back to him.

"You're my kind of sheila. You don't need to ask me twice." He took the glass from her hand and placed it down on the coffee table before pulling her to her feet.

The curtains were pulled closed before they started undressing one another. Catherine stood on her tip toes to reach Jake's mouth, his lips tasting of fine red wine.

The flames of desire quickly ignited as his hands explored her flesh.

Unfastening her bra, Jake grinned, letting the lacy garment drop to the floor. They left a trail of clothing in their wake before they fell onto her bed.

Catherine giggled when Jake flipped her over and ran his tongue down her spine, sending goosebumps up and down her back.

"You're not supposed to laugh when I make love to you," he admonished.

"Says who?" she retorted, then moaned with pleasure as Jake continued to glide his hand down her sensitive skin, leaving a hot trail everywhere it touched.

"You might make a bloke lose his confidence," Jake whispered in her ear. He delivered more kisses around her ear and along her throat as he made his way seductively to her lips. "Then where would that leave you?"

She turned back over to face him.

"In a very bad spot I would wager," Catherine replied. She felt breathless as his lips circled her breasts and continued downward to her navel.

"Yes, a very bad spot indeed," he grinned, looking up at her with a devilish smile before running his tongue lower.

Catherine arched her back and moaned as Jake licked and suckled.

"Oh, yes!" she cried.

He crawled his way up the length of her body, raining kisses along the way, and cupped her breasts. Catherine gasped as he nibbled her sensitive flesh until she cried out.

Weaving her fingers through his hair, Catherine pressed his head to her and begged him to take her.

Jake entered her in one slow, agonizing thrust before they began to move in unison, reaching their peak. Catherine cried out first, calling his name over and over again until Jake climaxed. They clung to one another until the world stopped spinning.

"How do you know just what I need," Catherine whispered against his skin once her breathing slowed back to normal.

Jake chuckled.

"It's as if we are two halves."

Catherine kissed him passionately and couldn't help but marvel at her good fortune.

"You're almost too good to be true," she murmured into his ear.

Smoothing back a stray curl, Jake pulled back to look her directly in the eyes.

"I'm just a man, my love."

"Tell me a story of your home, Jake. I want to know what you were like as a child and what it was like growing up in Australia."

Jake kissed her on her forehead as she snuggled herself into his side.

"I was a little devil, if you believe my older brother, Jesse. But Mum tells it differently," Jake said with a chuckle.

Eventually, they fell asleep in each other's arms, content, and happy.

CHAPTER 18

Catherine woke before her alarm and gingerly removed Jake's arm from her waist to slide out of bed. She padded to the bathroom quietly and began to take a shower.

She dressed, brushed her hair into a bun at the back of her neck, and put on her makeup. Then she leaned over to kiss Jake goodbye.

Opening his eyes, he yawned.

"Good morning, beautiful. Where are you off to so early?"

"I have an early morning meeting, but I wanted to say goodbye, rather than slink off without a word. Thank you for last night."

Jake wrapped his arm around her waist and pulled her back into bed.

"Why do you hide all of that beautiful hair, putting it up like that?"

"I don't know. Maybe because it looks professional?" she replied. "How would you have me wear my hair?"

Taking the pins out, Jake reached up and ran his fingers through her hair, sweeping it to one side.

"Like that," he said, giving her a satisfied smile. "Now you look perfect."

"Yes, but do I look professional?"

"Absolutely. One hundred percent," he exclaimed before letting her go.

"Well, if you're happy, I'm happy," Catherine said, giving Jake a kiss before walking out to the kitchen to fill her coffee mug. "I shouldn't be late, in case something blows up in my face today. Want to have a *barbie* tonight?" she inquired, trying to sound Australian.

Overcoming a yawn, Jake laughed.

"Of course, my little sheila."

"I'll call you later then," she said, with one last kiss goodbye.

It was hard to believe they had only been together for a few days. She felt euphoric. Jake was everything she wanted in a man. He was all she thought about. Up until now, her career had consumed every waking moment of her life. To her surprise, it was no longer controlling her.

As she walked into the office, the first thing Catherine noticed was everyone peering towards Russell Tillman's office. The next thing she noticed was the yelling, coming from said office.

"What's going on?" she asked. The staff exchanged looks. No one dared give an answer.

Russell's door opened and Patricia came running out with several tissues in her hand.

"Perfect!" Russell said, in an irritated tone, "Lawrence, I need to see you. Now! The rest of you, get back to work!"

Everyone immediately scattered. Catherine hurried into his office and closed the door.

"What happened? Why was Patricia running from your office in tears, Russell?"

Russell sat down into his chair. He emptied the contents of a large envelope that had been delivered to his office earlier by a courier. He spread the photographs inside, out onto his desk.

"This campaign is finished! I'm ruined!" he said. "And it's my own damn fault."

At first, she was dumbfounded. Then, careful not to get her fingerprints on the photos, she sifted through them, using the back of a pen.

"Did you touch them?" she asked, looking up at him.

"I took them out of the envelope, if that's what you're asking."

Picking up the phone, Catherine dialed an extension.

"Get me legal. Yes, I want them to call me on Mr. Tillman's line. And, Jane, this is important. Make sure they know that I need to speak with them immediately."

"What's going through that brilliant legal mind of yours?" Russell asked, looking hopeful.

"Do we know who sent them?" Catherine asked without answering his question.

"No! Or I would strangle them myself."

"I'm assuming these pictures came with a letter of intent, and that there are demands."

Russell opened then closed his mouth.

"Yes. But how did you know?" he stammered.

"It's standard operating procedure for blackmailers," Catherine answered without looking up from the photos. "There's a picture here of you and me having dinner last night..." she gasped. "And it looks as if some of these have been photoshopped, see? You and I were never together in Savannah. Boy, this guy may think he's good. But he's not good enough," she muttered to herself. "Do you have a magnifying glass?"

"Top drawer to your left."

Catherine pulled out the magnifying glass to examine a particular photo that had someone mirrored in the corner window.

She noticed that the person taking the pictures had accidentally taken a picture of his own reflection.

"Gotcha!" she cried.

Catherine picked up her phone and called her friend, Detective Peterson. She relayed the extortion attempt and asked him to send someone from his team to pick up the evidence.

He promised to send someone at once.

"Don't move from that chair," she told Russell as she stomped out the door and towards Patricia's office. Through the closed door, Catherine heard Patricia arguing with someone.

"How could you be so stupid?" Patricia hissed. "I told you to dirty up Lawrence, not to implicate me or Mr. Tillman in the process. How incompetent do you have to be to screw up such a simple plan?" she ranted. "What do you mean, you feel used? Of all the idiotic, pathetic excuses, that has got to be by far the lamest one I've ever heard."

Catherine had heard enough and flung open the door.

"And to think that I was foolish enough to—" Patricia stopped mid-sentence. She flushed red, a look of guilt on her face.

"I'm busy, Catherine. What is it?" Patricia said tersely with the phone still held to her ear as if she was unsure what she should do next.

"You can start by telling me who's on the other end of that call," Catherine demanded, stepping into the room and closing the door.

Caught off guard, Patricia did the only thing she could think of.

"I'll call you back," she said, before hanging up her cellphone and placing it face down on her desk. "I was having a private conversation. You have some nerve. What gives you the right to barge in here?"

Leaning over the desk, Catherine stared at Patricia.

"Being your boss, for starters. Besides, it was really a rhetorical question, Miss Grant. I know exactly who was on the other end of that call. *Chase Stoneman*," she said with emphasis. "I just wanted to see if you had it in you to be honest, for once in your life."

Patricia jumped to her feet.

"That is a bald-faced lie, Catherine Lawrence. Take that back!" she demanded. "Why, the audacity of you!"

Picking up Patricia's phone from the desk, Catherine redialed and waited for someone to answer.

"Hey, give that back to me!" Patricia insisted, stepping around the desk to retrieve her phone.

"It's about time you called me back, you back-stabbing—"

"Thank you for confirming my suspicions, Mr. Stoneman. You have a nice day," Catherine said, and hung up the phone.

Turning on her heels, Catherine walked to the door and opened it.

"Miss Grant, this phone is the property of this office. As such, it will be entered into evidence. And might I suggest, while you await security to escort you to the police station, that you clean out your desk. You're finished here. Your services will no longer be needed."

Patricia looked completely bewildered.

"You're wrong about me," Patricia said, plopping down into the nearest chair as if her legs would no longer hold her.

"No, I'm afraid not, Miss Grant," Catherine replied, from the doorway. "You had an endgame from the very beginning. I just didn't think that it included criminal extortion. The lawyers will be in shortly with a statement for you to sign, along with a non-disclosure agreement. If you cooperate with us, you just might get off with a few years of jail time. Mind you, that is if you are willing to roll over on Stoneman. Either way, your political aspirations are finished. And I'm afraid that you will no longer be able to practice law. But you already know that."

Patricia said nothing.

Catherine waited for the security guard to walk into the room.

"She is to stay put until you hear from me. Make sure that she only takes her personal belongings as she cleans out her office. I'll have a box sent in," she instructed, giving Patricia one last glance over her shoulder before walking out the door.

The attorneys were waiting for her when she returned to Russell's office. She explained to them what she had overheard when she went to confront Patricia. She also told them who was behind the extortion.

"Miss Lawrence, a Detective Peterson is here for you," Jane called over the intercom.

Catherine leaned over Russell's desk and pressed the flashing intercom button.

"Excellent, Jane, send him in."

Jane showed Peterson and his partner into the office, then idled by the doorway.

"Will there be anything else, Miss Lawrence?" She was clearly hoping for an invitation to sit in on their meeting, but when Russell shook his head, Jane quickly shut the door.

"It's good to see you again, Catherine," Detective Peterson said. "I wish it were under better circumstances. This is my partner, Detective Merrick. I filled him in on our drive over. Have there been any new developments?"

Catherine offered the two detectives a seat and didn't waste any time briefing them on what she had overheard, offering up Patricia's phone as evidence.

"You might want to offer Patricia a deal if she cooperates. She may have been the mastermind behind this entire debacle, but somehow, I feel Stoneman may have played her for the fool she is. Not that I'm saying she's a victim in this, by any means," Catherine clarified.

"Don't tell me you're feeling sorry for that...that miscreant!" Russell bellowed, as he paced back and forth, across the room.

"I am not feeling sorry for anyone who tried to sabotage this campaign. I'm just saying, let's be smart about this. I need you to take a step back from all of this, Russell. You're too close to it. If we get Patricia to roll over on Stoneman, it will be an open and shut case. One that could potentially be wrapped up before anyone is the wiser." She gave Russell a sour look. "If this gets out, it could ruin your campaign, and any future political aspirations you may have. Not to mention what it will do to your marriage."

"She's right, Mr. Tillman," the attorney advised. "If we can strike a deal and get Miss Grant to cooperate, it will be a done deal and over before it even gets started."

"I don't like it!" Russell bellowed. "She played me."

"You mean, you don't like getting caught with your pants down," Detective Peterson said.

"No one has been caught with their pants down, Detective."

"What Mr. Tillman is trying to say, gentlemen," Catherine cut in before Russell had the chance to continue, "Is that he is rather embarrassed by the entire incident and would like to put the matter to bed, so to speak, before this affects the campaign in a negative way."

"Just handle the matter and prosecute the two of them to the fullest extent. I don't want people to think that I'm soft on crime," Tillman ordered, "Keep this out of the public spotlight."

"Thank you, gentlemen. That will be all." Catherine dismissed the two detectives and walked them to the door.

"This matter is sensitive. Keep it between us. Secretaries and associates are not to lay eyes on any of this," she warned the attorneys.

In unison, the three men nodded their heads.

Catherine closed the door behind the attorneys and turned to study Russell, who had his back to her.

"So, I'm going to assume that you didn't tell Angela about the kiss last night."

He turned to face her.

"I didn't have the chance. She'd already gone to bed by the time I got home," he said, with a pensive expression. "She hasn't been feeling well lately and has been going to bed early."

"Have you asked her about it?"

"No…"

"And why not? You are her husband after all," she said. "What if there is something wrong with her?"

"Do you know something that I don't?"

"I know a lot of things that you don't, Russell. But for the answers you are seeking now, you will have to speak to Angela. I made a promise and I'm not in the habit of betraying a confidence."

"I'm such a fool, Catherine," Russell said.

Russell appeared deflated as he looked at her, so Catherine didn't see any need to kick him while he was down.

Catherine plopped down into a chair across from him.

"What were you thinking? You fell for the oldest trick in the book, Russell."

Tillman held up his hands.

"You can save the lecture. I've said it to myself at least a hundred times this week. I'm an idiot."

"You just made a bad choice. But now you have to fix it. If Angela catches wind of this scandal on the news tonight or from a third party, she'll be humiliated. I beg you, come clean with her."

"You're right, of course."

Jane knocked on the door and poked her head inside the office to gage the situation. Then she stepped inside and closed the door.

"What is it, Jane?" Russell asked in a tired tone.

Unsure, Jane shifted her weight from one foot to the other, looking ready to bolt.

"Sorry to bother you both, but there's a reporter at my desk requesting an interview. What do you want me to tell him?"

"Tell the little blood sucker..." Russell began as Catherine stood up and placed a hand on his shoulder to stop him from saying anything further.

"Give me five minutes, then show the man to my office. I will handle him," Catherine said, with a pleasant smile while she looked at Jane. "Offer him some coffee, tea, or water while he waits. I'll be there soon. Thank you, Jane. That will be all."

"Thank you, Miss Lawrence," Jane said with a grateful smile before closing the door behind her.

"I know I'm right, Russell," Catherine said, looking down at him before walking over to the door and resting her hand on the doorknob. "You have to call Angela this minute and meet her at the house. Work this out! You have to make things right with her, or your political career is over before it's even begun, not to mention your marriage. I will handle things here. Go home, Russell and tell your wife how much you love her."

"The only time I didn't listen to you, Catherine, is the only time I got myself into a tight spot."

Catherine watched Russell pull out his phone and dial his wife before she shut the door quietly behind her.

CHAPTER 19

*A*ngela locked eyes with Russell when he arrived home.

"What's going on, Russell? You haven't called me to meet you at our home in years," Angela nervously said, setting her bottle of water down on the table as she took a seat on the couch.

Russell had rehearsed everything he wanted to say to her on his way home in the car. Only, his words had sounded so trite, even to him: How does someone explain to their wife that they had been unfaithful, even if it was only in their mind?

He grabbed a bottle of water from the refrigerator and sat down next to her on the couch.

"I have something to tell you, and it isn't easy for me. I did something that was very stupid. I'm a complete idiot."

"You slept with her, didn't you?" Angela accused, tipping her head back. "I knew it was just a matter of time after that night at the aquarium. I knew this was going to happen." She got up and walked to the window with tears in her eyes.

"Angie, please, let me explain..." Russell pleaded, coming up behind her.

Angela turned and slapped him hard across the face, leaving a red hand mark.

"Save it, Russell," she exploded. "How many times?!"

"What?" he asked, stunned by the slap to his face.

"I asked you how many times..." she demanded. "Is that so hard to understand? Or am I speaking in a foreign language?"

"One kiss, and some inappropriate thoughts, Angela, that's it," he answered. "And it was a huge mistake. One which I deeply regret. I swear it."

"I asked you the night of the ball if there was anything between you and her, and you told me that I was crazy!" she screamed. "You had me believing that I was being paranoid for even thinking such a thing. But I was right!"

Tears welled in her eyes as she looked at the only man she had ever loved. They had had their problems—just like every other married couple—but Angela still loved him, despite it all.

"Why, Russell? Why did you do this to us?" she cried, burying her face in his chest. "I know things haven't been great since my last miscarriage. But this... this utter betrayal, why?"

"Angie, I was wrong. So terribly wrong for pulling away from you when you needed me the most. When you lost the last baby, I was so devastated. I tried to comfort you, but you just seemed to pull farther and farther away from me. I felt hopeless, abandoned, unloved. Especially when you started sleeping in the other room."

"So now this is my fault?" she cried, pulling back to wipe her tears with the back of her hand.

"No! No, my love. I would never put the blame on you. None of this is your fault. It was all me," Russell said, taking her into his arms. "I'm just trying to explain how... but none of that really matters. I made this mess. I will clean it up. I just need to know that there is a chance that you could one day find it in your heart to forgive me. Can you ever forgive me? Can we start again?"

"Your timing is impeccable as usual, Russell," Angela said, though she felt her anger cooling slightly.

"What do you mean?"

"I mean that I just came from the doctor's office this morning. That's why I wasn't in court today," Angela answered glumly as she pushed out of his arms and sat back down on the couch.

"I'm pregnant. We're having a baby," she whispered. "That is the reason I started sleeping in the other room. I didn't want to endanger the baby by us having sex in the first trimester. I also didn't want you to get your hopes up again, in case, well… just in case I lost the baby. I wanted to spare you that pain."

He stood there, dumbfounded.

She hurried on to explain further.

"The doctor has been monitoring me closely because I am so high risk. He has been giving me some new, experimental treatments that they have found effective in… in cases like mine."

"When?" he mumbled. "How?"

"I'm starting my second trimester. I was going to tell you tonight when you got home," she sobbed, grabbing a handful of tissues from the Kleenex box on the coffee table to blow her nose.

"Now I really feel like a complete…" Russell gasped, sitting down next to her.

"It isn't all your fault, Russell," she said, looking at him through watery eyes.

"Please, Angie. I'm begging you. Give me another chance. I'm an idiot. I will spend the rest of my life trying to make this up to you. I made a mistake, one for which I can never expect you to forgive me. All I'm asking is for you to try and forgive me."

She blew her nose into some tissues before softening her stance.

"I cannot lay the entire blame of our marital downfall at your feet. I pushed you away last year when I lost the baby and buried my sorrows at work. The only reason we are pregnant now is because we took that weekend trip to that island and drank too many Pina Coladas. Remember?”

His laugh was sad.

“Of course I do.”

“It would appear that I am partly to blame for our downfall—we are both idiots.”

“Oh, Angie, I would do anything to fix this. You name it, I’ll do it. We can see a counselor, or take a trip, or you can tell me to go to hell if you want,” Russell pleaded. “I love you, baby. I always have.”

“I love you too. You big dope. But what about Patricia?”

“She has been fired,” he assured her. “The woman is out of our lives forever.”

“I want to start over. I want us to be a family,” Angela said. “But I’m still going to be mad at you for a while longer.”

“You are perfectly within your rights to be so.”

“And I’m going to spend lots of money redecorating the spare room into a nursery.”

“I wouldn’t have it any other way,” he answered. “Whatever you want, it’s yours.” Russell put his arms around her. “Just please, don’t leave me. This fool loves you.”

“I love you too.”

Catherine eventually finished up with the lawyers, detectives, and the reporter. After she was done telling her side of the story, Patricia was painted as a pariah, Stoneman was portrayed as a disgruntled employee and a washed-up hack of a campaign manager who would never be able to work in politics again, and Russell Tillman looked like a choir boy.

Patricia had been led off in handcuffs and there was an all points bulletin out on Chase Stoneman. A statement was released to all of the local news outlets that a press conference would be held at ten o'clock the next morning to clear up any alleged wrongdoing on behalf of candidate Russell Tillman.

Catherine's job here was done for the day. She glanced down at her phone. It was seven o'clock, so no wonder she was hungry. Jake had left ten messages for her and she groaned. Her stomach was upset, and she'd promised Jake that she would be home early so that they could barbecue steaks.

On the way home, Catherine stopped at the store to buy some vegetables for a soup. She figured that it would be easy on her stomach.

Too much stress today, she thought.

Pulling into the garage she put her keys in her purse and entered the house. Hearing music outside, Catherine knew immediately that Jake had invited a few friends over, which was the last thing she wanted after the kind of day she had had.

Catherine quickly changed her clothes and began to chop the vegetables. She put all the ingredients in the pot to cook and sat on the couch to gather her thoughts. Her sliding glass door opened, and Jake stuck his head in.

"I saved you a burger, cooked just the way you like it," he said. "Hey, by the way, did you get any of my text messages today?"

Catherine grimaced.

"Yes, but only just before leaving work," she explained. "I'm really sorry. I had a horrendous day and I'm not feeling up to company. Besides, my stomach has been bothering me most of the day, so, I'm going to have to take tonight off."

"No worries, love. I don't think it will go long tonight. Most of my mates have to be off to work early tomorrow," Jake replied. "Why don't I just tell them the party is over. Once they're gone, I'll come over so we can talk."

"As appealing as that sounds, I don't want to be the party pooper," Catherine moaned. "I think I'll finish this soup, get a shower, and then go to bed. It really has been a bad day."

"All right, love. Whatever you say," Jake replied graciously, closing the door.

Catherine turned on the news but quickly found it all too depressing. She flipped through channels until finding an old movie and decided to watch the ending while she finished her soup. Once the credits started rolling, she cleaned up and went into the bathroom to shower.

Stepping into the hot water, she rested her head against the cold tiles and let the steam wrap around her like a soothing waterfall. She jumped with a start when the door opened. To her surprise, Jake stepped in.

"I thought you might need someone to scrub your back," he said with a grin.

Giving him a tired smile, Catherine turned back to the wall and didn't move as he washed her back. Then he rubbed the tight knots of tension in her neck and shoulders.

She slowly turned and smiled up at him.

"What happened to your friends?"

"They all went home."

"Are you sure you didn't kick them off the beach so that you could play scrub-a-dub-dub with me in the shower?" she asked. All the same, she felt extra special at the thought that he would rather spend quiet time with her than party with his friends.

"Maybe," he answered, lifting his eyebrows innocently.

She laughed and he gave her a smirk.

"Would it really be a crime if I did? Besides, I can see them any time, and I needed to talk with you about something face to face."

With a seductive grin, Catherine cast her eyes downwards and moved back. "Well, here I am," she said with a flourish. "All of me. What do you want to talk about?"

"I can see that," Jake chuckled. "It isn't important. We can talk later. Let's get your hair washed for you."

Pumping the shampoo into the palm of his hand, Jake began to massage her scalp, ignoring her momentary protest, before rinsing it out. Next, he conditioned Catherine's hair. Then, she soaped up her luffa and scrubbed his back.

"We make a very good team when it comes to this shower thing. I think if we practice a little more, we could become very skilled," he said.

"Is this your way of asking if you can come back tomorrow evening and do this little dance again?" Catherine asked. "Because my answer would be a resounding yes."

He playfully sprayed her in the face with water before pressing her into the wall and kissing her passionately.

"I'm sorry that you had a bugger of a day."

"Me too."

"Want to talk about it?" he asked, putting the shower head back up into its hook on the wall.

"Not really," Catherine said, feeling the weariness of the day evaporating from her body. She wanted nothing more than to simply be in Jake's arms. "I really just want to forget that it even happened."

Jake reached for one of the towels and draped it around her.

"I'm all right with that." He put the second towel around his own waist. She combed out her damp hair and twisted it up on top of her head, securing it with a clip.

Catherine slipped on a pair of lace panties and a large t-shirt. When she turned off the bathroom lights and walked into the bedroom, she discovered that Jake had lit several candles, creating a cozy ambiance. She smiled, wanting to pinch herself because she couldn't believe her luck.

He flipped back the covers for her.

"You are the best part of my day," she whispered to him, crawling into bed. "I'm really glad you're here."

"I can't think of any place I'd rather be," he answered, snuggling closer to embrace her.

CHAPTER 20

$\mathcal{C}$atherine woke early and leaned over to the night table to turn off her alarm before it woke Jake. When she rolled back, she found that Jake was already awake.

She flushed, realizing he'd been staring at her while she slept.

"How long have you been doing that?" she asked.

"Doing what?" Jake grinned.

"Staring at me?" she laughed. "Was I drooling? Oh no, please tell me I wasn't snoring?"

Jake leaned down and kissed her.

"No, you were not drooling or snoring. I just like the way you look when you're asleep. Your face is so peaceful when your eyes are closed—as if you were laying on a beach in some faraway place. You just looked so relaxed just now."

"Oh, I'm relaxed alright…" she started, only to look at her alarm clock and sigh. "I have a press conference to get ready for and I'm going to be late if I don't get up this instant." Catherine jumped out of bed and padded across the room to the bathroom.

Stepping out of the bathroom a few minutes later, she went to the closet and rummaged around before holding up two suits.

"Navy-blue or grey?"

"I would go with the navy-blue suit. It photographs better on the television," he said. He climbed out of bed, slipped on his shorts, and walked into the kitchen to fix them some coffee.

Catherine applied her makeup and combed her hair back instead of twisting it into a knot at the base of her neck. She decided that this time she would wear it down.

Maybe Jake was right about the hair, maybe I look better with it down for a change, she thought to herself with a smile. She dabbed on her perfume and slipped on a pair of navy-blue pumps.

She came out of the bedroom and kissed Jake's lips.

"Are you going surfing this morning?"

"And miss seeing you on the tele? Not a chance," Jake answered, pouring some coffee into Catherine's favorite travel mug. "Be careful not to spill this on your blouse." He handed her the mug after he made sure that he had screwed the lid on tightly. "It won't look good in high definition."

"You are most considerate," Catherine said, kissing him goodbye.

Jake wrapped an arm around her. He kissed her so passionately that she couldn't help but moan with pleasure.

"There will be more of *that* waiting for you when you return later," he grinned.

Catherine walked past the counter, then doubled back for her day planner before heading out the door to the garage.

"I'll hold you to that," she called over her shoulder, blowing him a kiss goodbye.

"Be safe! Eyes on the road while you're driving," he cautioned as he held the door open to watch her leave.

Catherine smiled and slipped on her sunglasses before closing the garage door behind her. She switched her mind to campaign mode, found the political talk show on her Sirius XM station and headed to work.

Arriving at the office without having spilled a drop of coffee on her white blouse, Catherine quickly jotted down talking points for Russell to go over. She then delved deeper into the brief talking points, fleshing out each one of the statements she had prepared for him to deliver during the press conference. It would be short and sweet.

She had just printed out her notes when Russell burst into her office.

"Is my statement ready yet?" he blurted out.

"I'm just putting the finishing touches on it now, and will have it ready in just a moment," Catherine said, still focusing on the words she had written. Then she looked up at him. "Why don't you take a seat? You're making me nervous."

"I can't. I'm too wound up."

"Fine," she said, turning back to the papers in her hand. It wasn't long before Russell's pacing became too much of a distraction and forced her to put the paper down.

"Is Angela going to be here for the cameras?" she asked. "I sent her a text earlier but didn't get any reply."

"Yes. And she's pregnant."

Catherine smiled.

"So, the two of you finally had your heart to heart and got everything out in the open. Good."

"Wait, you knew?"

"Of course, I knew—"

"And you didn't tell me?" he said, sounding very perturbed.

"Why do you think that I kept telling you that you both needed to talk?"

"That was your way of telling me that she was pregnant?" Russell said.

"No. That was my way of telling you that you both needed to talk and listen to one another. You both had a secret that you didn't want to burden the other with," Catherine said, taking a deep breath. She came out from behind her desk and took a seat next to him, taking his hand in hers. "I will never understand why married couples don't just talk to one another."

"Sometimes it's hard."

"Yes, Russell. But anything worth having is worth the extra effort. It's work, my friend, not some fairytale." Catherine smiled and released his hand. "So, I take it that you are over the moon about the news."

"Over the moon? I'm in the cosmos. I can't believe it."

"And how did she take the other news?"

"About as good as one would expect. But I'm not off the hook yet," he said, jumping up out of his chair and pacing across the floor. "I have a long way to go before I earn back her trust. Jesus, what was I thinking? I'm an idiot," he berated himself.

"Well, I could have told you that. How much coffee have you had this morning?"

"Three cups," he answered, almost before she'd finished her sentence.

"Maybe you should really consider drinking decaf the rest of the day. You are wired. Did you get any sleep last night?"

"Not really," Russell said, walking around Catherine's desk and taking a seat in her chair. "I couldn't stop thinking about how badly I screwed up. Then one thought led to another and before I knew it, the sun was coming up. Hence, the need for three cups of very strong coffee this morning."

"Yes, well, it shows," she said, pulling a makeup case from her purse.

"I'm not wearing makeup."

"I have some concealer and a light foundation," Catherine said, pulling a clean makeup sponge from her kit. "You look terrible, Russell, like a man possessed. And those dark circles under your eyes won't win you any votes. Now sit still."

In spite of his protests, she applied just enough makeup to hide the dark circles under his eyes. Then she handed him the compact mirror from her bag.

"What would I do without you, Catherine?" Russell said with a grateful nod, snapping the mirror closed and handing it back to her. "I really messed up this time."

"If you had slept with Patricia, then I would say that you had messed up, royally. But since you didn't, we will simply say that you took a walk down the wrong alley, then moved forward. Now, I really do need to get back to work and I can't possibly be expected to concentrate with you pacing back and forth in the office or sitting in my chair."

Russell fumbled awkwardly as he got up from her chair and walked out of her office, throwing a mere, "Thank you" over his shoulder.

Reporters and news outlets from the surrounding area were lined up in front of the campaign office. Their microphones, displaying logos from various organizations, lined the podium. Flashes began going off as Russell Tillman stepped up to the podium with his wife, who stood dutifully by his side wearing an expensive pair of sunglasses.

Catherine stood on the other side of him. She felt exhausted by the effort to prep Russell for his upcoming public declaration.

"Keep alert, boys," the head security personnel cautioned as the cameras began to roll.

Russell cleared his throat.

"I would just like to begin by thanking the authorities, our Police Chief, Mike Donovan, his detectives, and my Campaign Manager, Catherine Lawrence, for everything that they have done to contain this matter. I was sent an envelope yesterday with doctored photos, showing me in, uhm," he cleared his throat, "a compromising position." He felt his face redden with humiliation as he cast a look over his shoulder at his wife's stony face.

"We now know who the perpetrators of this blackmail scheme are: Patricia Grant, my former office manager and speech writer, along with Mr. Chase Stoneman, a disgruntled campaign manager who was recently dismissed. Both colluded to extort money from me and destroy my political campaign. But thanks to the fine work of these wonderful detectives," he said, pointing at the two men who stood near the front of the crowd, "and my campaign manager, their underhanded tactics were foiled. Make no mistake, this was nothing more than a personal attack perpetrated by two former employees of this campaign. Their efforts were thwarted yesterday. I will not be able to go any further into details in order to preserve the integrity of the ongoing investigation. So please don't ask. I simply wanted to bring the matter to the public's attention and to thank all of those who were involved for their fine work and discretion in this matter," Russell said.

"I also wish to assure the fine people of Florida that I am well, and that my campaign is going on as planned. My wife and I," he reached over and placed his arm around Angela's shoulder, "are thankful that this matter will be quickly resolved, and that those who were involved in this blackmailing scheme will be prosecuted to the fullest extent of the law. Thank you again for your time. I will now turn the rest of the time over to my campaign manager, Catherine Lawrence, so that she can answer your questions. Then we will hear from our Police Chief, Mike Donovan."

Angela and Russell stepped back from the podium so Catherine could take over.

She stepped up to the podium.

"Thank you all for coming out today. I want to keep my comments brief—" Catherine said.

"Miss Lawrence," a reporter cried, interrupting Catherine. "Miss Lawrence."

"Settle down Dan. You'll get your chance to ask questions when I'm finished," she said before continuing her speech.

When Catherine was finished, she answered questions, while skirting any sensitive ones. She expertly lobbed unwanted questions back at the reporters and wrapped the whole thing up within ten minutes by stepping away from the podium. A few reporters had tried to stretch things out, but Catherine quickly shut them down by turning the remainder of the press conference time over to the Police Chief.

Mike Donovan answered a few questions, clarified the situation, reiterated the matter at hand, and then closed the press conference by signaling to the security guards.

Two large men stepped forward, shielding Donovan from the press and any further questions they might have had. They all smiled one last time at the reporters and waved for the cameras and television stations before disappearing back into the building.

Angela immediately released Russell's hand and distanced herself from him.

"So, you think they bought it?" Angela asked Catherine the moment the police chief stepped away.

"We'll see in a couple of days when the voters have made their voices heard," Catherine said.

She looked anxiously at Angela and Russell.

"But the two of you have to keep it cordial, or it will definitely get out. I believe most people have already made up their minds about the matter, so this scandal will have little to no effect." Catherine paused. "But I have been wrong, once."

Angela seemed content with the answer and stepped away to talk with a few of the lawyers she knew from the campaign, while Russel seemed tense.

"You have to consider that a lot of people have already voted in the mail-in ballots, Russell. Those votes can't be changed. It's all of the people that will be going to the polls to cast their votes in a few days that concerns me. Either way, we will soon know how this all shakes out," Catherine said seriously.

Russell looked pale.

"For now," she said, "It will be business as usual. The plans for the celebratory party have been made, and I have the final meeting with the caterers this afternoon. Take care of Angela and, whatever you do, don't piss her off. I've seen her get mad before and it isn't pretty. Trust me, you don't want any part of that."

"You're preaching to the choir, Catherine," he said, lowering his voice so only she would hear him. "It's been minus ten degrees at our place ever since I had to come clean and I would wager that it isn't going to get warmer any time soon."

Catherine looked over her shoulder towards her best friend with a shake of her head.

"I'd take that bet. But don't worry, Angela loves you. She's just hurt by your actions and even worse, by the fact that it was with Patricia."

She whistled through her teeth, turning back to look at him.

"You're just lucky she didn't stick a steak knife through your heart."

"You're right, of course. And if I could take it all back I would, a thousand times over." His voice was raspy with emotion.

Catherine turned towards him. He appeared more concerned over his wife's distance from him than he did for his own campaign.

"I need you to keep your head in the game, Russell," Catherine said, "You took your eye off the ball once, and it landed us here."

"Yes," he said, nodding his head. "I'm really in the dog house."

"And you can expect to be there for quite some time, my friend." Her tone was sympathetic. "But if you ever hurt her like that again, I will be the one you will have to worry about."

"It will never happen again, I swear."

CHAPTER 21

𝒞 atherine needed an escape, a safe haven, where she could figure out her next moves. Everything was coming at her too fast. The past week had made her feel like she was being swallowed up by it all. She simply needed a minute to breathe.

Catherine had known exactly what she wanted her entire life, never giving it a second thought. Now, for the first time, she began to second-guess herself and doubt her plan.

"Is there another way? Perhaps a better way to achieve happiness?" she murmured to herself as she drove towards the place she liked to go when life became too much.

Going south on the freeway, it was as if her car knew the way. She was headed homeward to Deland and Kissimmee.

Her family was one of the original Florida families. Her great-great grandparents had settled these two small towns. Her lineage included a land developer, an architect, and one of the first pharmacists, as well as a teacher. Her ancestors would know what to do.

She drove for an hour in silence, her thoughts in disarray. She needed clarity. Somehow, her grandmother could always give her that, even if she was long dead and buried.

Catherine pulled onto the main road at the Kissimmee cemetery.

She grabbed the spare throw she always carried in the trunk, her notebook and pen, and a bottle of water. Then, she made herself comfortable next to her grandmother's grave.

Alice's grave site was directly in front of her parents' graves and surrounded by other members of her family. The rest of her family was spread out but still not very far.

The air was cool, but the sun warmed Catherine's skin. She had always felt safe being surrounded by the dead of her family.

She had only just begun to feel that way with Jake.

Jake.

Her relationship was so new, and yet, the thought of never seeing him again flashed through her mind, making her stomach tighten.

Despite it having only been a few days, Jake had awakened something inside of her. There was something beyond physical pleasure between them. He felt like home to her. He allowed her to explore herself and gave her the freedom to change, to become a different person. She felt like a different person every time he was near her.

"Hi, Grandmother. I know you don't like long-winded introductions, so I'll be brief. It seems I have come to a crossroad. And, please, before you judge me, remember that we are lawyers first. Innocent until proven guilty."

A gentle breeze kicked up, lifting a few fall leaves from the ground, landing one perfectly formed leaf in Catherine's lap. It had begun to change colors. Its soft gold and red tones brought tears to her eyes.

Her mind raced back to a time when she and her grandmother came to this cemetery and placed flowers on the grave sites in the spring, flags in the summer, and wreaths in the fall, just around Thanksgiving time. She and Alice would talk for hours.

Taking the leaf as a sign, Catherine began to speak, her words flowing out from her heart as if her beloved grandmother sat next to her.

Catherine felt as if she were receiving hugs and wisdom from beyond the grave from the many souls that surrounded her. She wrote her thoughts down in her notebook as she spoke.

"I'm not certain that I was cut out for politics after all, Grandmother. I know that we agreed on it, but that was ten years ago. Things change. I've changed. I want something more. I've met a guy. His name is Jake Ryan. He's from Australia, and before you start telling me all the reasons that he's a bad idea, I want you to know that I really like him. I know, I know, they come and they go, but Grandmother, this one's a keeper. He's tall, strong, and kind. He makes me laugh and rubs my feet. He sings and plays the guitar. Best of all, he makes me a better person when I'm with him," she said, making a note. "I did *not* chase after nor did I pursue Jake Ryan—the fates pushed us together," she paused, waiting. "I know you would like him. He truly is a kind man."

Catherine wiped the tears away from her cheek with her hand and sniffed loudly. Rising to her feet, she gathered her things. She ran a hand over her grandmother's headstone. Catherine kissed the tips of her fingers and touched the headstone once more.

"I love you, Grandmother."

She stopped by her father's headstone and repeated the act of leaving a kiss behind before she headed back to her car.

Somehow, communing with Grandma Alice always made Catherine feel better. It had been ten years since the last time, and it had gone by in the blink of an eye.

Getting home just after six-thirty, Catherine pulled her car into the garage and closed the door behind her.

She just wanted to close the world out for a little longer. The house was silent. Jake wasn't there. Catherine walked across the living room, stepped out of her front door and knocked on Jake's, but there was no answer. His surfboard was missing, so he was probably out surfing the last of the evening waves.

Quickly changing into her workout clothes, she put her earbuds in and started the treadmill at a decent pace. Fifteen minutes in, she was breathless but, instead of slowing down, Catherine sped it up for the last five minutes, pushing herself even more before her cool down.

By the time she was finished, Catherine was soaked in sweat. She stripped off her wet shirt on the way to the bedroom and dropped the wet clothes into the sink.

The warm water of the shower cascaded down her back, neck, and head, washing away the troubles of the last few days. After removing the makeup from her face, she began soaping her skin when she heard the front door close.

"Jake? Jake is that you?" she called out. Strangely, there was no reply.

She rinsed off the soap and turned off the shower, wrapping a towel around her as she stepped out. Concern began to rise within her. She pulled on a robe and wrapped a towel around her hair.

"Jake?" she called again, ignoring the sick feeling in the pit of her stomach.

Catherine looked around for something to use as a weapon, trying to recall whether or not she had locked the front door. She reached underneath the bed and retrieved the baseball bat she kept for emergencies, her eyes focused on the doorway.

Her skin prickled with fear.

She slowly crept towards the open bedroom door with the bat held high. She stopped, hands clenched tightly on the handle, when she noticed that her phone was no longer on the nightstand table where she had left it just a few minutes ago. That sinking feeling in the pit of her stomach suddenly turned sour.

There was no longer any doubt in Catherine's mind that someone else was in the condo with her, and it wasn't Jake.

Peeking around the corner into the living room, Catherine gasped. Someone was in her living room, sitting on her couch with her cellphone in his hand. The hooded figure looked down at the phone as a message came in and nonchalantly replied before looking up at her. Catherine cowered behind the door.

What was she going to do now? She couldn't sneak up on him. She couldn't possibly run past him to the front door, he would catch her at once.

She was trapped.

"I know you're standing there weighing your options, Miss Lawrence. As far as I can tell, you really have no options left to you but to come out of there," the figure called in a familiar voice.

"What is it that you feel I can do for you, Mr. Stoneman?" Catherine asked coolly.

She stood up and tightened the robe sash around her waist.

She took a deep breath and stepped out from her hiding place.

Chase stood as well, taking a few slow steps towards her. That's when Catherine saw the gun in his right hand.

"Nothing, Miss Lawrence. There is not a damn thing that you can do for me—except, maybe, die."

His words made Catherine's blood run cold in her veins.

"I'm certain your name will be forgotten months from now," he continued, "Perhaps you will simply be another name on a milk carton after you've disappeared."

Chase took another step towards her.

"A mere moment in history, which no one will even care to remember months from now because there will be no one left to remember you!" he growled. "Because everyone will have moved on with their lives and you will still be *gone*."

Catherine knew in her mind that Chase wouldn't hesitate to kill her if given the chance, but she couldn't move. She was paralyzed with fear. She hesitated a split second too long and then tried to run for the door.

Chase anticipated her move and lunged forward, cutting her off before she could reach the door.

Catherine jumped back as he pointed the gun directly at her heart, letting the bat drop back down to her side. She backed into the kitchen counter.

"Why don't you put that bat down?" he said.

"I'd like to…"

"I don't think you really want to finish that sentence, Miss Lawrence," Chase said menacingly as he waved the gun at her. "After all, you did just bring a bat to a gun fight. Now, drop it!"

She dropped the bat onto the floor before it clanked and rolled away. Catherine put her hands into the air like some old western movie. Her mind raced, searching for an escape.

Chase caught her by the waist and lifted her easily from the ground. She opened her mouth to scream for help, but he shoved the gun into her side.

"If not for the noise of the bullet, which will draw attention, I would shoot you right here," he said.

Catherine swallowed a cry.

"A few ground rules, if you please, Miss Lawrence," Chase continued, shoving the gun even deeper into her side.

"First off, no screaming because I will definitely have to shoot the first person who steps through that door. Then I will shoot you in the head and make a mess all over this lovely room," he said with a snarl, close to her ear. "And it would be such a shame to kill that good-looking Aussie of yours. And yes, I know about him. Who do you think I have been texting non-stop with since I've confiscated your phone? I would truly hate to ruin his day by killing him. So, you will cooperate with me and do just as I tell you to do or I will simply strangle you now and be done with it. Do you understand?" Chase said. Catherine nodded.

"Good."

Fear clung to Catherine like a blanket as bile rose in her throat, causing her to swallow hard.

"Please, Chase, there must be something—"

"Shut up!" he hissed, squeezing the air from her lungs with one arm. "I didn't give you permission to speak. Do you understand?"

She said nothing more, and nodded her head frantically. Tears burned in Catherine's eyes, but she refused to give him the satisfaction of seeing her cry.

Chase carried her across the room and threw her unceremoniously on the couch, where she landed with a thud.

He pointed the gun at her again.

"I'm in control here, not you!" his voice rasped with uncontrollable rage. He began to pace in front of her, scratching his head with the gun as if he were trying to think what to do next.

Catherine sat very still, studying his irrational behavior, praying that Jake wouldn't come through the door anytime soon. If he were hurt or killed because of her, she would never forgive herself.

She had to out think Chase. After all, he was an irrational man, prone to irrational behavior. That had been proven in the past.

"Tell me what you want," Catherine pleaded. "I can make it happen."

"Revenge," was all he said.

"I'm certain there is something that I can do to make this right. Come on, Chase!" Catherine said, gritting her teeth when he merely smirked.

"Can you get rid of the charges against me? Can you go back in time and make this all go away?"

"Yes. Yes, I could tell the police that I was mistaken—"

"Shut up!" he hissed. "By now, Patricia has turned on me. She wouldn't waste any time rolling over and giving the police exactly what they need to make a case against me."

"But I could tell them that it was all some kind of misunderstanding, please, Chase."

"It almost seems like you have real feelings, Miss Lawrence. Maybe you're not an ice queen after all. I could almost feel the sincerity of your words."

Her phone went off again as another text came through. Chase pulled the phone from his back pocket, looked at it, and with a sour face, texted something back.

"Your boy is quite persistent," Chase announced contemptuously, shoving the phone back into his pocket. "Get up!" he snapped impatiently, gesturing with the gun.

Catherine stood slowly and cringed when Chase grabbed her arm roughly, shoving her towards the bedroom.

"Get dressed," he said, pushing her from behind when she didn't move fast enough.

Stay calm, stay calm, she kept telling herself.

Catherine tried to stall for time.

"Where are we going?" she asked.

"Well, we're not going to the Governor's reception in a few days, if that's what you are concerned about. I'm sorry you won't be around to see all of your hard work come to fruition," he said, acidly.

He pulled a pair of sweatpants from the closest shelf and threw them at her before reaching for a random t-shirt.

Slipping the pants on under her robe, Catherine turned to retrieve a sports bra, disrobing so she could slip it on with her back to him.

"I forgot how modest you are, except when it comes to the Aussie. You're not really my type, so don't flatter yourself by being shy."

Catherine reached for the t-shirt he offered and noticed him ogling her breasts before she slipped the shirt on over her head.

She grabbed her green hoodie as she was shoved towards the door from behind. Catherine prayed that her spare cell phone was still in the zippered pocket and that it had some charge left in it. As she stumbled into the living room, she felt the slight weight on one side of the jacket and thanked her good fortune. If only she could find the opportunity to use the phone before it was too late.

"What's your plan, Chase? And how is kidnapping me going to solve your problems?" Catherine asked, while fiddling in her pocket, turning the phone on. Catherine pressed the panic button, crossing her fingers that it worked.

"Are you certain that kidnapping me is the best option, Chase? After all, don't you think that I will be missed if you dispose of the campaign manager of the leading Republican candidate for Governor?" Catherine raised her voice, ensuring that she could be heard, and hoped that the dispatcher could figure out what was going on quickly.

"What are you playing at, Catherine?" Chase asked, narrowing his eyes.

"Water?" she blurted out, making a beeline for the refrigerator to grab two bottles, and holding one out to Chase.

"Don't do that again!" he scolded, grabbing her arm in a vice like grip.

"Ouch!" Catherine cried, jerking her arm free with some indignation. "Do what? Get you a water? Where I come from that's considered common courtesy. Are you hungry? I could make you a sandwich or something else if you'd like."

She was scrambling to stall now. The last thing she wanted was to be taken to a second location. That was always a bad idea in the cases she had been involved in. It never ended well for the victim.

Her mind raced. What if she died without telling Jake how she really felt about him? What if her body was never found because Chase dumped her in some alligator infested swamp, hundreds of miles away?

She braced herself despite the shiver that went down her spine. She, Catherine Lawrence, was a survivor and she would out think Chase Stoneman and get herself out of this.

She had to.

"No! I don't want a sandwich or something else," Chase exploded. Catherine realized he was becoming easily rattled by all the questions as he snatched the water out of her hand and gulped it down.

Catherine took the opportunity to slip a fork from off the counter, tucking it up her sleeve. She glanced at him before peeking down at the phone in her pocket to make sure that the call had gone through and that it was still connected to the 911 operator. Seeing the call registered across her screen, Catherine let out a sigh of relief.

The phone in Chase's back pocket buzzed once again. Obviously irritated by the constant interruptions, he huffed, slamming the bottle of water down on the counter. Chase held the gun to her head as he pulled the phone from his back pocket and read the message before texting back. The phone buzzed again, and he growled in frustration.

"You really need to cut this one loose, Catherine. Honestly, he's a royal pain...what am I saying?" he chuckled sardonically. "You won't be around to cut anyone loose."

Chase had just shoved Catherine towards the garage when she heard a pounding on the front door.

"Catherine, are you alright?" Jake yelled.

Jake burst through the front door, eyes ablaze with rage.

"Look out, Jake," she shouted. "He has a gun!"

Chase swung the gun around, pointing it in Jake's direction, and fired. At the same moment, Catherine hit his arm upwards with her water bottle and stabbed him with the fork hidden up her sleeve. The shot went into the wall, causing Chase to scream in frustration.

Chase pointed the gun, eyes wild, at Catherine and fired. Jake leapt on top of him, knocking the gun from his hand, and began pounding his fist into Chase's face repeatedly.

"Jake!" Catherine screamed. "Stop! You'll kill him."

Jake's blood ran cold. He shook with uncontrollable rage as Catherine's voice penetrated his mind. The desire to kill this man coursed through his veins, and he wouldn't have stopped, if she hadn't called out to him.

Jake looked at the blood in front of him and it made him sick. He slowly turned until his eyes landed on Catherine.

She sat on the floor, not two feet away from him, holding her left arm. His hands shook. He crawled away from the stranger and took her in his arms.

"Catie, my love, you're hurt." His voice trembled as he frantically searched her body before pulling her hand away from her arm. "You've been shot!" he cried, seeing the blood still seeping through the small hole in her hoodie.

Desperately looking towards the opened doorway, he saw that people had begun to gather.

"Don't just stand there, call an ambulance! She's been shot!"

"It's just a flesh wound, Jake," Catherine whispered, touching his face tenderly with her bloodied hand, "You came for me."

"Of course, I came for you," Jake said, grabbing a dish towel from the counter and tying it around the wound.

"But how did you know I needed help?" Her teeth began to chatter, and she shivered in his arms.

"I could tell that it wasn't you sending me those texts. Then I heard all of that noise coming from your place."

His words broke off as he stared down into her face.

"I thought he was going to kill me..." she shuddered, "I thought I was going to die and never see you again," Catherine whispered, her teeth chattering as she buried her head in his chest. "I thought I would never get to tell you how much I loved you."

Pulling away from her, Jake cupped Catherine's face in his hand.

"I will never let anyone harm you, my love. I love you too."

He leaned down and kissed her.

"Oh, Jake, I was so scared," Catherine's voice warbled as she threw her good arm around his neck, kissing him passionately. "Don't ever leave me!"

"I would never leave you, Catie, my love. Never!" Jake crushed her to him, possessively, thankful that she was alive. "Never," he repeated softly in her ear. His hands still shook when he thought of how close he'd come to losing her.

He could hear the sirens from the police cars and ambulance as they arrived. People milled around the doorway to get a better look at the scene and gawked at them through the open door.

Even more people stood on the beach beyond the condo's railing.

"Is there anything I can do to help you, and what happened?" someone standing in the doorway asked.

"Was anyone killed?" another person asked, trying to get a peek inside.

It wasn't long before the police swooped in, clearing everyone away, forcing them to stand beyond the railing. Yellow crime scene tape went up, and two news crews quickly followed, asking questions and rolling footage for the ten o'clock news, just outside Catherine's door.

Officer Mark Sanchez was one of the first officers to respond at the scene, rushing through the open door with his gun drawn. He cuffed Chase and handed him off to his partner.

Officer Sanchez and Catherine had known each other for four years. They became friends after deciding that dating was not in the cards.

"Another wild party, Lawrence?" he said, breaking the tension in the room.

"You know I would never start the party without you, Officer Sanchez," Catherine replied, smiling up at him.

"By the look of things, I would say that you forgot to invite me."

A feeling of jealousy coursed through Jake's veins at the friendly banter between Catherine and Officer Sanchez.

"I don't think we've had the pleasure," he interrupted. "I'm Jake Ryan, Catherine's boyfriend."

Acknowledging Jake with a nod, Officer Sanchez knelt down to examine her.

"So, you went and got yourself shot."

"Between you and me, Mark, it was just a matter of time," Catherine said.

Mark began to chuckle.

"Well, this is a fine mess you've got yourself into. There's going to be a lot of reports and paperwork to file. This is going to take me half the night to write up. You could've just called if you wanted to see me," he teased.

Catherine looked up at Jake and smiled.

"It's alright, Jake. Mark...I mean, Officer Sanchez, is an old friend," she assured him, trying to defuse the look of jealousy she saw in his eyes.

"The EMT guys are ready to come in," another officer called out, "That is, if you have secured the scene?"

"Mr. Ryan, I need you to step aside, please," Officer Sanchez said. "She will be fine. My partner needs to get a statement from you as well."

Jake looked confused and didn't immediately move until Officer Sanchez insisted, handing Jake off to another officer while he remained with Catherine to supervise her care.

Jake hesitated, looking back at Catherine before he explained to the other officer what had happened.

Catherine informed Officer Sanchez that the man they had in handcuffs was a wanted felon, and that there was a warrant out for his arrest. They added attempted kidnapping and two counts of attempted murder to the warrant.

Catherine was wheeled out and taken to the nearby hospital where she was treated for shock and her gunshot wound.

The wound required a few stitches, a tetanus shot, and some antibiotics. Afterwards she was released to Jake's care.

Officer Mark Sanchez promised to stop by her condo the next day to take her preliminary statement. He insisted that it was purely out of respect for her political position and what she'd just gone through. Jake remained suspicious of the other man's motives.

Catherine simply patted him on the arm and assured him that he was the only man for her.

CHAPTER 22

$\mathcal{C}$atherine was up bright and early on election day. Jake hadn't left her alone for one minute since the shooting. They had become inseparable.

Catherine had taken two days off after nearly losing her life. Yet, she continued to pull all of the strings from home. She made all the final arrangements for the Governors' election celebration from the comfort of her couch, while Jake waited on her hand and foot.

Jake drove her to her various appointments to get her hair, nails, and makeup professionally done.

When the news broke about the attempted murder by her predecessor, Chase Stoneman, no one could seem to talk about anything else. In fact, the news feed had been on a continual loop since the story broke, which boosted Russell's numbers. It had turned out to be a blessing in disguise. Their every move was widely reported on TV and the early polls showed Russell in the lead by a wide margin.

She was dressed in her black Armani pantsuit with a white beaded bustier and a silver chain necklace that had a delicate crystal ball at the end, which dangled provocatively over her cleavage. Catherine wore matching earrings and her hair was fashionably styled atop her head with wisps of hair left out to frame her face. A pair of black Felicia crystal and satin pumps completed her outfit.

Jake wore a black Armani tuxedo with a silver pocket square. Catherine whistled between her teeth when she caught sight of his elegant outfit.

Jake helped Catherine into the car, buckling her seatbelt around her as if she were a child, which made Catherine smile broadly.

"You know that I can do that for myself, don't you?"

"Yes, but I like taking care of you," Jake said. "And you do remember the doctor warning you to not overdo things. He also told you to let your husband take care of you, his words not mine." Jake flashed her a rakish smile.

"And I also noticed that you didn't correct the good doctor's assumption."

"Why would I?"

"Well, I can see where the doctor might have gotten the wrong idea. You were telling the nurses what to do and ordering people around."

Catherine brought his hand to her lips.

"I rather enjoyed when they all called you Mr. Lawrence."

"I'm sure you did." He looked longingly into Catherine's eyes before opening the garage door and cautiously pulling the car out. He didn't want to run over any reporters who might be lingering, waiting for an update to give to their ten o'clock news spot.

Catherine waved to the two remaining reporters loitering about their news trucks and noted the dejected look on their faces as she and Jake drove past.

At the venue, Catherine walked past all the photographers and news crews vying for comments. Microphones were shoved into her face and rapid fire questions were shouted out in an attempt to get answers about what exactly happened at her place two days earlier.

Jake used his arm as a barrier between Catherine and the reporters who were aggressively pushing their way to the front of the line in an attempt to be heard.

Catherine saw an old friend, Janine Stanwood, and stopped to answer a question she posed to her. She was one of the news anchors from the local channel 10 station.

The two of them met as teenagers when their families had been vacationing in Fort Lauderdale at a resort fifteen years earlier. Catherine and Janine had both known that they were destined to be friends. That summer, everyone said that they were two peas in a pod.

After their vacation came to an end, the two of them continued to write and telephone each other regularly. They even communicated all through college. Even now, one or the other would reach out to make contact, but it was less frequent.

"Hello, Miss Stanwood. How have you been?" Catherine asked pleasantly, focusing all of her attention upon her friend.

Janine smiled broadly and kissed Catherine on both cheeks.

"Apparently, better than you, my dear," she said, looking concerned. "When your name came across my desk, I nearly fell off of my chair. I was worried about you."

Catherine took hold of Janine's arm and pulled her from the reporter's line. "How would you like an exclusive?"

"I was hoping you'd offer," Janine smirked. "After all, it's the least you could do."

"Why, you ungrateful..."

"Remember Bobby Ramos?"

"I've missed you," Catherine said, hugging her friends' arm. "We really do need to get together... and I believe we agreed to never bring him up again!" she laughed.

"What's the use of knowing someone so well if you can't drag out the skeletons in their closet from time to time?" Janine laughed. "I have missed you as well," she said, turning to wave for her cameraman to follow her. "The kids and husband really cut into my free time and keep me pretty busy these days. I truly miss the 'me' time with girlfriends."

"So many excuses," Catherine replied, giving Janine a sly grin. "When all of this is over, you and I will do some serious catching up."

"Promise?"

"I do!" Catherine crossed her heart with a finger, "I really mean it this time."

Catherine turned to Jake, who had been waiting patiently as the two of them talked, and pulled him forward.

"Janine, this is Jake Ryan, my boyfriend and the hero who saved my life."

Reaching her hand out, Janine gave Jake a warm smile and shook his hand. "It is wonderful to meet you, Mr. Ryan."

"Please, just call me Jake."

"Of course, Jake. And perhaps you and I should talk later," Janine smiled before turning back around and taking a hold of Catherine's arm.

Catherine and Janine walked arm-in-arm into the reception hall, laughing about old times, while Jake walked behind them, blocking the view of photographers and news reporters anxious to get a photo of Catherine.

Russell stood near the entrance with Angela by his side, greeting each individual coming through the door.

"You made it," Russell cried the moment he saw Catherine. "I was worried."

"I wouldn't miss this party for anything," Catherine responded. "After all, I did arrange every detail personally. You might recognize my friend, Janine Stanwood, from the local 10 news," she said, turning to Janine first. "We're old friends from way back."

"Well, I wouldn't exactly use the word *old*," Janine chimed in, presenting her hand to Russell and shaking it firmly. "That is what the news people call the kiss of death. It's a pleasure to finally meet you, Governor Tillman."

"It's not official yet," Russell humbly said, shaking Janine's hand. "Miss Stanwood, this is my wife, Angela Tillman."

Angela took Janine's hand.

"It's very nice to make your acquaintance, Miss Stanwood."

"You're also an attorney, I believe," Janine said, "and a good one, from what I hear."

"Yes, well, I won't be practicing much law in the next few years, it would seem," Angela said, putting a hand over her stomach.

"Congratulations," Janine said. "When is the happy day?"

"If all goes well, the second week in June," Angela announced proudly.

"And all will go well," Russell assured her, grasping his wife's hand and giving it a squeeze.

Catherine motioned for Jake to come closer.

"Everyone, I want you to meet Jake Ryan," she said. "He's my date this evening. Jake, this is Russell Tillman, your soon-to-be Governor of Florida, and his wife and my best friend, Angela Tillman."

Jake reached out his hand.

"It's a pleasure to meet you sir."

"The pleasure is all mine," Russell said. The two men began to talk politics while the women huddled together to have a conversation of their own.

"I thought I was your best friend!" Janine complained, accidentally elbowing Catherine in her sore arm and causing her to wince in pain. "Oh, damn it. I'm so sorry, Catherine, I forgot," she immediately apologized, crinkling up her face and looking embarrassed.

"Ouch!" Catherine complained, turning to her friend. "And, of course, you are, Janine, unless you do that again... It's just that Angela and I went to college together and—"

"Oh, Catherine, I'm just giving you a bad time," Janine cut in, reaching out to give Catherine another poke in the arm before she stopped, looking apologetic.

"Why don't you make spa reservations for the three of us? I bet Angela here could use a leisurely day at the spa after all of this."

"You aren't just whistling Dixie, Miss Stanwood," Angela said, rolling her eyes. "Is this him?" she asked, leaning around Catherine and extending her hand to Jake.

"Yes," Catherine answered pensively. "But you're not supposed to ask me like that in front of him, Angela." She looked up at Jake with a smile. "The man might get the wrong idea and think that we have been discussing him at great length, which, of course, we haven't."

"That's alright, honey," Angela said to Jake, shielding her mouth from the other two ladies. "I'll give you the scoop on this one," she indicated by throwing her head in Catherine's direction. "I know everything there is to know about Catherine Lawrence."

"Angie," Catherine protested.

"And I can tell you some stories of her early years," Janine interjected.

Catherine groaned.

"Oh, don't worry, honey. There isn't really anything to tell but I would be happy to make something up," Angela said.

"Turncoats!"

Jake squeezed Catherine's arm with a twinkle in his eye.

"Don't worry, my love, I promise not to listen to their gossip."

"You're a good man, Jake Ryan, and very diplomatic too," Catherine smiled up at him.

Russell and Angela made their way to the dance floor, while Catherine, Jake, Janine, and her cameraman made a beeline for the monitors to get an update on the election.

Russell's numbers were good. In fact, they were better than good. Catherine took a deep breath, relieved that the evening was going so well. People were eating, drinking, and dancing to the live band. Everything was finally going in the right direction. She was happy with Jake, the catastrophe that threatened the campaign was averted, and she was alive, even though a madman had tried to end her life only two days ago.

Catherine left Janine and her cameraman near the monitors as she and Jake stepped out onto the dance floor. Jake showed Catherine a few moves as he swept her into his arms and spun her around the floor.

"I didn't realize Australian men knew how to dance so well," Catherine said.

"We aren't a bunch of backwater Neanderthals, Miss Lawrence. We do have dance studios and professional competitions in Australia."

He looked down into her upturned face.

"Good to know," she smiled.

"My Mum made sure my brother, sister, and I were well rounded and grounded before she sent us out into the world," Jake said, adding tenderly, "My Mum is a great woman."

"Tell me something about her, Jake. You've never really said too much about your family."

"When I was about eight, my Mum looked me squarely in the eyes and said, 'When you fall in love, Jake, you will feel it in your very soul. Your soul always knows it before your brain. When you fall in love you will know it beyond a shadow of a doubt. Its pull on you will be stronger than the moon's pull on the tides, so don't you worry about love, because you won't need to. Love will find you,'" Jake quoted with reverence.

"She sounds like a very wise woman. I hope that I get to meet her one day," Catherine said, snuggling into Jake's shoulder as they danced.

"I always listened to any advice my Mum would offer when I was growing up. Her soft but serious tone always held the sound of truth to me, even at that age. It was rumored that my Mum's heritage included that of an aboriginal healer. They were given stewardship over important stories and interpreted dreams of others as well as their own. Like prophets, you know? Some ignorant people call them witch doctors, but that isn't what they are at all." He leaned down and kissed her on the forehead.

Jake smiled to himself.

"Life was so carefree back then, so many adventures."

"That sounds like a wonderful childhood, Jake," Catherine whispered, looking up into his eyes.

Jake chuckled and pulled her even closer.

Next, he told her about his older brother, Jesse, his younger sister, Jacqueline, and his father, Jack.

Catherine enjoyed the stories Jake told her as they danced.

"There is something that I have been trying to bring up to you for a few days now, but with everything that has happened, well, it's just gotten lost in the shuffle," Jake said.

Pulling back a little, Catherine looked up.

"What is it, Jake?"

"My Mum called me the other day to let me know that my Pops isn't doing well. I need to go home for a while to see if I can help out my family with the business and make sure my Pops is alright."

"Oh, Jake, I'm so sorry to hear that. Is it anything serious?" she asked.

"She seems to think that it is."

"How long do you think you will be gone?"

"I couldn't really say," Jake replied sadly. "That brings me to the real question I wanted to ask you."

"What is it?"

"I was hoping that you might consider coming with me to Australia."

"Oh, Jake," Catherine whispered with anguish. "There is nothing I'd like more than to travel with you to

Australia and meet your family—but right now, I have obligations."

"But I thought you were the campaign manager?" Jake said. "Doesn't that mean that your job is over after tonight?"

"Technically, yes. But Russell has asked me to stay on as his adviser," Catherine said. "I thought that we discussed the importance of my job. I thought you understood that my work comes first."

"No, I guess I really didn't understand that until now," Jake said, with disappointment. "Catherine?"

"Yes, Jake?"

"Is this political thing truly your dream—or is it your grandmother's dream for you?" he asked in a sincere tone.

Touching his face with her hand when he looked away, Catherine felt bad. "I'm sorry, Jake. I wish I had known—" Her words trailed off.

Jake was about to say something when Russell's booming, baritone voice stopped him, which left Catherine wondering what he was about to say.

Russell and Angela took the stage.

Russell cleared his throat.

"I wish to thank everyone for coming here this evening. Without your generous support and endless hours of time during my campaign this moment would not be a reality."

"Please give a round of applause to Catherine Lawrence, my campaign manager. Her tireless efforts on this campaign have made all the difference in the world. Everyone, please give it up for Catherine Lawrence." Russell's voice echoed throughout the venue as a spotlight shone on Catherine and Jake standing in the middle of the dance floor.

Catherine lowered her head modestly, then gestured towards Russell so as to bring the attention back to him.

"Some of you may not know this about Catherine Lawrence but she is one tough woman," Russell said, eliciting laughs from the audience. "She saved this campaign from collapse. She also faced down a gun-wielding ex-employee, took a bullet in the arm, and still managed to plan this evening's events while recovering from her injuries. She kicked my butt all the way to the finish line."

In response, the room erupted with clapping and cheers for Catherine and she turned to Jake. Her heart was breaking, because she wanted to continue the conversation with Jake, but was being pulled away from him in another direction—by her job.

"Let's see if we can get her up here to say a few words to us tonight," Russell suggested, motioning for Catherine to join him. "Come on up here, Catherine Lawrence. I'll even let you read the announcement I have here in my hand. I think she is going to require a little more encouragement, folks. Put your hands together for her."

He began to chant, "Lawrence, Lawrence," over and over, until the audience joined in.

The noise became deafening, and people patted her on the back, pushing her towards the stage, all the while chanting, "Lawrence, Lawrence, Lawrence."

Catherine glanced over her shoulder as she took the stage to see Jake clapping and chanting along with the crowd. He gave her an encouraging smile, but it didn't quite reach his eyes. She took a faltering step before losing him in the crowd. She turned around and finished climbing the steps up to the stage.

Catherine took the microphone from Russell's hand before turning around to address the very boisterous crowd.

"Well, it has been an exciting, albeit, wild ride up until this point," she joked, raising her voice, which made the crowd go crazy.

Catherine raised her hands to quiet down the crowd so she could be heard. She glanced down at the announcement Russell had put in her hands and grinned.

"It all was made possible by each and every one of you lovely folks, here tonight, and your generous donations and support of our newest Governor, Governor Tillman, and his vision for Florida!" Catherine announced.

The audience gasped in surprise.

"Yes, you heard me right, Governor Russell Tillman is your newest representative in Congress and the voice of the people of Florida!" she repeated, causing the crowd to erupt into another loud round of applause, hoots, and ear-splitting whistles.

"And it is all because of you!" Catherine shouted, swept up in the excitement of the crowd. "Give yourselves a big round of applause, folks!"

Handing the microphone back to Russell, Catherine wanted to put the spotlight back on him. After all, he was the man of the hour. Catherine hugged Angela and then Russell before leading the audience in another loud, rambunctious round of applause by lifting her arms up into the air and clapping.

She started to leave the stage when one of her interns ran up and yelled into her ear that she needed to announce the Governor's first dance before exiting the stage. Catherine quickly walked back and took the microphone from Russell.

"I do apologize, folks. I forgot to announce that the Governor and his wife will be having their celebratory dance," she announced dramatically. "Strike up the band, boys!"

Catherine left the stage to search for Jake, which was made difficult by the sheer volume of people who stopped her with congratulations on running such a successful campaign. Even as she graciously accepted everyone's well wishes, Catherine's eyes never stopped roaming the room.

She spotted Janine Stanwood standing near the monitors and waited for her to finish her segment for the ten o'clock news.

"Janine, have you seen Jake?"

"I saw him heading towards the food and drink table earlier," Janine answered.

"Thanks Janine." Catherine turned to leave as Janine grabbed her hand, stopping her.

"Hey, where do you think you are going, my friend? You can't drop an announcement like that and then run off. I need a statement from you for my segment."

"I have to find Jake," Catherine said before letting out a large sigh and agreeing to a quick interview before resuming her search.

She found him staring morosely into the crowd with a glass of beer in his hand.

"You are a hard man to track down," Catherine joked, trying to elicit a smile.

Jake obliged her with a halfhearted grin.

"You just need to know where to look for a man like myself. I'm a simple man. I need food to sustain myself and a drink to comfort what ails me," he said, tipping his glass of beer towards her.

"Are we all right, Jake?" Catherine asked, taking a step closer. "Because I really am sorry that I can't go with you to Australia right now."

"We're cool. Anyway, it probably wouldn't be the best time for you to meet my family with my Pops doing so poorly."

"Oh, Jake, I'm so sorry. Why didn't you say anything to me yesterday?"

"Yesterday was about me taking care of you and your needs. Not about me." He leaned down to kiss her on the cheek. "Are you hungry?"

"No, not really. But I could use another dancing lesson from someone as good as you," Catherine said.

Finishing the contents of his glass, Jake set it down on the nearest tray.

"It would be my pleasure to teach a pretty little sheila, such as yourself, just what an Aussie can do on the dance floor."

Jake led Catherine out onto the dance floor and they took their place next to Russell and Angela as the band began to play a waltz.

Jake executed a flawless spin. She looked up at him, and the room fell out of focus for her.

When the music stopped, Jake and Catherine paid no attention to the applause around them. She stood gazing into his eyes, lost in a world of her own. It was as if they were the only two people in the room.

"I think we are creating a scene," she said to Jake out of the side of her mouth.

"They're definitely not watching me, love, since you are, undoubtedly, the most beautiful woman in the room," Jake said, still looking lovingly down at her.

"Ha! Just goes to show how little you know," she protested.

Jake offered her his arm.

"I know more than you think."

Catherine smiled politely to people as they passed them before looking back up at Jake.

He was still gazing down at her.

"See," he insisted, "I told you so."

"How would you like to get out of here?"

"I thought you would never ask," he said, "but don't you have duties to fulfill?"

"I'm feeling a little worn out by all of the festivities."

"Is your arm hurting?" Jake asked. "I told you to slow down or you would overdo it."

With a heavy sigh, Catherine elbowed him in his side.

"No, silly. That's just our cover for getting out of here early."

Jake quickly caught on and took a hold of her hand.

"Just play along, and if anyone asks you any questions on our way out the door, you know what to do," Catherine said under her breath.

"Gotcha," Jake said, a mischievous twinkle in his eye. "You are a fatigued sheila that I have to take home and put to bed. Have I told you lately that I like the way you think?"

"No, you have not," she said with a shake of her head.

"I have been remiss in my duties, Miss Lawrence," he said, tucking her hand in his.

"Good. So, I'll leave instructions with my interns and then we can leave. Hopefully, no one catches on and needs another interview."

"I will just run interference and block them all from getting to you."

"Perfect," she purred, looking up at him with desire.

CHAPTER 23

*T*he ride home felt like it took forever. At last, Jake pulled her car into the garage and pushed the button to lower the garage door behind them.

Jake immediately leaned over and took her into his arms, kissing her passionately. Catherine ran her hands over the fabric of his tailored jacket, relishing the feel of his muscles. The heat radiating from him ignited her passions.

"Let me kick off my shoes right here before we have at it," Catherine said.

"Race you to the bedroom. First one there gets to be on top!" He grinned boyishly before jumping from the car and running toward the door.

Catherine jumped out of the car, shoes in hand.

"No fair. I'm injured," she protested over his laughter. "And besides, you have to call out your challenge before taking advantage of little ol' me."

Jake turned with one hand on the doorknob.

"You're right, I wasn't playing fairly. Is there any way that I can make it up to you?"

Catherine leaned into him and kissed his lips.

"You could carry my shoes in for me," she said coyly, placing her shoes in his hands as she pushed the door open.

Stepping over the threshold, Catherine took off running towards the bedroom, laughing the entire way. Seconds later, she threw herself onto the bed. "Ha! I won," she shouted, "whoo hoo!"

Jake knew that he'd been duped, but didn't care. He enjoyed this version of his Catie, fun, light, and playful.

He lifted his eyebrows in mock disapproval, depositing her shoes and his jacket on the nearest chair of the bedroom.

"Well, it would seem that I have been played for a fool by the master manipulator. Even so, I still consider myself a winner."

He kicked off his shoes.

"You better believe you're a winner," she said breathlessly. "Because I'm not wearing any underwear."

Jake playfully gasped with a look of surprise.

"What? You mean this entire evening you weren't wearing any undergarments?" he feigned a look of shock. "Why, Miss Lawrence, you are simply scandalous! I need to alert the news media."

"Before you do that, come over here and give me what I deserve," she said, unbuttoning her pants and kicking them onto the floor.

Ripples of desire ran up her spine as he stepped towards her. The look in his crystal blue eyes seemed to turn obsidian, darkening with desire. His playful expression changed to one of intensity as he reached the bed. He crushed her to him, their mouths molded together as his probing tongue explored hers, tasting, demanding. Catherine's pulse pounded in her ears. She took in his intoxicating scent. It took every ounce of willpower she had not to tear his shirt from his chest.

Instead, she removed his belt, fumbling with the buttons of his trousers as Jake rained kisses down her throat, cupping her full breast in one hand and skimming his other hand up the length of her thigh.

Catherine sucked in sharply as Jake's index finger found its mark and she felt his chest reverberate when he found the spot that drove her crazy. She moaned and dropped her head back.

He brought his head down to capture her delicate breast in his mouth, suckling it through the thin material of her blouse. Sighing, Catherine brought her hands up to pull him closer.

"You are driving me...oh yes," she cried, "that's the... OH!"

The rest of her unintelligible words were lost to her as she felt her entire body go taut with pleasure and she cried out with her sudden release.

Jake's eyes flared with triumph.

Catherine's heart raced. She kissed Jake while reaching her hand down his pants to grasp his swelling member.

"Someone wants to play," she whispered seductively in his ear.

Jake slowly unbuttoned his shirt and slipped out of his pants, taking her face between his hands. He kissed her slowly, slipping his tongue between her teeth and probing her mouth as if he had all the time in the world.

Catherine panted.

"Jake," she moaned. "Please—"

"Please, what?" he asked.

"I need you. Now!" she demanded, breathlessly.

"If you want this party to continue, we need to slow it down."

"Oh no. That would be terrible."

Catherine wrapped her leg around his waist.

"Let me help you," she added sincerely, pulling him over on top of her.

Jake growled as he slipped inside of her, hearing her sharp intake of air. His hands crushed Catherine to him as they fell into rhythmic thrusts. He rolled onto his back, pulling Catherine with him. His large hands grasped her backside and pulled her towards him over and over again.

Catherine knew that she was pushing him to the brink of his self-control, but it felt so good. Suddenly, she cried out as she felt her body approaching its climax. The moonlight shone through the window, lighting the room with its soft glow as Catherine threw her head back, rejoicing in the ecstasy of it all.

The emotion and pleasures were so close to pain that the lines became blurred. She cried out his name, panting as her body went taut with ecstasy. She gasped, clinging to Jake while he thrust into her twice more before his own body reached its climax.

Lights strobed behind Jake's eyelids as he closed them to the exquisite pleasure that washed over him, his breathing coming in and out like a steam engine. He was powerless when it came to this woman.

His fingers twisted in her hair, pulling her mouth to his. Catherine collapsed on top of him, her muscles slack with fatigue.

Catherine brushed her finger through his dampened hair as her lips brushed against his neck.

"That was…"

"Amazing," he finished her sentence, letting out another ragged breath.

"Yes," she agreed, picking her head up to stare down at him. "Jake…"

"I know."

"What do you know?"

"I'll miss you too, Catie," he muttered.

"But how did you…"

"Because, my love, we are connected," he said. "I can feel you even when I'm not with you."

Catherine bit her lower lip and felt tears sting the back of her eyes.

"Oh, Jake." She buried her face in his neck. "I will miss you so very much."

"I'll be back before you know it," he assured her, rubbing his hand up and down her spine. "You will be fine."

"You and I happened so fast."

"Yes, but when you know that someone is right for you. Well, you just know."

Catherine took a deep breath, relishing the scent of him. Jake smelled of salty waves and expensive aftershave. It was heavenly to her. She wanted to memorize everything about him—the feel of him, his touch, his smell.

"I tried to tell you about the trip weeks ago," Jake said with a deep sigh, "But the time never seemed right to bring it up. Then everything went sideways..."

"I'll be alright, Jake. As long as you come back to me. You are coming back, right?"

"Of course, love. I just don't know how long it will be."

He was flying home to Australia tomorrow, she didn't know how long for. The only thing she knew for certain was that it would feel like an eternity until he held her in his arms again.

When did I become that woman? The person who needed that special man in her life to make her feel whole and alive? Catherine asked herself. She could feel her heart breaking as tears escaped her eyes.

"Hey, hey, now what is this?" Jake asked, when he felt a tear touch his skin. "I'm not gone yet. And I swear, I'll be back for you!"

"I know, I know. I'm just being silly," Catherine confessed. "It'll pass. I just need a minute."

"The offer to come with me is still on the table," Jake said, kissing her on the nose. "It would be great to have you to talk to on the long flight."

"I wish with all of my heart that I could just pack up and go with you, Jake, I really do. But I can't."

"If you change your mind, you just let me know and I'll send the plane for you."

"Wait, what? You have a plane?"

"I didn't tell you that my family has a private jet service? I must have forgotten. It's not really something that one leads with. Anyway, the offer is there."

Catherine studied him as he got out of bed.

"Would you like water?" he asked.

"Yes, that would be wonderful," she responded, watching him walk from the room to retrieve two bottles of water, unashamed of his nakedness.

She pondered what else she didn't know about Jake Ryan.

CHAPTER 24

*C*atherine felt Jake stir two hours later as his phone buzzed on the nightstand. He reached over to check it, then rolled back over, kissing her on the forehead, before sitting on the edge of the bed.

Catherine reached out and touched his back gently.

"It's still early, Jake. Come back to bed," she said sleepily.

"I can't, love. I have an early flight."

He slipped a shirt over his head then leaned over to give her a kiss.

Catherine saw his sadness as their eyes met.

"I'm not ready to say goodbye. It's too soon."

"The driver will be here to get me in an hour. I still haven't packed," Jake said, smiling down at her with an understanding look.

He smelt himself and turned up his nose.

"Besides, I could really use a shower." He turned away to grab his clothes. "I'll put the coffee on since you have to get to the office soon. You told me as much last night, when we made love."

"Which time?" she asked, a provocative smile on her lips.

"The second...no, it was definitely the third time," he insisted, while pulling his pants on and fastening them. "Now, get yourself up and pop into the shower, love. Unless you want everyone in the office to know what you were up to the entire night."

"Are you joining me?"

"I'm afraid not, or we will both be late."

Catherine heaved a sigh and tossed the covers back.

"Perhaps you're right. I am smelling a bit ripe," Catherine muttered to no one in particular. "It would be unprofessional of me to show up smelling of," she paused and turned to look at Jake with a seductive grin, "You!"

Jake walked into the kitchen and turned the coffee maker on before heading out the front door to his own condo for a shower. After his shower he threw his clothes into his suitcase.

When he returned to Catherine's place he found her standing by the sliding glass door watching the sunrise with a cup of coffee in her hand. She turned when she heard him approach and smiled.

"I leave for Washington, D.C. in a couple of days. I'll facetime you when I get settled," Catherine said, walking over to the counter to pour him a cup of coffee.

"If you changed your mind about joining me, the offer still stands," he said, touching her hand as he waited for her to look up at him.

When she finally did, unshed tears shimmered in her eyes and she quickly turned away.

"I told you before, I made a commitment..."

"I know, status quo and all," Jake said, resting his hand on her arm to keep her from pulling away. "I'll miss you." he whispered softly.

His phone chimed to signal that his ride had arrived to take him to the airport. Setting his cup down on the counter, Jake took her in his arms.

"Oh, Jake!" Catherine cried, putting her cup down beside his as she tried to hold back her tears. "I will truly miss you, every minute of every day," she whispered, wrapping her arms around his waist and burying her face in his chest.

He took her face in his hand and tipped it up to his to kiss her.

"Stay out of trouble while I'm gone," he said, wiping the tears from her cheeks with his thumbs. "And keep my side of the bed warm. I'm just a phone call away so don't hesitate to call if you need anything."

Catherine swallowed the lump in her throat and tried to give Jake a reassuring smile.

"I will. I promise."

Turning from her, Jake pulled his favorite t-shirt from his bag, the one she liked to wear when he wasn't there.

"I'll be back for this," he said, handing her the shirt. "It's my favorite."

With a large smile, Catherine took it from him and held it to her nose.

"I know. And, Jake, I'll be fine."

"There was never a doubt in my mind, my love."

He leaned down to kiss her again.

A horn sounded, announcing that the impatient driver was getting tired of waiting. Taking out his phone, Jake texted him that he was on his way.

"Doesn't he know that I have to say goodbye to my girl?"

Catherine wiped her eyes and stepped back from him.

"It's alright, love," Catherine said, in her best Aussie accent. "The bloody wanker has to make a living too."

The two of them stepped out onto the front landing and took one last look at the view with the sun cresting over the horizon.

"It sure is a beautiful sunrise," she said.

"The view is nothing compared to what I'm looking at," he said, gazing down at her.

Jake slowly leaned down for one last, slow, passionate kiss. She closed her eyes and wished it would never end, but knew that it had to.

"I just have one last question for you, love," Jake quietly said into her ear. "If you knew that you only had a year to live, would you still choose the life you have—or would you chuck it all and run away with me?"

Jake didn't wait for her answer. He kissed her cheek before letting go of her, then grabbed his suitcase and walked away.

She followed him as he reached the end of the condos and handed his luggage to the driver. Jake opened the car door and turned to give her a wave and one last smile, before climbing into the waiting vehicle.

Tears fell from Catherine's eyes as she watched the car pull away. She continued to stand there, twisting the antique wedding ring on her finger, long after the car's tail lights faded. She wiped the tears from her cheeks with the backs of both hands and slowly walked back to her condo, knowing that she would have to reapply her makeup before leaving for work. Jake's parting question repeated over again in her mind, haunting her. She had lists to make and details to pin down before leaving for Washington D.C. in a few days. How could he expect her to concentrate on such matters when he posed such a question to her?

She felt emotionally drained, but knew that she would have to force a smile to her lips when she faced Russell and her other coworkers. After all, they had a big move coming. People were depending on her. It would be all hands on deck while she made living arrangements for their stay in D.C. for the next two months.

Jake's driver made good time and got them to the airport ahead of schedule. They drove through the private entrance leading onto the tarmac. A sleek, white and silver twin-engine turbo jet sat in front of them, glistening in the early morning sunlight.

From the window of the car, Jake caught sight of the pilot inside the plane's cockpit going through his final checklist in preparation for departure.

Traveling usually left Jake feeling exhilarated, but today he felt less than enthusiastic about his impending trip. However, he was grateful that he wouldn't have to fight anyone for the armrests or leg space, since he was traveling in style.

Leaving his bags at the bottom of the steps, an attendant quickly retrieved them and stowed them below.

Jake climbed the steps of the sleek jet and entered the fuselage. He was greeted by a lovely blonde woman with crystal blue eyes. She was dressed in a smart navy-blue crew members' pantsuit, scarf, and two-inch stacked heels.

"G'day to you, sis," Jake said, bending over and giving her a kiss on the cheek. Jacqueline was the baby of the family and three years younger than him.

"It's Miss Ryan to you for the duration of this flight, if you don't mind, Mr. Ryan," Jacqueline said, rather curtly.

"You're not still mad at me about last time, are you? Because it wasn't my fault, Jackie. We hit a lot of turbulence and you know how I get when that happens."

"Well, it better not happen again, I'm warning you. You will be cleaning up your own mess this time, Mr. Ryan," Jacqueline said, punching him in the arm.

"Ouch, Jackie. That's not very professional of you."

"And you better not be a bloody wanker and cheap out on me with the tip this time because I work hard on these flights. Expensive shoes don't buy themselves."

"You are way too uptight. You need to lighten up, sis." Jake pulled out his wallet and tucked a hundred-dollar bill into her pocket. "Don't say I didn't ever give you anything. And my service on this flight better be exceptional."

"Thanks, Jakey. Nice doing business with you," she smiled cheekily.

"Any other passengers tagging along?"

"We picked up a businessman in Atlanta, and we are waiting on a couple headed to Sydney for their honeymoon."

She took his coat from him and placed it on his seat.

"I sat you up front in your favorite spot. Oh, and the pilot would like a word with you before we take off."

"Of course, he would." Jake tapped on the cockpit door with a rat-a-tap-tap-tap, the signal he always used to let his brother, Jesse, know that it was him.

The cockpit door quickly swung open. A large, burly man with dirty blond hair, neatly cropped, military style, grabbed him and gave him a bear hug. Jesse was the oldest child, being two and a half years older than Jake.

Jesse had decided to go into the elite plane service business five years ago and he came to Jake and his father to ask if they wanted in too. Jake had been a successful financial consultant at the time and was looking for a tax shelter as well as an investment that could make him money. So, the three men went into business together.

"How are you, little brother?" Jesse said, his voice booming in the small space. "I was expecting your call two weeks ago. What happened? Wait, don't tell me. It had something to do with that girl you told me about. Is she here?" He peered over Jake's shoulder.

"No, she isn't here," Jake answered, a sullen tone to his voice. "And yes, I was delayed because of Catherine, but she has a very important job and couldn't get away."

"Well, don't keep me in suspense, you bludger. Tell me everything there is to know about her," Jesse said.

Just then, the co-pilot stepped onto the plane.

"Hey there, little Jake. I heard you were going to join us today. You want to climb in the jump seat behind me and catch me up on everything you've been up to?"

Zackery McLeroy had been Jesse's best friend growing up. They had done everything together, including getting in to trouble at school. When Jesse had started his business and became a pilot, Zackery became his co-pilot.

It wasn't long before Zack began to invest his earnings into the business and had become a fully vested partner in the last year.

"Jake, here, has a girlfriend," Jesse said, motioning for Zack to squeeze around them. "He was just about to spill the details on his newest sheila that has been taking up all of his time."

Zack perked up.

"Well, don't keep us in suspense, old man. Spill."

"No, no, boys. I don't think I was about to divulge any such thing to the likes of you. Besides, it's a long flight and I think I'll stretch out my legs right over here." Jake walked to his seat and sat down. "And I think I might even close my eyes for a few winks, since I got precious little sleep last night. So, this time you mates will have to fly this beauty of a plane without me."

"Ah, come on, Jake," Jesse said, sounding disappointed. "You know how I live vicariously through you, ever since my Molly became perpetually pregnant for the third year in a row."

"And who's fault is that, big brother?" Jake shrugged as he reclined his seat and placed his arms behind his head. "Didn't Pops have the talk with you?"

"Jake, come on, man," Zack said.

"All right, all right," Jake relented. "Jackie?" he called out, peering down the row of seats to the back galley with a mischievous look.

Jacqueline poked her head out from the galley.

"Yes? Did I hear someone calling my name?

Sitting his seat up so that he could face his sister, Jake asked, "Could I get a preflight drink? Surprise me."

"Coming right up, Jakey."

"So, Jackie tells me that we have a honeymoon couple joining us today." Jake turned back to face his brother and Zack. "If it gets too mushy out here, and the windows start to fog up, I'll be joining the two of you in the pit," he said, buckling the seatbelt over his lap and pushing his seat back. Then, he closed his eyes.

"I intend to catch up on some sleep."

He stretched out his long legs and crossed them at the ankles.

"So, if the two of you don't mind, bugger off!"

"Fine," Jesse muttered under his breath as he turned to disappear back into the cockpit. "But I suspect you'll be joining us sooner rather than later, if this couple is anything like the last honeymooners we had aboard this plane a week ago. Oh wait… weren't they doing it in Jake's favorite seat?"

"I'm going to assume that you sanitized the seats properly after they deplaned," Jake said.

"Don't listen to him, Jakey," Jacqueline said, bringing him a scotch and water, which she presented on a silver tray. "He's just joking with you. They actually did it in the restroom."

"That is disgusting! Honestly, do people have no respect for this fine aircraft?" Jake said, taking his drink from her.

She stepped back towards the cabin door to greet the newlywed couple, along with the businessman they'd picked up in Atlanta.

Jake laughed to himself. It was wonderful being around his family again. They always managed to step right back into exactly where they'd left off.

They were always close growing up and made a pact long ago that they would always be friends.

Nothing could take the place of a sibling, Jake mused. Absolutely nothing.

They had a family business going and it was making money. Jacqueline begged her brothers to get in on the family business because she said that she wanted to see the world. In truth, Jackie had a crush on Zackery McLeroy and wanted to keep an eye on him.

Jesse and Jake had always known about their little sister's fondness for Zackery from an early age. She had followed them around when the three boys used to hang out. So, it came as no surprise to either of them when Zackery and Jackie became entangled romantically and got engaged shortly after.

Their mother, Matilda, was their flight scheduler. She also collected the payments and kept the books, while their father, Jack, made sure that their permits, visas, and logbooks were maintained properly. Jack also managed the ground crew and made sure that the regular maintenance reports were kept up to date and filed on time.

Jesse's high end, private jet service had become so successful that they were adding another plane to the fleet in two weeks. That was before their father had become ill and was now in the hospital.

Jake knew from the start that he would be called upon to take over for their father if anything should happen to him. Yet, it didn't make leaving Catherine behind any easier for him.

Jake's family needed him, now more than ever, and he wanted to be there for them, for as long as it took. In the back of his mind, Jake hoped it wouldn't be long before he could get back to Catherine.

.

CHAPTER 25

*C*atherine drove into work early, beating the rush hour traffic. She couldn't get that stupid question of Jake's out of her head. What would she do if she only had a year to live?

She shook her head to clear her thoughts. She needed to be clear minded and this was not helping.

After she arrived and opened the offices, she went straight to work making phone calls. She arranged for the leases to be sent over for signatures and double-checked that their flights were taken care of.

And although it was highly unusual that a new governor would take up residence in Washington, there was impending legislation coming up that would greatly impact Florida and its economy, so Tillman needed to make regular trips back and forth for extended periods of time.

Catherine needed to make this move as seamless as possible for everyone involved, especially for Angela, who was in no condition to take this on in her current state. Catherine knew Angela would worry about every little detail until she made herself sick, so Catherine had volunteered to take care of everything. After all, that was what she did best.

She'd been working with a realtor in Washington for over a month to arrange suitable housing for the three of them, plus four of their staffers. She was confident that she would have everything wrapped up by today. Catherine was certain that she'd found the perfect home for the three of them. It was a large home with a guest house in the back. The agent had also sent over information on several apartments, all of them centrally located, for the three interns. Catherine was leaning towards the three-bedroom apartment that they could all share. For her, Russell, and Angela, the move would merely be temporary. But for the four staffers, at least some of them would be staying in the Washington office. One of them would serve as the D.C. Office Liaison, with the others providing administrative and technical support.

Then there were the staffing positions she would need to fill permanently once they reached D.C. Catherine knew that there was a long list of eager interns and newly graduated college students looking to pad their resumes. The five to six positions she needed to fill wouldn't be a problem.

Russell and Angela would retain their current home in Florida. They liked where they lived and didn't need more space, even with the new baby coming. They would renovate the spare room into a nursery. Angela would see to the Florida home nursery, and Catherine would take care of the Washington D.C. nursery.

On Catherine's to do list was the task of hiring someone to check in on her own condo as well as the Tillman home. She'd decided to hire a professional firm that managed properties to check in and make sure that no squatters had moved in while they were away.

Catherine typed everything up for the morning meeting. She had sent out for danishes, bagels, an assortment of fruit, had a fresh pot of coffee on to brew, and was placing the agenda papers out on the conference room table when people began to file into the room.

At ten, Russell entered the building and dropped his things off in his office.

"What did you do, Catherine, stay up all night prepping?" Russell said. His jovial voice boomed as he entered the conference room.

Louisa, one of their fortunate interns who would be going to Washington, nervously jiggled her leg under the table.

Conner, who also would be going to Washington, looked in Catherine's direction. He'd been asking her incessantly about living arrangements and if she knew where they would be staying while in D.C. Catherine shot him a reassuring glance and pointed to the paperwork in front of him. He gave her a grateful smile and began to leaf through the pages. When he gave her a thumbs up and a toothy grin, Catherine knew that she had made at least one person in the room happy.

The three interns were thrilled with the apartment Catherine had rented for them. They would be near the Pentagon in a secure building that had a work-out room, indoor swimming pool, and a jacuzzi. The three of them would commute together on the train each day and walk the few short blocks to the offices.

She had thought of everything.

The house she found for Russell, Angela, and herself to rent was in Georgetown, twenty miles from the offices. She and Russell would hire a driver and commute together so that they could discuss the day's agenda and get work done on the way to work.

Russell, meanwhile, fixed himself a coffee and put a few things on his plate before taking a seat at the head of the table. Sipping from his cup, he gave a satisfied sigh, then rubbed his hands together. He felt like a child who'd just gotten his heart's desire, all wrapped up in a pretty box with a great big bow on top.

"I want to thank everyone in this room for all of your hard work. As you know, some of you will be going to Washington with us, and the rest of you, who have been retained permanently, will work out of the Florida office. It is also important to acknowledge our ever steady campaign manager, Catherine Lawrence. She has been working overtime to make housing arrangements and airline reservations."

Russell made a big show of it by clapping his hands and gesturing towards Catherine sitting to his right side.

"We couldn't have pulled this off without her tireless efforts and quick thinking. Thank you again, Catherine. And with that I will turn the rest of the time over to her, as she will be running the meeting today."

Another round of applause went out and Catherine smiled politely and begrudgingly accepted the attention.

"As you well know, I prefer to work in the background and all of this attention is somewhat disconcerting, so if you will all hold your applause, I would really appreciate it," Catherine said, giving a small smile. She added, "That being said, may I direct your attention to page one."

The meeting went well. Russell was pleased with the numbers, the slush fund, and living arrangements in Washington, D.C.

Her day seemed to have flown by as Catherine headed home just after six-thirty. She felt exhausted. She hoped that she wasn't coming down with anything.

After stopping in at her favorite Chinese Restaurant to pick up dinner on her way home, Catherine sat down to eat her dinner with the news on in the background. When she was finished, she needed to pack for Washington.

"It's going to be a long night," she muttered, looking out the window at the ocean and stars.

She wondered if Jake had made it home to his family yet and if he was thinking of her at that very moment.

CHAPTER 26

*T*wo days later, Catherine sat in the Elite Day Spa with her two best friends. Her mind was wandering as she tried to relax but she couldn't stop thinking of all the things left for her to do.

It was the day before the big move to Washington, and her last chance to unwind before moving her entire life to another state for a couple of months. She had been in an agitated mood since Jake had left and found it difficult to pull herself out of it. Everything just felt wrong since his departure. Catherine wasn't even sure that she wanted to continue with her current plans to move and start a political career in Washington.

The plan was that Angela would join Catherine and Russell in Washington in two weeks, giving her ample time to close up the house in Florida. Russell was understandably anxious about leaving Angela behind. He'd hired two full-time bodyguards to watch over his pregnant wife and get her to Washington safely.

"Hello, Catherine? Earth to Catherine. Did you hear me?" Janine asked, waving a hand in front of Catherine's face.

"What? No, I'm so sorry Janine. I was thinking about something else," she admitted, with a sense of shame.

"Girlfriend," Janine said, "how could you have let that man get on a plane and fly away without you? He was yummy."

Catherine laughed.

"I'm an idiot. That much is clear."

"I'm glad that you said it and not me, but I would have to agree," Angela said under her breath.

"So, what were you thinking about and why do you have that perplexed look on your face?" Janine asked, taking a sip of her herbal tea.

Their day at the spa was scheduled so that the three of them could spend some time together. They booked the group massage first, followed by a pedicure, facial, and manicure. Then they would finish out the day at the hair salon. They were currently waiting to be taken back for their massage.

Catherine hesitated before confiding in her friends.

"What was I thinking about? It's something Jake said to me at the victory celebration the other night."

"What did he say?" Angela and Janine asked simultaneously.

"He asked me if I was living my grandmother's dream for my life or if this was the life that I had chosen for myself. Then, before he left, he asked me another strange question."

"Don't keep us in suspense," Janine said.

"He asked me, if I knew that I only had a year to live, would I still choose the same life or would I chuck it all and run away with him?"

"Well?" Angela said, sitting on the edge of her seat.

"What did you tell him?" Janine also asked, sitting forward in her chair.

"To the first question, I told him that I wanted to leave my mark behind, long after I ceased to exist," Catherine answered with a heavy sigh.

"What is wrong with that answer?" Angela said, leaning back in her seat.

"Rookie move," Janine said. "The man just wanted to know that he mattered more than the job. So, what was your answer to his second question, the one about only having a year to live?"

"I didn't answer him."

"What do you mean, you didn't answer him?" Angela asked.

"I was caught off guard and didn't know what to say. The truth is, I just don't know if it's true anymore," Catherine said. "Is this enough? Is the path that I have chosen for myself still enough for me?"

"What do you mean, Catherine?" Angela asked, quickly sitting forward in her seat again and placing a hand on her friend's knee. "What is it you truly want out of life that you don't already have?"

"A life!" she said with a groan. "I want a life with a husband to love and children to cherish. I don't think that I thought about those things before. They were always in the back of my mind, but they didn't seem that important to me before."

"You mean, before Jake came along," Janine said.

Angela smiled and reached over to take Catherine's hand in her own.

"They are all excellent desires, my friend."

"Look at you, Janine. You have a career, a husband, and kids. Is it worth it?" Catherine said, looking over at her friend.

"I think it is," she answered. "I'm not saying that it's easy. We have our struggles but I wouldn't have it any other way."

"I suddenly find myself wanting to have it all as well. But I fear that the political arena isn't the best place to have everything I desire," Catherine said.

She took a sip of her tea as her eyes welled up with tears.

"It is such a cutthroat business. Maybe he's right and I'm still trying to make my grandmother proud of me."

"Only you know the answer to that, Catherine," Janine insisted.

A woman appeared in the doorway to take them to the massage room.

"When we are finished here, I say we have dinner and discuss it until we come up with a suitable answer. And I warn you, there will be a copious amount of wine involved. For medicinal purposes, of course," Janine said.

"Maybe for the two of you," Angela answered indicating her stomach, "but I will be having water or something non-alcoholic."

"I will second that," Catherine said. "I've been feeling out of sorts and would prefer to keep a clear head."

"Then I will join the sober brigade," Janine added. "There is strength in solidarity."

Catherine continued to question her life's plan and the motivation behind it. She had managed to survive the loss of her grandmother and father by allowing herself to go numb. To feel nothing. Did she have it in her to change course?

CHAPTER 27

"So, what you are really trying to say, little brother, is you're an idiot," Jesse said.

"That's a little harsh, don't you think?" Jake fired back over the telephone.

"Well, did you or did you not come clean with her?"

"Not exactly," Jake admitted. In his heart, he knew that his brother was right.

"So, you didn't tell Catherine, the woman you can't stop thinking about, might I add, that you are a successful businessman as well as a pilot and financial advisor?"

Jake could almost see the dry smile on his brother's face.

"You're right, I'm an idiot. She thinks that I'm nothing more than a free spirit, going around riding waves for prize money. And here she is with her life all planned out, probably wondering if I have anything to offer her," he said with a groan.

"You have to make this right, Jake. You have to tell her the truth before it's too late."

"That's why you are the older, wiser brother, Jesse."

"No, that's why I'm Mum and Pops' favorite," Jesse said. "Besides, with all of our dealings, do you have any idea how vital a solicitor in the family would be? Does she have any barrister experience?"

"Yes. She definitely does. Why?"

"Because, the way I see it, someone has to keep the family out of jail," Jesse said. "You know I'm just joshing you, little brother, but you do have to tell her the truth."

Jake thought for a moment before answering.

"You're right, of course. I will. It's just a matter of working out the time logistics. After all, we are fourteen hours ahead of her. She told me her schedule before I left but I didn't write it down. So, now I have to figure out how and when to call."

"How indeed," Jesse replied. "Well, I've got to fly. Get it? I've got to fly."

"Yeah, yeah, pilot humor," Jake grumbled. "And it still gets me every time."

"Talk to you later, little brother."

"Back at you, Jesse. You guys be safe out there. I hear the skies over the straights are going to be rough tonight."

"All part of the adventure, Jakey, it's all part of the adventure. Signing off now."

"See you when you get back, Jesse."

"Ten-four, good buddy. Over and out," Jesse answered.

Jake sat in the office in Sydney, pondering over his conversation with Jesse before turning out the lights and heading to the hospital to check on his father. Maybe he'd have some good advice for him.

Jack Ryan had taken a turn for the better since Jake arrived home. His mother said that it was because he was back and his father could stop worrying now.

Jack seemed to be doing a lot of sleeping, in Jake's opinion, since his return. Jake even wondered if it had all been a ploy to get him back home. Not that his father was faking his illness, only that his father had wanted him to come home and take over the business but Jake had been reticent.

It didn't take much imagination for Jake to see that his father was getting older. Jake didn't remember the lines in his father's face being so deep. In the six months that he'd been away, Jack seemed to have grown older overnight. His once strong hands were now white, unsteady, and thin. Every vein protruded and he'd developed a tremor when he sat still. His father shuffled his feet when he walked across the room and shook with the effort of getting out of a chair.

Why shouldn't Jack turn the reins over to the younger generation to run the day-to-day operations of their growing family business? Jake had even been seriously contemplating returning home to the business before he met Catherine. But falling in love with her had changed everything for him. She was like the air he breathed. The two of them had never discussed his family's business, let alone moving to Australia as a couple.

What should I do? he wondered.

"Pops will know what I should do," Jake murmured to himself. "He's always known the right thing to do."

CHAPTER 28

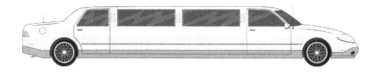

*C*atherine felt tired and anxious. She'd barely slept in three nights and suddenly wanted to call off the move and next five years of her life that had been planned out for her.

What had she been thinking?

What's wrong with me? she asked herself, standing in the airport with a coffee in one hand and a bag containing a bran muffin in the other.

This isn't like me. Get ahold of yourself, Catherine Lawrence, she thought.

She had sent her clothes ahead by two-day shipping to cut down on the number of bags she would have to carry, and now she was having a nervous breakdown in the middle of the terminal.

She found the nearest bathroom, set her cup down and placed her muffin in her handbag. Then, splashing water on her face, Catherine looked into the mirror at her bloodshot eyes. She took a deep breath and dried her face and hands with the rough paper towel before walking out of the restroom, armed with a new determination.

"Is everything all right, Catherine?" Russell asked as she walked up to him while he stood in the line to board.

"Yes, of course it is. Everything is great. Couldn't be better," Catherine lied as they showed their boarding passes and walked down the ramp to board the plane.

When they arrived in Washington, the three interns took an Uber to their new apartment while Catherine and Russell had a private car waiting to take them to the rental home in Georgetown.

They discussed strategy as they drove and stopped at a store to pick up a few essential items before they arrived at their new residence. They took that same car to Capitol Hill for a tour of their new offices then went out to dinner with their small, intimate group to celebrate.

Catherine excused herself, went to the restroom, and found herself taking deep breaths of air, letting it out slowly. She had never had a panic attack before, so it was not the first thing that came to mind as her heart pounded in her chest. She found it difficult to catch her breath, which made her even more anxious.

Catherine pinched her pale cheeks and returned to the table as the party was coming to an end. They said their farewells and she and Russell climbed back into their private car and headed for the rental home.

On the way, Russell called Angela to check on her. Catherine found herself staring out the window, trying not to eavesdrop on his conversation. She wondered about Jake, about how his father was doing. Just then, her phone began to ring.

Checking the caller ID, she immediately answered the phone.

"Hey, I was just thinking about you," she said, wishing that she could crawl through the phone and curl up next to him.

"I told you before, we are connected," he said. "How was the big move? Are you all settled into your new place?"

"Not exactly," she admitted. "I haven't had time to unpack yet. We have been on the go ever since we landed earlier today."

"I bet you have the next seven days all planned out, down to the last minute."

"Yes, but after that it's a free-for-all," she laughed. "How did you know?"

"I know you, Miss Catherine Lawrence. Maybe even better than you know yourself."

"How's your father?" she asked somberly after her laughter faded.

He took a deep breath.

"The nurse said he had a good day and that he was improving."

Catherine could tell he was not telling her everything.

"Oh, Jake, that's wonderful."

"Tell me that you wished you'd come with me. Tell me how much you miss me...Tell me you love me, Catie, because I miss you so much," Jake said, letting out a heavy sigh.

In a heartbeat, she responded.

"I do love you, Jake. Words alone cannot express the way I miss you." She was unable to keep the sadness or longing from her voice.

She cupped her hand to the phone.

"I hate being here without you," she whispered, as a lump formed in her throat.

"Me too," Jake whispered back. "Then come to me now, Catie, my love. The world be damned and just come."

"I can't," she said, feeling her heart breaking in her chest. "Hey," she added, forcing a lightness to her tone, "I'm in the car with Russell right now, and we are on our way home from dinner. I'll call you back in fifteen minutes so we can talk."

"That sounds good," he answered. "But let me call you back in twenty. The phone bill can get rather exorbitant at the end of the month. Besides, I have a few connections at the phone company."

"Well in that case, by all means, you call me back," Catherine said. "Talk with you in a few minutes then."

"Yes, in a few," he said and hung up.

Catherine turned the phone over in her hand a moment while staring out the window.

"You really like this guy, don't you, Lawrence?" Russell said.

She turned to him and nodded.

"Yes, Russell, I really like him, but we are thousands of miles apart. I just don't see any way for this thing to work out."

"If it is meant to happen, it will."

"That's what people say when they want to give you hope," Catherine answered glumly. "I just don't see how it can work with me here in Washington half the time and in Florida the rest. Then there is Jake. He has family obligations in Australia…" Her words tapered off as she shook her head.

"Chin up, Lawrence," Russell said, trying to sound positive. "One way or the other it will work out."

"Nice, Russell," Catherine said, in a sarcastic tone, "That makes me feel so much better. Good talk."

"I just meant to say, things work out the way they are meant to," he offered. "Look at me and Angela for example—"

"Let's not," Catherine countered, cutting him off.

She leaned over and tapped the driver on the shoulder and instructed him to stop.

"I'll walk from here," she said before jumping out of the car. "Don't forget that we have a 10 A.M. breakfast appointment. So, please set your alarm this time. I'm your advisor, not your Momma... Oh, and don't be late."

"Are you sure that everything is alright with you, Lawrence?"

"Yes, I'm fine, Russell," she replied, giving him a puzzled look. "Why do you ask?"

"Because you seem...well, different lately," Russell said with a smile, obviously dismissing the whole thing. "See you in the morning."

Catherine closed the door and the driver tipped his hat to her before driving Russell up to the main house. She ran into the guest house the moment they were out of sight. It was a modest, thousand square foot cottage that was perfectly designed and decorated. Luckily, she didn't have to wait long for Jake's call.

The two of them talked for over an hour. When it was time to hang up, neither wanted to be the one to say goodbye first, but Catherine was exhausted and could barely keep her eyes open.

"I wish you were here to tuck me in and just hold me," she told him with a sigh.

"I know. Me too."

"Jake?"

Her voice sounded small to him and he couldn't put his finger on what was wrong but, in his gut, he knew there was something bothering her.

"Hmm?"

"We can do this, right?"

"Of course, we can do this," he assured her, swearing quietly under his breath. "I will be back before you know it."

"I'm just trying to be practical."

"Well, stop it," he said in a joking manner before turning serious again. "I don't know how often I'll be able to call you in the next few weeks, but you can text me any time and I *will* get back to you when I get a free moment."

The silence between them felt heavy.

"I miss you, Jake."

He smiled a little.

"I miss you more. I wish I was there with you right now, Catie."

"I know you do. I'll keep your side of the bed warm for you until you return."

"Sleep tight, my love."

CHAPTER 29

hree weeks dragged by. Catherine and Jake exchanged text messages, but had not spoken since his last call. Catherine texted Jake during her meeting that she missed him and that they needed to schedule a phone call for later that day.

After pushing send, Catherine interjected a particular point that needed to be made at the meeting. Afterwards, she stood up and moved to pour herself another cup of coffee.

Why do I feel so tired lately?

Catherine stifled a yawn before taking her seat again. She listened patiently to the other side's argument. They were from the democratic party, attempting to get more funding for one of their pet projects. They were attempting to sidestep certain rules approved by lawmakers to earmark funding for a bill that had questionable wording in it. The document they were trying to pass off as good for the Florida people hid grants and contracts to key groups that weren't actually good for their state at all. They hid the truth in the rather wordy, small print and Catherine's interns had discovered it before it was too late.

"You are wasting my time and yours, gentlemen. We are not going to budge on this particular point of view. Not now, not ever," Catherine said, abruptly interrupting the one man, who just happened to be a blow-hard. "And I speak for Governor Tillman when I say that, gentlemen!"

She shuffled her paperwork around and placed it back into her briefcase with a flourish.

"Please, let me know when you have come to an appropriate consensus that includes a solution and we can revisit this matter, particularly when it comes to the wording on page one-thousand-twenty-two. I have made a few notes," she added, laying out three small green binders upon the table. "I'll be waiting for your call," Catherine stood up and headed for the door. "But for now, I have another meeting to get to."

"That's it? You're just going to leave?" the blow-hard said with a slight whine to his voice.

"Unless you are ready to concede the point and do the right thing, we are done here!" she stated emphatically. "I have other pressing matters to attend to and I don't have the time to waste arguing with you any further. And let me be perfectly clear, gentlemen," Catherine said, glaring at the three men, "I'm not really accustomed to having my time wasted. Have a nice day."

To their astonishment, she left the room.

Mindy, Catherine's personal assistant and intern, was waiting just outside the door for her.

"Giving them hell again?" she asked.

"Of course. What else would I be doing in there with that bunch of knuckleheads?" Catherine grinned.

"I was about to come in to get you as you instructed but you were too fast today. Do you think they will come around?" Mindy asked.

Pulling a five-dollar bill from her jacket pocket, Catherine handed it to Mindy.

"I have five-dollars that says they will fold by three o'clock today."

"I'll take that bet but I say they don't come around until tomorrow at noon!"

"It's a bet then," Catherine said, with a devilish glint in her eye. "Winner buys coffee. You can start a board and take some bets quietly in my office. Just don't make it too obvious or we'll all be in trouble."

"Deal," Mindy agreed, quickly snatching the five-dollar bill from Catherine's fingers. "I'll just keep this safely tucked away," she added, tucking the bill into her top for safekeeping.

"And I mean the good coffee," Catherine clarified, "not that sludge they try to pass off as coffee in the lounge area."

She made a face as if she had just eaten something distasteful.

"I'm with you on that one," Mindy agreed quickly. "Governor Tillman is waiting for you in his office. Oh, and Mrs. Tillman has just arrived and was asking about you."

"Yay!" Catherine exclaimed excitedly, clapping her hands. Suddenly, a dizzy spell washed over her and she grabbed Mindy's arm to steady herself.

"Are you alright, Catherine?"

"Give me a minute," she gasped, bending over and resting her hand upon her knees. She breathed in and out until the spots dancing before her eyes disappeared.

"Let me get someone for you," Mindy said, nervously.

Catherine straightened slowly, still clutching Mindy's arm, and forced a smile to her lips.

"No, no! I just didn't eat this morning," Catherine lied, trying to sound convincing. "I'll be alright!"

Mindy gave her an uncertain look.

"Well, if you're sure. Let me know if you change your mind. I have an excellent doctor on speed dial."

"I'll keep that in mind, but for now, stop worrying so much, Mindy. Honestly, I'm good. I just need something in my stomach besides more coffee," Catherine said. "Does Russell have anything to eat in his office?"

"No, but I'll order lunch early and have one of the new interns pick it up and deliver it right away," Mindy said, still looking concerned. "In the meantime," she added, pulling a power bar from her pocket, "eat this."

"Thanks, Mindy, you're a lifesaver," Catherine said, opening the power bar and taking a bite out of it, realizing that she was starving.

"Would I be cherry or pineapple flavor?" Mindy teased.

"Oh, no, you are definitely grape flavored. That's the best lifesaver as far as I'm concerned," Catherine said, her mouth full of power bar, which made them both laugh. "Are those the notes I need for the next meeting?" Catherine continued, pointing at the stack of files in Mindy's hands while covering her mouth to keep from spitting out pieces of food.

"Oh, yes." Mindy fumbled with the stack of files she was balancing, pulling the green binder out and giving it to Catherine. "And here, take this," Mindy added, placing an unopened bottle of water under Catherine's arm. "I'll get another bottle from the office."

Saluting Mindy with the partially eaten power bar in one hand, and the bottle of water and file in the other, Catherine started down the hallway before turning around to call back to Mindy.

"Tell Angela that I will have dinner with her this evening," she said, stopping in front of Russell's door. "Wish me luck."

"Will do, and good luck."

"Good morning, Governor, gentlemen, and Miss Hastings. I hope I didn't keep you waiting long. Let's get started, shall we?" Catherine forced a note of cheerfulness to her tone as the door closed behind her.

Jake Ryan sat at his desk in Sydney, having just completed scheduling another flight. His cell phone started vibrating across the desk.

"Hello?" he answered absently.

"Mr. Ryan?" the female voice on the other end said cautiously.

"Yes, this is Mr. Ryan," Jake muttered, still processing the reservation on the computer in front of him.

"This is Dr. Hill from Macquarie University Hospital." The doctor paused, giving Jake time to process her words. Then she continued, "Your mother asked me to phone you… I'm afraid I have some bad news to deliver."

Jake's eyes began to burn and he felt sick even before the doctor said anything more.

"Sir, I'm afraid that your father passed away suddenly this afternoon," she concluded sympathetically.

"What? How?" Jake gasped, staring straight ahead at the computer screen, disbelief causing his mind to grow numb.

"As you know, your father's lung infection was severe, but he was responding well to the medication. We aren't certain but believe that it could have been a blood clot that broke off and settled in his heart. We did everything possible to revive him, but unfortunately, our efforts weren't enough," Doctor Hill said. "I am terribly sorry for your loss, Mr. Ryan. We will know more after the official autopsy."

"How is my mother?" Jake asked quietly, pushing his own grief aside.

"She is understandably distraught," the doctor said, "and asked that I deliver the news to you. She said that you would know what to do."

Jake cleared his throat, choking back a sob.

"Tell my mother that I will be there as soon as I can."

"I will pass the message on to her, Mr. Ryan. And again, I am sorry for your loss," she added in a well-rehearsed, yet soothing tone before hanging up.

Jake sat frozen in disbelief for another moment, the phone still held up to his ear. Tears began to fall from his eyes. Jake debated whether or not to radio his brother while he was still in the air or simply wait until he'd landed to deliver the news. Jake finally settled on the decision to wait until his brother and sister landed before delivering the bad news to them in person.

Looking at his phone as if it were some foreign creature sitting in his hand, Jake pushed the button to hang up. Jesse and Jackie would be landing in about four hours, giving him time to go to the hospital and see to his mother first.

Jake felt stiff getting up from his seat. Every muscle in his body felt strange, as if he had swallowed something that caused him to move in slow motion. Wandering into the break room, Jake found Camilla fixing herself a cup of coffee. He mumbled something about the hospital and needing to go, then simply walked out the door.

Arriving at the hospital, Jake realized that he had no recollection of driving there. He was in shock as he walked through the hospital doors and then took the elevator up to the third floor.

His mother collapsed into his arms, weeping. He did his best to console her.

"Oh, Jake, what will I do without him?" Matilda sobbed. "I don't know how to be without him."

"I know, Mum. I'm here now. Everything will be alright." He began crying into her hair as he cradled her head in his hands. "We'll take care of everything. I don't want you to concern yourself with anything."

"Oh, Jakey..." Her mournful cry could be heard throughout the entire third floor.

"Hush now, Mum. I'll take care of you."

CHAPTER 30

Catherine found it strange that Jake hadn't replied to her text yet. She told herself that he must be swamped. Dialing his number for the second time that day, she became concerned when he didn't pick up.

"Why do you have that look on your face, Catherine?" Angela asked, with a concerned look on her face.

The two of them had decided to dine at a fine downtown restaurant for dinner to catch up while Russell attended a last-minute meeting.

"Something is up with Jake," Catherine said, looking puzzled. "He hasn't answered my text from today and now he isn't answering my call."

"You don't think he's avoiding you?" Angela narrowed her eyes. "Oh, I never trusted that foreigner."

"You are so dramatic, Angela, you always have been."

"But what if I'm right?" Angela countered. "He did have shifty eyes."

"Oh, Angela, he did not have shifty eyes. Jake has beautiful, kind eyes and you know it."

"You're too trusting, Catherine. If he hurts you, I will personally fly to Australia and punch him in the nose," she insisted.

"Angela, you are ridiculous. First of all, you don't know where he lives," Catherine pointed out. "Then there is the long plane ride, which you cannot make in your condition." Her eyes traveled to Angela's stomach. "And for what? My feelings? Pish, Angela, I'll survive."

"Well, only if you are sure that you don't need me to go over there and kick some Aussie butt," Angela narrowed her eyes again.

"I appreciate the gesture but, I assure you, I am quite capable of fighting my own battles."

"Remember Kyle Campbell?" Angela said suddenly. "And what he did to you?"

"Yes, Angela, and I also remember what you did to that poor boy for breaking my heart. Please swear to me that you aren't planning to do anything drastic to Jake if this thing goes south. I still feel bad for Kyle. His hair and eyebrows fell out because you put hair remover in his shampoo. And, if that wasn't bad enough, you got three members of his own rowing crew to turn against him. They put itching powder in his jock strap and laced his t-shirt with the stuff. I still remember his humiliation. He couldn't stop scratching himself during rowing practice the day the recruiter was there. He was devastated, and he dropped his oars into the water before jumping out of the shell and into the water."

"Yes, but you were vindicated," Angela said proudly, looking very self-righteous.

Catherine eyed her friend.

"But it was wrong, Angela."

Angela picked up her menu and pretended to study it.

"And the twerp got exactly what he deserved."

"He was kicked off the rowing team!"

"That was the icing on the cake when you think about it," Angela gloated, giving no indication that she was in the least bit remorseful. "I certainly didn't lose any sleep over it." She closed her menu abruptly. "I believe I will have the salmon."

"Salmon sounds wonderful," Catherine said, closing her own menu. "And, Angie, stay out of this relationship, understand?"

"I merely wish to help."

"I don't need your brand of retribution. I'm a big girl and can handle my own affairs."

Angela shrugged her shoulders and gave Catherine an innocent look. "Well, if you are certain..."

"I'm certain. No interference!"

"Well, alright then."

"I'm glad we settled that," Catherine said, laying her menu down on the table as the waitress came over to take their order. "I will have the glazed salmon, rice pilaf with the mixed vegetables, and a small Caesar salad."

Angela nodded her head.

"I'll have the same."

"Very good. Will there be anything else?" the waitress asked.

"No," Angela answered, "I believe we have ordered enough to fill us both up for a week."

She waited for the waitress to walk away before continuing their prior conversation.

"I get what you are saying, loud and clear, Catherine but—"

"But, nothing," Catherine cut in, "I don't need or *want* help in this matter, just so that we are clear."

"Crystal clear!"

"Look, I'm barely holding it together with duct tape and a prayer at the moment and I'm nearly out of both right now, Angie."

"I get it. Let's change the subject. I'm certain hunk-a-hunk-a-burning love will call you eventually. He probably got busy," Angela said.

Not wanting to think about Jake anymore, Catherine asked about the new nursery and what baby names Angela and Russell were considering.

The two of them spent the rest of the evening deep in conversation about babies, the impending sleepless nights, and how excited they both were that Angela was going to get what she had always wanted—to be a mother.

Jake was too busy with funeral arrangements and taking care of his Mum to check his phone and missed the two calls and text messages from Catherine. His father had been the strongest man he'd ever known and just like that he was gone, taken from them by a blood clot.

Four days had passed since his father's death. Funeral arrangements still needed to be made, but the autopsy had been performed and just as the doctor had suspected, a blood clot had lodged in his fathers' heart.

Jake couldn't get that fateful day of his father's death out of his head. It stuck in his mind on a continual loop, playing over and over again. After taking his mother home and getting a neighbor to come over and stay with her, he'd gone to the airstrip to meet his siblings.

Jake had waited for Jesse and Jacqueline for an hour and a half before they finally landed. He'd rehearsed over and over what he was going to say to them. Jesse and Jacqueline took one look at his face as they stepped off the plane and both knew what had happened before any words came out of his mouth. The three of them hugged one another and cried for their loss together.

Seven days later, Jake had found it difficult to get out of bed in the morning. His mother and sister tried to comfort him but all of their wise words fell on deaf ears.

Jake had called Catherine to tell her what had happened to his father, but he found it difficult to even speak without a large knot forming in his throat, which made him end their conversation quickly.

Catherine assured Jake that with time, his heart would heal, but he doubted that his soul would ever be whole again. He felt like he was in a black fog, as his mother called it, and he couldn't see his way out.

The only time Jake felt like himself was in the water. He took his surfboard out into the large waves and sat there for hours in the middle of the ocean where it was quiet. It was his only solace.

Jake only felt at peace with the sound of the seagulls above him and the breeze in his face. Sometimes Jesse would grab his board and follow him out, sitting near him in the waves. They didn't really talk, but sat quietly for a time before a large wave would come along. Then Jake would take off, disappearing until the wave subsided.

It was a difficult time for them all to come to terms with the large hole Jack's death had left in their lives.

CHAPTER 31

*C*atherine felt extremely tired as another dizzy spell hit her. She took Mindy up on her offer, allowing her to schedule a doctor's appointment.

The doctor was thorough. He did a full exam and ordered a comprehensive blood panel to rule out anemia. It was just possible that she was working too much.

A phone call from the doctor's office came later that same afternoon. Mindy answered it and had taken a message for Catherine to call the office as soon as possible. The nurse even gave Mindy the number for their backline, in case it was after hours.

The nurse had made it sound urgent, so Mindy had stuck her head into the conference room and placed the note, marked URGENT in big red letters, into Catherine's hands.

"Is there anything I can do for you, boss?" Mindy asked, seeing the concerned look on her face.

Concern and dread filled Catherine, but she gave Mindy a reassuring smile and shook her head.

"You worry too much, Mindy. I'm fine. Probably, he just wants me to get more rest and take some iron pills. I'll most likely call it a day and go home early. I'm still feeling a bit tired." She nervously fidgeted with her phone but smiled before excusing herself and finding a quiet spot to make her call.

"Yes, this is Catherine Lawrence. I received a message from your office to call you back. I'm assuming it's about my lab work," Catherine said to the receptionist, then waited a few minutes on hold for the doctor.

When he came on the line, the conversation lasted for exactly four minutes and twenty seconds before Catherine hung up.

She took a seat in the nearest chair and had to take several deep breaths, placing her head between her knees for a few minutes as tears filled her eyes. The news stunned her. She stood up, headed outside, and stepped into the waiting car, still in shock.

She ordered the driver to take her to the doctor's office while sending Mindy a message to tell Russell that she had gone home for the day.

A message quickly came back, asking Catherine if she was all right; to which she replied with two thumbs up.

Yet, Catherine wasn't feeling so sure of how she felt about what the doctor had just told her.

The next day Catherine did something very out of character. She called in sick to work even though she wasn't actually sick. She had some heavy decisions to make, and she needed the time and space to do that.

Catherine sat in bed in her pajamas and turned off her phone, contemplating her life. She'd tried to call Jake last night but he hadn't picked up. There were so many things she wanted to tell him.

She wondered if Jake had changed his mind about them and didn't have the heart to tell her. Then she remembered when she had lost her grandmother and then her father, how she didn't want to talk with people, how she had closed herself off from the world for weeks, barely sleeping or eating.

For the first time in a long time, things were not going according to plan. Here was a decision she would have to make entirely on her own. There was no time for wallowing in indecision and self-doubt. This matter was entirely up to her and no one else.

She lay back down and pulled the covers over her head, letting out a primal scream. Tears flooded her eyes once again. Catherine reached for the tissue box and pulled it under the blankets with her. She gave into her basic instincts and allowed herself to cry long and hard, until there were no more tears left. Then she crawled out of bed and did what her grandmother had taught her to do when facing a difficult decision. She made a list of the pros and cons and worked it out until she came to a logical decision.

An hour later, Catherine decided that she would inform all those who needed to know tomorrow morning. For now, all she wanted to do was eat an entire pint of her favorite Haagen-Dazs ice cream straight out of the carton.

Early the next morning, Catherine was met by Mindy as she stepped off of the elevator.

"Good morning, Boss."

"How do you always manage to know exactly when I'm coming in?" Catherine asked, taking the cup of tea Mindy stuck in her hand.

"I have my spies," Mindy said, with an impish grin. "Now, getting down to business... Oh, I'm sorry. Where are my manners? How are you feeling?"

With a confident smile, Catherine took a deep breath.

"Better, now that I'm certain that I've made the right decision."

"Decision?" Mindy narrowed her eyes with suspicion, fumbling for her phone to pull up the calendar. "Decision about what? And what did you forget to tell me about?"

"Relax, Mindy. You haven't missed anything on my calendar. The decision I'm speaking of is of a personal nature."

Looking relieved, Mindy put away her phone and gave Catherine a questioning look.

"Well?"

"I think you are ready," Catherine said cryptically before starting down the hallway.

"Ready for what?" Mindy asked, trailing behind Catherine, still trying to make sense of her mysterious words.

"Is the big guy in his office?" Catherine asked, heading in the direction of Russell's office without waiting for an answer. "What am I talking about? Of course, he's in his office. Where else would he be?" she said, giving a cursory knock before opening his door.

"There she is," Russell said as Catherine entered. "How are we feeling, now that we had a day to rest and recover?"

"I don't know about "*we*," but I'm feeling better today," Catherine responded. "I have some good news and some bad news. Which would you like first?"

Looking puzzled, Russell tilted his head.

"The good news. Of course."

"Mindy is ready to step up and play a bigger part in this organization," Catherine announced.

"I am?" Mindy responded, turning to Catherine with a look of astonishment on her face before quickly recovering. "I mean, I am, sir. Ready to step up, that is."

"Excellent," Russell said, stepping out from behind his desk to shake Mindy's hand. "Excellent," he repeated giving Catherine a quizzical look.

Catherine simply smiled at them both before she reached into her briefcase, slung over her shoulder, and produced an envelope.

"I regret to inform you that I will be taking a medical leave of absence," she said, placing the envelope into his hand.

Taking a step back to take a seat on the corner of his desk, Russell looked shocked.

He and Mindy simultaneously gasped.

"What?"

"I'm sorry. I realize this isn't ideal, but I am certain that Mindy is ready."

"No. I wasn't asking about Mindy. I was concerned about you," Russell finally said.

Catherine saw the bewilderment in Russell's face. She could read him like an open book after working with him all this time.

"I know you have a million questions, but at the moment I need you to respect my wishes. I need to remove myself from this stressful environment and concentrate on myself," she said. "I'm not saying that this will be permanent."

"Sure...sure. Whatever you need, Lawrence." He glanced down at the envelope in his hand as if it would provide him with more information. "Have you told Angela yet?"

"No, not yet, but I will call her today, I promise."

"Good. She'll need to hear this from you."

"I know, and she will," Catherine said, taking a seat next to him on the desk. "Do you want to talk about it?"

"If you have a minute," he replied, looking up from the envelope at her.

"If you will excuse me," Mindy said, making her way to the door, "I'll just be…rescheduling appointments."

"Of course, Mindy, and welcome to the big league," Russell said.

He directed Catherine to the couch and sat across from her.

"Please, take a seat and talk to me."

"Only for a moment," she said. "I have so much to do before I pack up my office. I have a flight back to Florida tonight."

"So soon?" Russell sounded surprised.

Their conversation lasted for over an hour behind closed doors but when Catherine stepped out of Russell's office, they had parted on the best of terms.

Catherine headed straight for her office and sat down with Mindy. The two of them went over the resumes of applicants to fill Mindy's job. They settled upon Michael Fenton, a Stanford graduate with a degree in Political Science as well as a first-year law student.

Next, they went over procedures. Catherine stopping at one point to assure Mindy that she would be a phone call away and would make herself available to answer her questions for as long as it took.

By four-thirty, Catherine was spent. Her office was packed up and Mindy would ship her personal effects to her Florida address. The belongings at the house were already boxed up and ready for shipping as well. The only thing she would be taking on the plane with her was one small carry-on bag which she had brought with her.

When everything was said and done, Catherine was relieved to be going home. It was as if a heavy burden had been lifted from her shoulders. She couldn't understand why it had taken her so long to understand that she had been living someone else's dreams for so many years.

CHAPTER 32

*W*aking up in her own bed had felt amazing. It felt like she had been away longer than a few weeks. For the first time in years, Catherine was at a loss. Not having something to do or someplace to be was a new experience for her. She was happy to finally be home, and yet, she was unsure what to do next. Her mind was a jumble of emotions, not the least of them being her feelings for a certain Australian who wasn't there.

Taking time off from work or her career wasn't a money issue, considering she had a tidy sum saved along with some healthy investments. She knew she would be fine financially but the prospect of tackling life without a plan freaked her out.

Catherine looked at her bag sitting by the closet. It was very uncharacteristic of her not to have unpacked yet. She reasoned that it was because it had been late when she finally made it home. But deep down, she knew that there was a deeper reason she hadn't unpacked yet.

Catherine went around the house opening all of the windows to air the place out. Then she made her bed and had breakfast. She left the unpacking until later. Right now, she wanted to feel the sand between her toes and the sun on her face.

Catherine put her bathing suit on and grabbed a magazine, a towel, and a beach chair before heading for her favorite hideaway.

Once she was tucked away and sure no one would find her, she began to relax, telling herself that she would make a plan tomorrow. But today would be all about frivolity and nothing more.

She stopped to watch a couple of surfers riding a wave and squinted her eyes trying to see them more clearly.

"Oh, who am I kidding, he's not out there," she said, setting up her chair and placing her towel upon it. Then she settled into it and closed her eyes, allowing her thoughts to travel back in time to when she and Jake first met. She remembered how he would wait around, waxing his board for more than an hour until she stepped outside, just so he could casually wave to her as if he just happened to be there at the precise moment.

Catherine picked up her magazine and attempted to read an article that had caught her interest, but instead sat staring at the same page for a while. She couldn't get Jake out of her mind. The way he smiled at her when she said something that made him laugh or the way he smelled first thing in the morning.

Catherine had it bad, she was lovesick. At least that's what her grandmother would have called this awful feeling that now resided in the pit of her stomach.

She eventually made her way back to her condo, stopping in front of Jake's place, hoping that somehow, he would magically appear.

She noticed his surfboard sitting on the deck next to the front door, and her heart jumped out of her chest. She tried to figure out what she would say to him. She held her breath after knocking on his door, waiting for it to open.

When Catherine heard footsteps, she was giddy with anticipation.

"I've been trying..." Catherine began crossly as the door opened but then stopped short when she saw Jake's best friend, Mick, instead.

"Hey," Mick said, "well I'll be hanged. Ow ya doin'?" His thick Aussie dialect threw Catherine off for a moment. Half the time she couldn't understand whether he was greeting her or telling her to shove off. "Look who it is, Midge," he called over his shoulder, "it's Jake's Catie, she's come to pay us a visit."

"That pretty little sheila from next door?" Midge called from the kitchen, poking her head around the corner to take a quick look. "Oh, ye, love. G' day to ya," she greeted cheerfully before ducking back into the kitchen. "I haven't seen you since the beach party."

"I'm so sorry to barge in on the two of you. I've been unable to reach Jake and I really just wanted to talk with him. But then I saw the surfboard and thought..." Catherine began to explain but stopped short. Tears stung the back of her eyelids as she tried to put on a smile. "Oh, I don't really know what I thought."

"Come on in, sit awhile," Mick insisted, taking Catherine by the arm and pulling her in, despite her reluctance. "Midge," he yelled, "get our guest something cold to drink."

"Oh, no. I couldn't—" Catherine protested.

"Sure, you can, love. It's no trouble at all," he persisted, showing her over to the couch. "Now what's this about our Jake not calling you?"

"I'm just being silly," she said, feeling awkward for even bringing up the subject. "I really should go."

"What can I get ya to drink, sweetie?" Midge called out from the kitchen. "I've got beer, wine, juice, and water."

"I really can't stay," Catherine said, looking towards the door.

"Nonsense," Mick said. "If Jake knew we turned you out without being hospitable he would be ashamed of us."

Midge came out of the kitchen with a bottle of cold beer in one hand and a bottle of water in the other. "It's no trouble at all, see, I have one of each."

Catherine smiled and took the bottle of water.

"Thank you, Midge. You're too kind."

Midge handed Mick the bottle of beer.

"Then you haven't heard," he said solemnly, then opened the bottle and took a drink.

"Jake did tell me about his father. I only wish that I'd gotten to meet him before he passed," Catherine said, putting her head down as a tear slid down her cheek.

"Jack went suddenly and Jake has been very torn-up over it," Mick said, taking another swallow of beer as he stared out the window. "That Jack was a good man and he will be missed."

"The distance between us has been hard on me," Catherine said, standing up to look out the window at the ocean. She took a drink from her bottle of water before continuing. "Sometimes I wonder if it was meant to be? If we are meant to be?"

"Our Jake has it bad for you. You're all he talks about," Midge said, coming up behind Catherine and standing next to her.

Catherine's phone buzzed as a text message came through. Pulling the phone from her pocket, she saw that it was from Jake.

I feel like I'm drowning without you.

"I've got to go to him," Catherine said suddenly, turning to look at Midge and Mick. "He needs me. Do I need a visa? How hard is it to get a flight to Australia?"

Midge put her hand on Catherine's arm.

"You don't need a visa and Mick and I will help you get there. Mick, make the call," Midge said, giving Catherine a reassuring squeeze. "He's got connections. Don't ya, Mick?"

"Ah, yeah, yeah! I got connections." Quickly getting to his feet, Mick pulled out his phone and pushed a few buttons.

When someone on the other end answered, he wandered into the other room to make the arrangements. Catherine strained to hear what he was saying but Midge nudged her shoulder.

"Ol' Mick will take care of everything, sweetie. Don't you worry about any of it," Midge assured her.

When Mick poked his head around the corner and gave Midge the thumbs up sign, she smiled broadly.

"Now then, we should go next door and get you all packed up."

"How can Mick get me a flight so quickly?"

"I told ya, he's got connections."

"How much will it be?" Catherine asked. "I'll need to go to the bank and get some money to pay Mick back—"

"I'm sure they will give you the friends and family discount," Midge said and patted her gently on the arm. "You won't need any money and you can stop worrying about paying anyone back. It will all be taken care of."

Catherine was puzzled by Midge's statement but decided to let it go for the moment. She would be sure that she made it right with them. For now, she needed to get packed. She was going to Australia to make sure that Jake was alright.

CHAPTER 33

Nick stepped out of Jake's condo just as Catherine unlocked her door.

"We're in luck. The plane is scheduled to leave tonight at seven, so there won't be any time to dilly-dally."

"That is good news," Midge said. "But we won't have any time to waste."

Catherine picked up her suitcase and dumped the contents out onto the bed. She sorted out the dirty from the clean.

"What kind of clothes will I need? Warm or cold?"

"Warm," Midge replied, taking a seat on the edge of the bed. "You will definitely need some warm weather clothing. This is our summer."

"Perfect."

Catherine began placing underwear, shorts, a couple of bras, some shirts, three sundresses, and a bathing suit in her bag. Next, she packed toiletries, hair brush, comb, toothbrush and sandals in the bag.

"If I may? Is this your closet?" Midge asked before showing herself into Catherine's walk-in closet. She pulled a few more things off of hangers and carried them over to her.

Catherine nodded her approval and Midge handed them to her. Finally, Catherine zipped the suitcase up, carried it out of the room and set it by the front door.

"Thank you for all of your help, Midge. I can't thank you enough."

"Me and Mick would do anything for our Jake. He's like family to us. And that makes you practically family as well. When you are ready, Mick and I will take you to the airport."

"Are you sure? I can call an Uber."

"I wouldn't hear of it," Midge said. "When you're ready, just come next door.

"I should have just enough time for a quick shower and freshen up a bit before we have to leave," Catherine said. "And Midge?"

"Yes?"

"Tell Mick I said thank you."

"Will do. Be sure to dress comfortably for the long flight. The plane is quite spacious and you will be able to walk around, but you still want to be comfortable."

An hour later they were in Mick's Jeep and headed for the private airstrip near the main airport. Catherine felt as if she were in a dream.

When they'd reached the airstrip, Catherine pulled out her wallet and offered them money for gas and thanked them for driving her to the airport, but they refused to accept any compensation.

Mick pulled up to the secured gate and flashed a card. The gate lifted and he was waved through. He drove onto the tarmac and pulled up to a private jet.

Catherine was beside herself and felt like a carp stranded out of the water as she opened and closed her mouth several times without any sound coming out.

Mick got out of the car and took Catherine's suitcase from the trunk, walking it over to an attendant who was waiting by the cargo door.

Midge stepped out of the car followed by Catherine, who straightened her sweater. She wore black knit pants, a high-end, black t-shirt with a black cashmere sweater over top and a pair of black, one-inch slip-on shoes. Layers were always good on a plane. She felt she looked elegant in her ensemble, for which she was grateful for now as she stared up at the sleek, silver jet she was about to board.

"How much is this ride going to set me back?" Catherine asked.

"Not one red cent," Midge said. "I told you that you would be getting the friends and family discount. Now, go make sure that our Jake is alright."

Catherine gave Midge a goodbye hug and turned to look up the ladder to the opening where she saw a beautiful young woman waiting for her.

"Well, go on, now," Mick said.

Catherine hugged him.

"Thank you so much, Mick. I won't forget your kindness."

"Go on now, Jacqueline won't bite you," he said.

"That's Jake's sister?"

"Yes, and I wouldn't keep her waiting."

Catherine climbed the steps and was greeted at the door then shown to her seat up front.

"My name is Jacqueline but you can call me Jackie. I'm so glad you could join us," she said pleasantly. "Jakey is going to be so surprised when he sees you. If there is anything I can get for you this evening, please don't hesitate to ask. I have put a blanket, pillow, and eye shades next to you for your convenience. The lights will be dimmed as soon as we begin our taxi down the runway. If you would like a movie, I have placed a menu next to your chair. I hope you enjoy your flight."

"Thank you so much, Jackie. Jake forgot to mention that you were so stunning," Catherine said. "I promise not to be a bother. Truth is, I just flew in from D.C. last night and I'm feeling very tired. I will probably sleep most of the way."

"Please, don't consider your comfort or needs a bother to me. I'm really very happy that I've been able to meet you, Catherine. Jake had nothing but wonderful things to say about you. And you're even prettier in person than he said you were." Jackie flashed Catherine a dazzling smile as two men appeared from the front of the plane. "Let me introduce you to our pilot, who also happens to be my other brother, Jesse Ryan. And this is our co-pilot, as well as my fiancé, Zackery McLeroy. Fellas, this is Miss Catherine Lawrence, Jake's girl."

Catherine smiled and shook the two men's hands.

"It is a pleasure to meet you both."

"G' day, Miss Lawrence. It's a pleasure to meet you as well," Jesse said, arching an eyebrow. "And may I say that you are even more lovely than I was told."

"Thank you. You are very kind."

"Did you have a nice stretch and get something to eat?" Jacqueline inquired of Zackery.

Zackery leaned over and whispered something in Jackie's ear before saluting Catherine with two fingers and heading towards the cockpit.

"He's a sly one," she said.

The flight was long but Catherine slept most of the way. Once or twice she woke with a start before realizing where she was. It was ten hours into the flight when Catherine decided to watch a movie. She picked *The Art of Racing in the Rain*.

The beautiful story made her cry. She was already feeling emotional but she couldn't stop watching. When it was over, she was happy that she didn't turn it off because the ending was worth it.

When the plane touched down in Sydney it was one o'clock in the morning the next day. Since she had slept a good portion of the flight, Catherine felt rested and jet lagged all at the same time. But Jesse, Zackery and Jackie were ready to hit the sack.

"Come on," Jesse said, motioning with his hand for Catherine to follow him. "We have a ride waiting to take us home."

"And I have an extra bed for you, if you like," Jacqueline said. "It's so comfy, you'll go right back to sleep, I promise."

"That's quite an endorsement," Catherine teased. "Are you sure that you're not over selling it?"

"She's not," Zackery said, "I've slept on the guest mattress once or twice."

"Oh, go on, now," Jackie said, giving him an elbow to the ribs.

A dark SUV was waiting for them with the engine running. Soothing music played as the four of them climbed inside and buckled up. The driver placed their bags in the back and slammed the door before climbing in behind the steering wheel.

"Take us home, James," Zackery said when everyone was settled.

The driver drove for more than an hour. Jacqueline, Jesse, and Zackery fell asleep in the first ten minutes, but

Catherine couldn't. She was a bundle of emotions and far too excited and fascinated by the scenery outside her window to sleep.

While they drove from Sydney to the Central Coast, she had time to ponder many things about the last ten years. Catherine had spent far too long merely sleepwalking through life. Now, all she wanted to do was begin living it with someone who loved her for who she was. And she believed that someone was Jake.

Before falling asleep, Jacqueline told Catherine that they normally stayed in the city, a mere fifteen minutes from the airport. But since they had a few days off, they would be staying at the family compound along the coast.

Arriving at the compound, there were four houses, built side by side, with a mere fifty to sixty feet between them. They were each individual homes of similar design, yet each one had a distinguishing feature that set it apart from the rest. Even in the dark, Catherine could see that they all had front porches that looked out towards the ocean. The front porch lights were shining as if someone was expecting them. She thought that it was quaint. It made her feel welcomed, in some small, yet strange way, to this foreign land.

Jacqueline bid Jesse farewell as she, Catherine, and Zachery got out of the car. "Kiss the wife and kids for me in the morning, Jesse. We'll meet up around noon if I can drag myself out of bed by then," Jackie told him.

"What she really means to say is she will try to drag my sorry ass out of bed by then," Zackery said, nudging her with his elbow.

Giving him a playful shove, Jacqueline giggled. "He's right, that's what I meant to say."

The driver exited the car, carried their bags up to the front porch, and said goodnight as they passed him on their way to the house.

"Don't we need to tip him?" Catherine whispered, picking up her bag as she followed Jacqueline into the darkened interior of the house.

"Nah," Zachery said. "James is on retainer and we tip him all at once at the end of the month when we pay him," he answered with a pleasant smile as he passed her. "I'm going to bed," he called over his shoulder with a big yawn.

A very sleepy Jacqueline ushered Catherine up the staircase and down a hallway.

"Best room in the house," she told Catherine. "You'll see what I mean when the sun comes up in the morning. You even have your own private bathroom," she said, flipping the light on in the bedroom and then the bathroom.

"I don't know if I can sleep anymore," Catherine said, setting her things down on a luggage rack in the brightly decorated yellow and white room.

"There's a television over there," Jacqueline said, pointing to a cabinet. "Just open the doors. The remote is in the nightstand next to the bed. And I guarantee, Zackery and I will never hear a thing." She turned toward the cabinet. "Once he and I fall asleep after a long flight, we are dead to the world. I must warn you, however, Australian television is quite different than what you might be used to. Oh," she exclaimed, turning back around, "we do have movie channels. You'll find them…" Jacqueline yawned, "I'm sorry but I can't keep my eyes open another minute or I would keep you company for a little while."

"That's alright," Catherine said, looking around the room as she rummaged through her suitcase. "You can go to bed. I'll be fine. I'll see you in the morning."

"If you get up before us, which is a good possibility, there is a coffee maker and food in the cooler, I mean, refrigerator," Jacqueline corrected herself. "And if you feel like it, you can wander down to the beach."

Catherine nodded and smiled.

"Good night."

Closing the door behind her, Jacqueline made her way downstairs and climbed into bed, snuggling up next to Zackery, giving him a kiss on the cheek while he softly snored.

"Love you, you big lug."

Catherine settled in, opening the window to get some fresh air. She breathed the salty sea air in deeply, and looked up at the stars, wondering which house belonged to Jake.

Turning the television on, she turned the volume down and flipped through the channels until something caught her attention.

Before long she felt herself unwinding as she curled up on the bed and pulled the blankets up to her chin. Snuggling down in the bed a little deeper, she realized that Jacqueline was right. This was the most comfortable bed she'd ever laid in. Catherine felt completely relaxed for the first time in years. There would be no deadlines to meet or conferences to prepare for. She was living her life without a plan for the first time that she could remember and it felt freeing.

If this is what it's like to improvise, I think I could get used to it, she thought before sleep tugged her under.

CHAPTER 34

*J*ake rose early, unable to sleep. He'd had a long night, tossing and turning as a particular redhead continued to invade his dreams and every waking thought. He'd wanted to reach out to her for days but every time he picked up the phone to call her something stopped him. He knew how important her job was to her and didn't want to burden her further by whining about his sorrows or pointing out the inevitable.

There was nothing she could do about the situation anyway, he thought as he grabbed his surfboard and headed out to catch some early morning waves. Jake needed to ponder over a few matters before he called Catherine, later on today.

Catherine was a workaholic, and they had had a discussion or two about how she saw her future. Jake wasn't sure if he would fit into those plans. In fact, there wasn't much about life at this point that Jake felt sure about any longer.

He'd forgotten how much he loved being home around his family, and the last few weeks had shown him just how important they were to him. Besides, he couldn't leave his mother alone now. She needed him. His family needed him.

Matilda had been devastated by Jack's sudden and unexpected death. The two of them weren't exactly in their prime, but they weren't that far from it. They had plans. Plans that got put on hold when Jack became ill. The two of them were certain that they still had time to do all of the things they'd dreamt about doing. So many dreams had been put on hold when they were raising their kids. But sometimes plans don't work out the way that you plan them. Then one thing led to another, and before they knew it, they were out of time. They'd put their lives on the back burner until it was too late.

Jake felt responsible for his mother now that his father was gone. How could he explain this to Catherine? She was an independent, strong-willed woman who lost her own family years ago. Would she understand the need to be around family when she didn't have one?

He'd been racking his brain for days, trying to work out a plan that would accommodate everyone's needs, but in the end, the only thing he managed to do was make himself miserable. He couldn't see any way around it. Two people couldn't make a relationship work from two different continents. That was just a basic fact, and he was sick about it.

The early morning sun came through the gauzy white curtains and shone directly into Catherine's eyes. At first, she was annoyed, then she breathed in the salty sea air. She opened her eyes and remembered that she was in Australia and that she'd traveled halfway around the world just to see Jake.

Suddenly Catherine couldn't wait to hold him in her arms. Stepping to the window, her breath caught when she saw the ocean for the first time in the light of day. It was a moving experience for her as the sun glistened off the waves. She felt drawn to the water, like a magnet to a metal pole. She needed to feel and touch the sand.

She fumbled through her luggage, pulling out a bathing suit and a coverup, then raced to put them on. Next, she washed her face and combed her hair back into a high ponytail. Catherine felt simply giddy as she dabbed on a sheer lip gloss and pronounced herself ready.

She walked quietly down the stairs, trying not to wake up her host and hostess as she opened the front door and stepped out onto the front porch. There was a hanging swing for two and two rocking chairs that she hadn't paid attention to the night before. They appeared so inviting in the light of day she thought as she headed towards the rocky bluffs. There, she found the path down to the shore below.

Steps leading down to the beach had been painstakingly cut into the packed dirt and rocky cliffs. Someone had also gone to the trouble of putting up a wooden railing. It had been sanded, and a clear coat of resin had been applied on top of it to keep anyone using the path from getting splinters. For some reason, this made her smile as she ran her hand over the well-worn wooden railing on her way down.

Her life's plan was much like a railing that hadn't been varnished. It served to keep people at arm's length. And to think that she had clung to this plan for so many years as if it were a life preserver. Instead of letting her live, it had merely served to hold her back.

Catherine had never felt freer in her life than when she made the decision to let it all go, let the chips fall where they may. Until a few days ago, she felt anxious all the time as if something terrible would happen if she didn't stick to the master plan. Yet, when she laid in bed that day, contemplating the meaning of life, something profound happened. The world didn't stop turning. Everyone managed just fine without her. And most of all the sky didn't fall. That was the beginning of the end of Catherine's so-called life's plan.

Stepping onto the sand and feeling the powdery grit between her toes, Catherine took a deep breath and looked up at the sky.

"Well Grandmother, this is a new beginning," she said aloud. She walked out into the water up to her knees. It was refreshing and crisp, and Catherine felt alive. All of her senses had suddenly awakened.

She cupped her hands over her eyes to shade them from the bright morning sun and searched the ocean until a lone surfer came into view. He was sitting on his board looking away from her, towards the horizon. Catherine knew it was Jake by the way he was sitting upright on his surfboard. She would know that profile anywhere.

Finding a tall rock to scale, Catherine stood on top of it and waited for Jake to turn around and notice her.

Jake turned to catch a wave, paddling hard before he stood up, cresting a wave. He then dropped down to do a backdoor maneuver, a term he'd taught her about.

Catherine's mind went back to the time Jake had taught her all about surfing. She would never forget any of the moves or terms because of the way he'd demonstrated them with his hands. They were in bed, during pillow talk, and he described to her each of the moves by running a finger along her belly.

Catherine watched as Jake carved sharply to the right, dropping into the tube of the wave while skimming his hand along the back of it until he emerged on the other side. Then cutting sharply back, Jake glanced in her direction and in a heartbeat fell off the board.

Jake thought he was seeing a mirage when he looked toward the shore and saw a woman standing up on a rock. She reminded him of Catherine. A second later he fell off of his surfboard like a rookie.

Jake felt dazed as he climbed back onto his board. He looked up towards the rocks again and saw the woman waving to him. Quickly finding a wave that would take him to shore, Jake frantically paddled towards the rock.

He caught a wave the surfers called a floater, where you first surf on top of the wave then drop back down into it, so he could get to shore quicker. Then Jake picked up his board and raced in, shaking the saltwater from his hair.

He unleashed from his board the moment he hit the dry land and dropped it to the sand before racing towards the rocks. Jake felt his heart beating out of his chest as his breath caught in his lungs.

"Catie," he called out. "Is that you?"

"Jake, I'm here," Catherine called back as she quickly came around the rock, throwing herself into his arms.

"It is you. Oh, Catie, how I've missed holding you." His eyes filled with tears as he hugged her to his heart. "I dreamt of you and of this moment, not two nights ago," he whispered into her hair while he breathed in her scent.

He pulled back to look into her eyes.

"What are you doing here?"

Catherine felt drops of water clinging to her skin.

"I came because you needed me."

"But how did you know I needed you?"

"I guess you were right when you said that we are connected."

"What about your job? I thought your career was everything to you."

"I couldn't be without you a minute longer. I realized that I don't want to love you halfway, but with all of my heart. I don't know how to do it any other way, and if I had to choose just one thing in my life that I couldn't live without, it would be you, Jake Ryan. I don't want to go another day without having you in my life. I also realized that plans can be changed, and the world won't fall apart," Catherine confessed.

Tears streamed down her cheeks, and Jake gently wiped them away with one finger.

"I love you, Jake Ryan."

"You don't know how I've prayed to hear those words from you. My world was falling apart and I felt like a drowning man. Then like magic, you appeared before me, just like in my dream. You have saved me, Catie, my love," he said, kissing her again as if it were their first time. Jake led her up the stairs before abruptly turning to face her.

"Wait, how did you get here?" he asked, staring down at her as if he half expected her to disappear in a puff of smoke.

"Mick made the arrangements, and Midge helped me pack. Oh, and I met Jesse, Zackery, and I really love your sister, Jackie. She's a kick in the pants."

"I can't believe that you're really here," he said, crushing her to his wet body again.

"I can't believe I'm here either. This place is amazing—" she began to say as Jake leaned down, kissing her on the lips. The anxious weeks, filled with so much pain and doubt, were behind them. He finally felt as if he could breathe again.

"I have missed you more than you will ever know," Jake whispered, before his lips captured hers again.

Catherine cried tears of joy at hearing his words. She couldn't have dreamt this moment up, even in her wildest dreams. She felt that she had finally found her home, right here in Jake's arms.

Jake took her hand and placed it on her heart.

"Can you feel that?" he asked. "You are the reason that my heart beats. I would climb the highest mountain, swim across the deepest ocean to be with you. I just needed you to know that," he whispered, leaning down near her ear and kissing her neck before placing another gentle kiss upon her forehead. Then he gazed down lovingly into her eyes. "Do you believe that one moment in time or one spontaneous decision can change your entire life?"

Tears welled up again in Catherine's eyes as she tried to swallow the lump in her throat.

"Yes, because a spontaneous decision has changed mine. Oh, Jakey—"

"You've already been around my sister too long—"

"Jakey, my love, as far as I am concerned, you hung the moon and the stars in the sky. I love you, now and forever."

Jake kissed her again then pulled back.

"So, you met Jesse and Jacqueline," he said casually, "Tell me, what did you think of our little operation?"

"I was impressed, but don't forget about Zachery and James," she corrected. "They were amazing too."

"Who could forget about Zachery and James?" Jake said. "Do you know that I have been friends with those two guys since I was in nappies?"

"You don't say."

"Honest. I wouldn't lie about that. Well, I suppose they approve of you or I would have gotten a heads up by now," he said, giving her a glance out of the corner of his eye. "So, the only real test you have to pass now is the Matilda test."

"What is the Matilda test?"

Looking concerned, Jake shook his head and grimaced.

"Well, you could say that it is the most difficult screening process you will ever go through. I did tell you that my mother has the gift of sight, right?"

She stopped walking and looked up at him to determine if he was being serious.

"Your mother can tell the future?"

He nodded.

"Yes, she certainly can."

"Oh, Jake, I'm not—" she started to say while backing up.

Jake took her by the hand and tucked her beneath his arm.

"Everything will be fine," he said, with a knowing smile. "You will see."

"How can you be certain?"

"Because, I think that I've inherited the family gift. Besides, if she says I can't marry you, we will run away and join the circus."

"What?" she cried, pulling away to look up at him again.

With a shrug, Jake gave her a kiss on the forehead and began walking again. "Two nights ago, I had a dream that you were standing on that very rock," he said, turning to point at the rock she'd been standing on a few minutes before. "You were waiting for me."

"How could you have—" she began to say, then stopped.

The two of them continued to walk towards his mother's home, each pondering their own thoughts as they stepped up onto his mother's porch.

At the same time, Matilda opened the door.

"What took you so long?" she said, looking directly at Catherine. "I've been up for hours, just waiting for your visit."

Catherine and Jake looked at one another and began to laugh.

"See, I told you."

Matilda threw her arms around Catherine's neck.

"I'm so happy you're here." Then touching her stomach with one hand, she whispered, so that only Catherine could hear her, "And *they* will be a welcome addition to the family too."

Catherine stiffened with shock. She and her doctor were the only two who knew that she was carrying twins. In fact, the reality of her situation hadn't truly settled in yet, and Catherine wanted to wait another four to six weeks before telling anyone about the pregnancy, just in case something went wrong.

"But we shall keep this between you and me," Matilda said, before pulling back with a large grin as she brought a finger to her lips.

Matilda took Catherine by the hand and led her into the house, turning to give Jake a contented smile.

"This one is the one. She is definitely a keeper, my son."

"Somehow, I knew you would think so, Mum," Jake said, following behind the two most important women in his life. "Did you hear that, Catie ? Now, we don't have to run away and join the circus."

"A fact that I am very grateful for, my love," Catherine replied.

CHAPTER 35

Central Coast, Australia
4 years later

Jake dropped in on a large wave, making a bottom turn before performing an Eskimo roll as the wave faded, washing him up close to shore. He enjoyed surfing these days, but loved spending time with his growing family even more. If someone had told him three years ago that he would be this blissfully happy living with another person, Jake would have told them to nick off, because they were crazy. Yet, in the end, his mother was right. When you find the right person, your souls become one and life is even more fulfilling. And that was exactly how Jake felt now, more fulfilled.

He stepped out of the water, carrying his surfboard. He leaned it against a large rock as his three-year-old twins came running.

"Daddy! Daddy!" they shouted in tandem. "Jack found a crab, Daddy," Alison said as she wrapped herself around Jake's leg.

Handing his precious find over to his father, Jack smiled proudly, wrapping himself around Jake's other leg.

"Give us a ride, daddy," he squealed.

Their adorable antics were impossible for him to ignore.

"One of these days the two of you will be too big for me to lug around like this."

"Faster, faster, daddy!" they both shouted.

Lifting each leg as if he were a giant stomping along the beach, complete with roars and loud grunts, Jake made his way towards his beautiful wife.

Catherine had dropped her formal name, for the simpler, more intimate name of Catie.

She felt it was only right, since she was starting her life over in a new country. But to the most important people in her life, she was simply, Mommy.

Catie never regretted her decision to stay in Australia with Jake and his family. She still used her law degree from time to time. After all, she had spent a great deal of time and effort acquiring it. But now, she used her knowledge to further the family business.

Catie laid on her side on a large towel spread on the sand, cradling her expanding belly as Jake and the twins clambered up the beach, giggling and squealing.

"Mommy, Mommy, look at us!" Alison shouted.

"Daddy's a big, bad giant and he's going to stomp all over you," Jack growled.

"Not if he knows what's good for him," Catie said quickly, giving Jake a playful glare before smiling up at him sweetly.

With a wicked grin, Jake peeled the twins off of his legs.

"Why don't the two of you go collect your toys and put them in the basket so that they don't wash out to sea? Hurry before the tide comes in."

"Then what, Daddy?" Alison asked. "Then what are we going to do?"

"Well, I thought that we could go to The Reptile Park. That is, if Mommy is feeling up to it," he said.

"Yaaay!" the twins shouted, jumping up and down with excitement.

"Can we, Mommy? Can we go?" they pleaded, turning to her with a look of anticipation.

"Why don't you two pick up your toys and Daddy and I will talk about it," she replied.

Alison and Jack clasped hands and ran down the beach, quickly picking up their buckets, shovels, and sand toys.

"You know that the park will be packed today," Catie said while watching her children happily play in the sand.

"I thought I'd ask Jesse and Jacqueline if they wanted to go as well, but if you're not up to it—" Jake started to say with an understanding tone.

"I want to feed the kangaroos and koalas, Daddy," Alison said, depositing her sandy toys in the plastic basket beside her father.

"I want to see the cranky crocodile, Mommy. Can we, please?" Jack begged.

Catie tried to look serious for a moment before breaking into a large smile. "You bet we can. But first, Daddy needs to help Mommy get up the hill."

A chorus of, "Yaaay!" went up from all three of them before the twins started up the steps to the top.

Jake took Catie by the hand and helped her climb the steps slowly.

"I am truly a blessed man, Mrs. Ryan."

"I am the blessed one, Mr. Ryan."

They stopped halfway up the hill, taking a moment to gaze lovingly into each others' eyes when Jake leaned down to kiss his wife.

"I will always be grateful that you loved me enough to get on a plane and travel to another continent for me."

"And I will always be grateful that you came into my life and taught me that there was another way to live it," Catie whispered.

They could hear the children chanting, "We're going to The Reptile Park, we're going to The Reptile Park," in unison as they reached the top of the cliff and marched to the house.

"We had better hurry before we have a mutiny on our hands," Catie said.

"I definitely don't want to be responsible for cleaning that mess up. Remember what happened last time we left them alone in the house for twenty minutes, while we...? Well, you know..." Jake grinned, looking down at her stomach.

"Oh, I remember," she laughed. "How can I forget?"

They continued up the steps, arm in arm, as quickly as they could, chanting, "We're going to The Reptile Park, we're going to The Reptile Park," laughing like teenagers, all the way to the top.

An Important Message From
Author Diane Merrill Wigginton

Thank you for reading my book. I have some fun, exciting news for those of you who enjoy my writing. Soon I plan on putting out a newsletter that will give my wonderful readers the opportunity to learn what I'm up to and what is going on with me. And when I say, "News," letter I really mean it. When you just give me your name and email address you will not only receive my newsletter, but you will also learn about upcoming "events," such as my new books, past books, upcoming contests (how would you like to spend a day with me in person for example), personal appearances and much more. Just include your name and email address to one of these landing pages: https://mailchi.mp/dianemerrillwigginton/as-landing-page [1] or here https://BookHip.com/FFJRKAT [2] to sign up.

I look forward to connecting with you.

Romantically Yours,
Diane